An assassination plot that could lead the
human race to extinction.

A child who holds our only hope.

A mother who has seen the horror the future holds.

And the horror itself, an emotionless cyborg killer. . . .

TERMINATOR ™ 2: JUDGMENT DAY

T2 ™

TERMINATOR™ 2
JUDGMENT DAY

A NOVEL BY
RANDALL FRAKES

BASED ON A SCREENPLAY BY
JAMES CAMERON
AND
WILLIAM WISHER

BANTAM BOOKS
NEW YORK • TORONTO • LONDON • SYDNEY • AUCKLAND

TERMINATOR 2
Judgment Day

A Bantam Book / July 1991

ISBN 0-553-29169-6

Published simultaneously in the United States and Canada

For William Wisher

They don't make friends
like him anymore.

DAY ONE TWENTY-SIX

BUENAVENTURA, MEXICO
July 19, 1984
Thursday—8:58 A.M.

Sarah Jeanette Connor was driving across a vast and lonely landscape of cacti and sand toward a brooding range of mountains, shadowed by swollen rainclouds. Sheet lightning fired behind them like giant strobes. The promise of a storm was in the air.

In a way, the Terminator *had* killed her, Sarah was thinking as she checked the load in her .357 Colt Python revolver, then slipped it back into the holster hidden under the dash of the open Jeep. She was certainly no longer the naive nineteen-year-old waitress she had been just a few months ago. That person had died when the two people she loved more than her own life—the father of the child now growing in her, and her mother—had been brutally murdered. Their deaths still haunted her, even though lately she had been learning how to lock the feelings into a place where they would not interfere with her survival. Because she must survive. For now, Sarah Connor was the most important human being in the world.

Sarah raised a Walkman to her ear and listened to something she had recorded a few minutes ago when she's stopped to get gas. "Should I tell you about your father?"She glanced down at her swelling stomach. "Will it change your decision to send him here, to his death?"

She imagined a point in the future when that choice would have to be made, and she shuddered. "But if you don't send Kyle, you can never be."

The crazy thought swirled in her head. Kyle Reese, a young soldier who had volunteered to be sent through time to protect her from the Terminator, had made her pregnant with the son who would one day order the father back through time to make her pregnant, so one day the son would order the father back in time to make her . . . a circle of events, bending infinitely back on itself. She remembered what her high school science teacher, Mr. Bowland, used to say about paradoxes: the universe was one big python, feeding on its tail. It made her feel as if she were a puppet of Fate, a mere link in the causal chain. On the other hand, her will to survive had seemed to determine the outcome of events. Or maybe human will was merely another element in the preordained design? The whole of the rest of her life might be the answer to *that* paradox.

Her voice continued on the recorder. "I suppose I will tell you about your father. I owe him that. And maybe it will be enough for you to know that in the few hours we had together, we loved a lifetime's worth."

She snapped off the recorder. The words sounded so trite, so pale when placed next to her blazing memories. Sarah wanted her son to one day love his father as she now did. But she never was any good with words. . . . Frustrated, she popped out the cassette, slipping it into the glove compartment next to a growing stack of C-90s. "The Book," she called it; an audio chronicle of information her son would need to survive. That morning Sarah had recorded the story of the arrival of the Terminator one hundred and twenty-six days ago. How it had been "killed" three days later. And the lifetime of changes that had happened to her in those three days . . .

The Sarah Connor who went to junior college, dreamed of marrying a nice man and having a simple,

snugly life tucked somewhere in the pruned, green sub-
urbs, had been obliterated by the gleaming death that
was the Terminator. It had taught her to hate beyond
any capacity she could have imagined by killing those
she loved. Sarah had avenged herself by crushing the
cyborg in a hydraulic press. But it gave her no pleasure
to think of it. Because when she had punched the button that sent the press crashing down like the iron fist
of God, Sarah had died, too, and been reborn in blood
and sorrow into a world where everyone was doomed
to a future of mass destruction and universal suffering.
She knew what no one else did: One day the computer
designed to automatically control the U.S. nuclear
strike force would become "alive," and Skynet's first
sentient decision would be that mankind was obsolete.
It would launch a first strike, riding out the firestorm
of retaliation to follow, safe in a hardened underground complex in Cheyenne Mountain, while on the
surface men, women, and children would writhe in
their death throes. Civilization would grind to a halt
as nuclear winter set in. Before long, the machines
Skynet had built to be its eyes, ears, and weapons
would spread out across the earth to claim its prize. It
wanted a world populated only with endless mechanical refractions of itself, the ultimate egoist, with direct
control linkages to automated factories to realize its
scheme. That was the future Kyle Reese had told her
about. And the Terminator's arrival had convinced her
of.

She reached over and scratched the dog behind the
ears. The sleek, muscular German shepherd poised on
the passenger seat turned its hyperalert brown eyes on
her for a brief moment before returning their gaze to
the narrow highway, scanning the horizon protectively. If anyone else tried to touch the animal, it would
most likely ruin their day, unless Sarah commanded
otherwise. The animal was not just a dog. It had been
trained by experts to be a weapon. And it hadn't been
cheap. Sarah had emptied her meager bank account
and cashed in her mother's life insurance to buy the
attack dog, the Jeep, and the gun. She was carrying out

The Plan, driving south, all the way down the continent if necessary, to find a hiding place from the gathering storm of Fate. She would raise her son in safety, protect him from the thousand possible accidents that could rob the world of its savior before his time. That was her whole life now, and the only hope for the rest of humanity.

She had enough food and water for five days, a full tank of gas, a Spanish-English dictionary. She would go as far as she could until supplies ran out, then somehow find a way to provide for herself and the baby. She wasn't afraid. Sarah found in those three terrible days that she had hidden resources she never dreamed existed, a vast secret cache of courage that had gotten her this far, against impossible odds. The casualties had been devastating, but she had won the battle. And, even if there were other Terminators that had been sent back to finish what the first could not, she would make herself ready to fight them. Because no machine was going to hurt her son. The yearning, aching love she felt for him propelled her past the horrible knowledge that she could never trust anyone again. Because *anyone* could be a Terminator, programmed by Skynet to stride across eternity and rip her soul out.

Kyle Reese had taught her this paranoia, learned from years of scrabbling in the postwar ruins, fighting off killer cyborgs and renegade humans. He'd been a soldier most of his life, he had said. It was the only way to *have* a life, up there in the future. Upthen, he'd called it. Where huge war machines rolled over the bones of millions; the dead, the flash-burned or the irradiated-out-of-existence. But John Connor had rallied the pitiful survivors into a threadbare resistance force. And little by little, humanity began to take back territory from the metal masters. Until one day the tide of battle turned, and Skynet, in a desperate burst of brilliance, devised time displacement, the first tactical time weapon. It sent a lethal emissary back through time to find and eliminate Sarah, so that John Connor might never be born.

But John's forces took control of the time displacement device and sent Kyle through, to stop the Terminator, if possible. It was essentially a suicide mission, and yet he had volunteered for it. He was a simple soldier about to walk point into the gaping maw of history because he loved Sarah.

At first Sarah couldn't comprehend how she could inspire such fierce passion. She was a relatively ordinary-looking girl, with brown hair and eyes, pleasant enough features, but nothing startling. Kyle, however, had worshipped her. No, that wasn't quite true. He adored what she was to become: the mother of John Connor, the tigress who would keep him safe through the cataclysm. So, Kyle had ridden the banshee maelstrom of time into an impossible world, so whole and rich and teeming with life, a world he could only half imagine from stories the old ones told him when he was a child. He snatched her out of the Terminator's sights and made love to her with gentle awe. And in that burning moment in each other's arms, Sarah had merged body and soul with Kyle, and only then did she believe his love was real. They had made it real, unknowingly seeding John Connor, who would grow up one day to send his father back through time so that Sarah could survive the Terminator and become pregnant with John Connor who . . . the python circling back on itself.

As the Jeep went into a turn, something fell off the dash into Sarah's lap. It was a Polaroid photo of herself. At the forlorn gas station a few miles back, a Mexican boy had run up and taken it, demanding five dollars. Taking pity on the poor waif, she had given him four, then casually tossed it on the dash. She glanced at it now, surprised to see an older woman staring out at her. Her face was still creamy-smooth with youth, made even more flush by the pregnancy, but her eyes were ancient, as old as the wrinkled gas station attendant's had been. Ancient because she had looked back into the painful past and forward into the terrifying future. But what aged her even more than that was the sadness under the Mona Lisa smile. At the instant the boy snapped the picture, she had been thinking about

Kyle. She wouldn't know until much later that this was The Photo, the one Kyle said John Connor had given him a long time ago, when they were crouching in some dirty hole together while the night sky thrummed with Skynet's aerial armada. Sometime in the future, Sarah would give it to John, and he would give it to Kyle. And Kyle would fall in love with her enigmatic, wistful smile, always wondering what she had been thinking, but never knowing that it was inspired by love and mourning for him. This, perhaps, was the beginning of the circle. But of course, circles have no beginnings or ends. But she couldn't think about Kyle now. She had to think about the road ahead, and finding a safe haven from the storm and the night to follow.

It started to rain; a hot, stinging downpour that made her eyes water. She pulled over and hastily put up the canvas top. But when she got in again, her eyes were still filled with tears. She grimly wiped them away and gunned the Jeep higher into the mountains.

UPTHEN

The moon had risen, but thick layers of slightly radioactive cumulus, black as iron, prevented any light from coming through. Cars were stopped in rusted rows, still bumper to bumper, a frozen sculpture that someone might have called "The Last Rush Hour." Buildings that once towered over the freeways had been shattered by some unimaginable force, like kicked-down sandcastles. Wind blew through the desolation, keening with the sound of ten million dead souls. It scurried snow into drifts, stark white against the charred rubble. Here and there were heaps of fire-blackened human bones, and beyond, a vast tundra of skulls amid shattered concrete.

At a nearby playground, intense heat had half melted the jungle gym, the blast had knocked the swing set on its side, and the merry-go-round had sagged in the firestorm. The faint hieroglyphs of hopscotch lines were still visible, seared into the asphalt. And next to them, the dark silhouettes of little bodies, flash-burned into the concrete in midplay. Near a burnt and rusted tricycle, the tiny skull of its owner stared up accusingly out of the drifts.

7

Three billion human lives had ended on August 29, 1997. The tenacious survivors of the nuclear fire called the war Judgment Day. Those with endurance had lived through unimaginable hellfire and then arctic cold, only to face a new nightmare. . . .

A metal foot crushed the child's skull like china, as a chromed skeleton stopped for a moment in the cold blast of air, hefting a massive battle rifle. The ruined city was reflected in the cyborg's hydraulically actuated endoskeleton that was the combat chassis of the Series 800 Terminator, unadorned by the usual covering of organic skin grown for camouflage. This was the primary antipersonnel weapon controlled by Skynet, designed to penetrate the warrens and hiding holes of the city, where the human prey huddled. The endoskeleton's glowing red eyes swept the dead terrain without emotion, all its intelligence focused through its visual and thermal sensors, hunting. Suddenly, they locked on a target.

It saw the distant, running figure on a digitized geometric map overlaying its scanners. Symbols and graphics rapidly appeared on the center display as the machine's complex wafer-circuit brain projected several possible trajectories for the target. The most likely path was highlighted. The endoskeleton swiftly raised its rifle, a Westinghouse M-25 forty-watt phased-plasma pulse-gun. A compact burst flashed from the barrel.

The figure, a young boy in rags, was centerpunched. His chest erupted outward, vaporizing into red crystals in the freezing air. He sprawled into a smoking heap on the blackened sludge.

A guerrilla soldier, hefting a battered RPG rocket-launcher, suddenly rose up behind the endoskeleton.

As the cyborg started to snap around, the soldier fired the rocket, which screamed toward the humanoid machine, and in a bright blast of orgasmic energy, tore off the top half. The endoskeleton took a few uncertain steps, then toppled, its legs spasming in the snow. The soldier strode up and spat on what was now just very expensive scrap-metal, then motioned to someone hunkered down in the shadows. It was a shivering, ten-year-old girl, nearly frozen in her tattered pullover sweater. She tentatively approached her father. Glanced down with fear at the endoskeleton in the snow. He put a reassuring hand on her shoulder and said, "I told you, it's not over till it's over." She nodded gravely. It was a saying John Connor had used as a slogan for his army. It gave people hope and strength to carry on the fight.

To Skynet, human stubbornness made no sense. They fought when logic told the synthetic intelligence they were beaten. They relentlessly poured out of the rubble like a bacterial plague, their patterns of counterattack clever and difficult to predict. And humans reproduced at an alarming rate, their sexual appetites evidently fanned high by the threat of total annihilation. Even though it took at least eight years before the human young could be made ready for battle, they were beginning to outpace Skynet's manufacturing capabilities. And they were quickly learning to find the soft spots in the metal vanguard, decimating Skynet's army of killing machines. Soon, there would be more human soldiers than nonhuman. The hypercomputer had miscalculated gravely on something it was still furiously analyzing: human will. So far, it had not come to a conclusion. And the war was grinding into its thirty-first year. . . .

The rising sound of roaring turbines caused the man to grab his daughter and dart across the uneven terrain for cover. Searchlights blazed down as a formation of flying Hunter-Killer machines on patrol passed overhead and moved on toward the jagged horizon, which was lit up by intermittent flashes and the distant thunder of a pitched battle.

At the intersection of what used to be Pico and Robertson, the desperate combat raged. The ragtag guerrilla army consisted of Doberman-mean young men and women. They came from Southern Hemisphere countries, mostly Africa, South America, a few from Australia. Most of the survivors of the nuclear war between the Northern Hemisphere superpowers lived below the equator. Under John Connor's leadership, they had come to the ruined cities to reclaim them from Skynet's steel legion.

Energy bolts crisscrossed the field of battle, revealing the ranks of advancing machines in nightmarish flashes. The computer's forces consisted of tanklike mobile robot gun-platforms called Hunter-Killers; four-legged, running gun-pods called Centurions; aerial HKs; centipedelike bombs called Silverfish, which snaked into human emplacements to explode; and the humanoid terminators in various stages of camouflage.

Beam-weapons fired like concentrated lightning, arcing out to burst buildings, earth, metal, and flesh in gut-pounding explosions. A battered pickup truck, covered with customized armor plating, bolted into the open, the gunner in the back rising to target an aerial HK above with a hand-launched Stinger missile. The HK's turret gun angrily whirled just as the human fired. The missile cut through the night like a hot knife, striking one of the HK's turbines. The sky flared into flame as two halves of the huge flying machine fell onto the battlefield, one flattening what little was left of a burning building, the other pounding a small squadron of Centurions into the ground.

The gunner yelled triumphantly, but turned as a ground-shaking rumble rose up behind him. A massive HK tank suddenly smashed through a pile of debris and rolled toward him like a wall of iron. He only had time to scream as the treads slammed into the truck and crushed it like a beer can.

A few blocks away, in the dark nooks and crannies of the collapsed rock pile that was once the Westside Pavilion shopping mall, an intense firefight with terminator endoskeletons raged. The human soldiers there were like most of John Connor's army: bleeding, frostbitten, wrapped in rags . . . this was Valley Forge, with better weapons.

Cowan, a seventeen-year-old guerrilla, leaped from cover and fired a handheld grenade-launcher directly at three charging terminators, blasting them off their feet. They lay still, their skulls punched through, their circuits fried. The boy rapidly fumbled to reload.

A man stepped out of the shadows. "Let me help you," he said calmly, and reached for the grenade-launcher. Cowan instinctively knew something was wrong. The stranger was wearing the guerrilla armband, all right, but it was *last week's* color. Cowan jammed the huge shell in the firing chamber and pulled the trigger, then leaped behind a large chunk of fallen concrete.

The back of the boy's head was singed by the heat of the shockwave. He sat up, groggy, stemming a trickle of blood that ran out of his left ear. Cowan realized with growing horror that he could no longer hear anything on that side. But he smiled with satisfaction when he saw what the grenade had done to the "man." He was on the ground, nearly cut in two, his flesh torn open, revealing patches of chromed-metal underneath. The thing's "spine," or neuron trunk, had been sheared, one sparking end of it showing through the twisted flesh. The Terminator spasmed insanely, like a puppet tangled in its own strings. In a moment, the joint servos ground to a halt and the glowing eyes winked out. Cowan took no time to gloat over his kill. He was too busy reloading.

A Silverfish scuttled out from under a pile of rubble and stopped between his legs. The boy looked down and screamed. He twisted his torso and flung himself away. The Silverfish erupted, spraying the area with razor-sharp and sizzling-hot shrapnel. Cowan hit the ground, immediately rolling back onto his feet in a ready crouch, managing to get another grenade in the launcher as he did.

The area was thick with smoke and dust. Cowan rose and stumbled over a new pile of debris into a corridor, his eyes stinging from the acrid fumes. And now he couldn't seem to hear very well. Also, a chunk of muscle and skin had been torn out of his forearm by shrapnel. In another moment, the pain would hit him hard. Still, he counted himself lucky. Just how lucky, he was about to discover.

As he reached an intersection, a blur suddenly lurched up from a hole in the floor. A terminator endoskeleton. Its steel fist jackhammered his ribs and he flew back against the wall. The grenade-launcher skidded down the corridor, out of reach. The boy gasped for breath, realizing by the pain each one cost that at least one of his ribs must be broken. The cyborg rose up and stood over him, swinging its battle-rifle barrel toward Cowan's head.

This time there was no escape. The black cavity of the Terminator's barrel welled to an infinity of endings. This was death, then, the boy thought. The machine would blast his head off in the next second, and then . . . but strangely, time seemed to slow to a crawl. Cowan looked into the Terminator's "face." Its lipless mouth revealed enameled titanium teeth set in a perpetually grinning jaw. The gleaming skull seemed to be laughing at him. A high-tech reaper, come for his soul. The glowing red demon eyes were fixed on him. It couldn't miss. And yet, *it did not fire.* The boy took a breath, amazed he was still capable of it. It seemed now as if many seconds had passed. Then, he realized the Terminator *was not moving.* In fact, the thing's eyes *had gone dark.*

The boy painfully pulled himself up the wall to stand on shaky legs. The cyborg was still staring at the space where he had been sitting. Hesitantly, he stepped up to the chrome skeleton and pushed against its chest. The Terminator teetered, then toppled on its side with a loud thud.

A guerrilla appeared at the end of the corridor.

Cowan looked up. It was Bryn. They had fought together many times. But he could not say anything, only gape, his senses pounded by shock and the pulsing ache of his wounds. She cautiously approached and looked down at the inert endoskeleton.

He finally managed to croak a few words. "It just . . . stopped."

"They never just stop," Bryn said. She put his arm around her neck and gingerly led him back toward what was left of their squad. A few minutes later they would both discover the reason why the endoskeleton in the corridor had indeed just stopped.

In a makeshift gun emplacement at the edge of battle, a man too important to be risked in the line of fire watched the distant combat with field glasses, standing still as a statue among running, shouting techs and officers. He wore the uniform of a guerrilla general. Sadly, he lowered the binoculars, revealing forty-five-year old features made severe by constant stress. The left side of his face was heavily scarred. Yet he was still an impressive man, forged in the furnace of a lifetime of war. The name stitched on his jacket read CONNOR.

Behind him he could hear the scratchy chatter of radio traffic, the voices hyped with the adrenaline rush of combat, calling in position reports. They were coming in from other battlefields, as well, from other cities, other states: San Francisco, Seattle, Albuquerque, Chicago (New York had been overrun by the machines years ago). The voices spoke in many languages; Spanish, Swahili, Japanese and English. This was the first truly international army. The volunteers had come from countries least damaged by the war. They came together to survive.

Today, there were battles against Skynet's forces all over the world. But the two most important ones were happening in Cheyenne Mountain, Colorado, where Skynet's mainframe was housed. The other was here, in the Westside, where the real prize was; the site of Skynet's second largest and most guarded underground complexes. The vast conclave was encircled with a lethal concentration of defensive machines. In the last two days, human casualties had been very high. But John knew that eventually they would win. They now had the firepower, and more importantly, the will. But the loss of lives tore at him. So many young men and women desperately needed to start over after the blood of battle had dried. To see the soldiers who had fought alongside him for years slaughtered by the metal motherfuckers so near the end of the battle was, to John, infuriating. It wasn't a fair universe, nor a kind one. If there was a God, his love and forty-five cents would buy you coffee. No one seemed to be at the cosmic controls anymore. It was every man for himself, until Skynet became alive and filled the void left by a seemingly disinterested God. Its vision was very controlled. The ultimate dream of man, carried out by one of man's lowliest tools: eliminate evil men. But there was a touch of evil in all men, and Skynet was having trouble separating the worst of them out. So the totality of humanity, with all its biologic messiness, wasn't wanted. And to this machine-god, forgiveness just did not compute. Only cold retribution for the sins of the past.

John ached to end this war and start over, to correct the mistakes of history. But, like other generals from other wars in the past, he wasn't sure what kind of world he was making possible. He had time only to strategize this war. It hadn't occurred to him until recently that there would be a life after the conflict. It seemed so far away, the horizon of it always out of reach, no matter how long you traveled toward it.

Something was happening over on Pico and Robertson. John raised the glasses again and zoomed in on an aerial HK, suddenly spinning out of control like a Frisbee, slicing down to burst into a massive fireball that lit up the ravaged terrain all around. Somebody had just made a good kill. If they survived, John would decorate them. But two other HKs suddenly tilted at a crazy angle and dropped to the earth, without being hit. In the bright flare of the flaming debris, John saw a bizarre sight; a squad of endoskeletons, standing nearby, oddly frozen in place like toy soldiers, their metal surfaces burnished by the blaze. The flashing of beam weapons lessened, then, miraculously, ceased altogether.

John's forces were cautiously emerging from their emplacements and approaching the frozen machines. Another aerial HK, about a mile beyond the battle, hurled down to a fiery death. John was astonished to see the sky suddenly clear of gunships. He scanned the battlefield. *None of Skynet's machines were moving!*

And then an awesome thing happened.

It grew quiet.

Now all John could hear was the high wail of the wind. No guns. No explosions. No turbine whine or grumbling engines. Even the radios behind him fell silent, until one voice spoke out, the awed emotion detectable under howling static: "This is New Orleans Division. They're not moving! They . . . just stopped!" Another voice came on the line, more excited: "This is Chicago. HK₃ are falling . . . my God, they all crashed—" Another voice overlapped: "—San Francisco reporting. I don't get it. The terminators are just standing there—" Another: "—nothing came out to stop us. We're inside the factory now and—" Then all the radios from all the battlefields began to babble the news. But John already knew what they would say. Had known it for most of his life.

Lieutenant Fuentes approached and stood alongside John, gaping at the scene beyond. He spoke so softly John almost couldn't hear. "Just got confirmation. . . . Skynet has been penetrated and destroyed."

The two men looked at each other, their faces blank with shock and the awareness of how inane the monumental can seem. "The war is over, John. We won."

Fuentes took a breath, for him, seemingly the first in a century. With the oxygen came emotion. It began as a trickle, then built up pressure until it tore through the restraints of duty and burst out his lungs as a triumphal shout. It was a shout that in moments would grow to a thundering cheer, repeated long into the day and the following night, as the victors raised their eyes to a sky devoid of machines, and knew that the long war was indeed . . . over.

For now, all John Connor could do was sink to his knees. But there was still more work to do . . . a lot more, before he could really take a breath. And it would begin in the belly of the Beast. He grabbed a radio mike and began to give orders. Orders he had been born to give . . .

THE MINISTRY OF FATE

They didn't just walk in. Although the mainframe computer in Colorado had been destroyed, there were hundreds of autonomous terminators not under direct link command, still free to seek out human targets, and eliminate them. Their internal power cells would keep them lethal for over a hundred years. John realized that the casualties would continue to mount, even after the war was won, until all the terminators could be eliminated.

They had to fight their way past a dozen wild card terminators into the complex. Three hours later, the place had been cleared out. John's handpicked sapper squad formed a protective phalanx for John and the tech team as they rode a huge freight elevator deep into the bowels of the building. They were tiny figures on the open platform that descended at a forty-five-degree angle into the concrete-lined tunnel, rapidly becoming a speck in the overscaled industrial landscape.

Minutes later, the lift clanked to a stop and the men stepped into a bizarre world designed by machines for machines. The architecture was alien, without aesthetics, without even such human basics as doorknobs and lights. And yet, John was thinking with a thrumming in his chest, I've been here in my dreams many times. All my life I've tried to imagine what it would look like. Now I'm actually here. . . .

John led the uneasy men past statuelike terminators, deactivated like the ones on the surface. Along the way they passed techs moving through the endless corridors with awe, stationing themselves like parasites in the guts of the now lifeless Skynet. When they passed John's team, they would grin as they saluted him, even though John wore no insignia of rank. Everyone knew him. He was one of the few commanders in all the wars that have been fought who truly earned his troops' respect as a man. When most of the survivors were cringing in the shadow of the colossus called Skynet, John Conner had stepped into the light with a pincer grenade and blasted the tracks of a rolling HK. Instead of darting back undercover, he stood in the flaming wreckage and siphoned off the unburned fuel to power his armored car. There was nothing John had asked his army to do that he had not already done, and more importantly, he knew with uncanny accuracy *what had to be done.* This created a loyalty and trust that no machine could ever inspire.

Even so, John was a hard man to get to know. Fuentes, who had fought alongside his commander for the last five years, felt the distance between them. They were comrades who could trust their lives to one another, but they were not exactly friends. John had been more charismatic and accessible years before, when he was first forming the army, building a relationship between himself and a growing legion of strangers. One got the impression his friendliness was part of the recruitment technique: heartfelt, but expressed more out of necessity than desire. But when he was in his mid-twenties, a personal tragedy caused him to withdraw even more into that gray prison of responsibility that had always been his. Fuentes had brought him the news. John had been crouched in a blasthole crater, giving final instructions to a squad of soldiers still in their teens. They were bright, eager, and dispensable. They would all later die in a diversionary battle that would lead to a major victory. As he watched them snake out into the moonlit ruins, Fuentes turned to John, struggling to remain calm as he gave his nightly field report. The supply convoy from Mexico had been ambushed by a squad of HKs. There were no survivors.

John had listened, then only nodded. After all, this was simply one more defeat in a war filled with them. The supplies were important, but there were backups the army could use. And John had steeled himself to loss over the years. People were always dying in this war. Like the squad of teenagers John had just sent out on patrol. Even the horror of death could become routine if it happened often enough.

All this Fuentes knew. And in normal circumstances, Fuentes would not have found John's reaction strange. When he wasn't needed, the general would often go off by himself to brood, especially after he had ordered hundreds of men into hopeless battle, just to buy time to build the army. But he would get over it quickly, eager to continue the struggle, driven by a certainty of their eventual victory. The loss of lives was necessary to achieve that victory. But Fuentes also knew what John knew. . . .

Sarah Connor had been leading that convoy. She had been ordered out of the action, but Sarah went her own way, and few people had the rank or the balls to stop her. Even John was in awe of her. Not only was she a superb combat soldier, she was also an expert tactician. But sooner or later, even the best soldier can be overwhelmed by superior firepower. As in this case.

So Fuentes found it strange that John simply nodded when he told him his mother was dead. When the news became common knowledge, people who only knew and respected her by reputation would be weeping. Sarah Connor had been almost as legendary as her son.

But all John did was thank Fuentes for the information and stride off.

Later, Fuentes walked in on John, bent over his cot, sobbing. He quietly backed away, not wanting to intrude. It was the only time he had seen the great man cry. Since that time, John had never talked about his mother. It seemed his soul had seeped into the threads of his uniform.

Fuentes loved John Connor, but he was not all that comfortable with him, and he certainly did not want to *be* him. When Fuentes looked closely, he could still see sadness in John's eyes, as if the price of victory were too high, the wounds suffered far too deep to easily heal. In fact, the deeper they went into this place, the more depressed John seemed to get, as if there were something down here that he dreaded. Something terrible still to be done.

They came to a huge open vaultlike door. There was a bustle of hurried activity inside the vast chamber beyond. It was the size of a high-school gym, comprised totally of incomprehensible machine surfaces. Techs knelt like priests in prayer before the altar of the machine-god, inserting probes into the wafer-circuit terminals, stacked like skyscrapers of thought throughout the enclosure. They were furiously downloading systems files, and crossreffing the data with what they had already decoded, double-checking information John had already given them, had, oddly, already known.

John and his men approached a busy hive of techs who had pulled up several floor panels and tapped directly into the cabling of the machine, using portable terminals that they had wheeled in. Many of the soldiers in this war against machines were technical specialists; child-geniuses who had gotten their education in bombed-out libraries and on the battlefield. Men who not only had to think on their feet, but as they ran. John had gathered the best of them to break Skynet's machine code, read its thoughts and plans, and analyze its data. Fighting fire with fire, John thought as he proudly watched his techs moving with rapid assurance. It was one of the main reasons why they had won.

Tech Specialist Winn looked up. He was a quivering reed of a man, who had shown enormous stamina and intelligence in supervising the chrono team. He ner-

vously greeted John and told him they were almost
ready.

"Is he here?" John asked, a catch in his voice. Winn
nodded and indicated a group of techs at the far end of
the room. A young soldier stood among them, being ad-
ministered to as if he were royalty. John closed his eyes
and held his emotions in check. It was Kyle Reese.

John started walking toward him, feeling a resonant
sense of *déjà vu*. His body seemed to become insubstan-
tial, floating above a pool of grave sadness. He had
yearned for this day of sweet victory and dreaded it for
the bitter sting of what he was about to do, *had to do*.

Kyle was finishing stripping off his battle uniform.
The techs started smearing his body with a sour-
smelling jelly.

Fuentes wrinkled his nose. "What's that?" Winn
turned to him and answered. "Conductance jelly, so the
time-field will follow his outline."

Fuentes didn't know what the hell that meant, but
then he didn't know what the hell this whole time-
travel angle was about. John had tried to tell him, but
it sounded like tech babble to him. Fuentes hated being
here, surrounded by the machine he had fought so hard
to defeat. He hated all machines, except the simple device slung over his shoulder. Weapons were the only
good machines. He knew his hate was irrational. John
had patiently told him machines were neither good nor
bad. People were. Skynet had been built by men. Men
who had been too terrified of each other to trust themselves with their own weapons. So they built a tool that
simply carried out *their* paranoia to the nth degree.

Okay. Fuentes still wished they could get out of here.
Up top his squad was celebrating with homemade brew
and the new cache of canned food they'd liberated a few
days ago. His woman was probably up there now, too,
waiting for him. John had said there was more work to
do. Fuentes agreed. But it wasn't down here. It was up
there, beside the warm fires of victory. But Fuentes,
more than any man, had seen John's wisdom before,
and struggled to endure a growing claustrophobia.

John was watching Kyle's face. It was so strange, to

look into the smooth face of a younger man, and know that he was your father. Kyle was breathing deep and slow, showing supreme control, prepping for something that could never be prepared for: time travel. Only John could sense the utter terror behind Kyle's grim expression as a med tech hyped his arm, pumping his veins full of synthetic adrenaline, making his muscles pop out, combat-ready.

The techs moved aside and suddenly John was beside Kyle. The two men looked at one another. They weren't friends. If there had been more time, perhaps they would have been. But John had only seen Kyle Reese five times before this day. And it wasn't until the second time they had met that John heard his name and realized with a shock who Kyle really was. He hadn't said anything then. Although John's mother had told him about his father, and what was destined to be, he hadn't really wanted to accept it. In fact, for a time, John had rebelled against the whole idea of "his destiny." Until the war came, that is, and the machines rose, and everything Sarah Connor had told him came heartbreakingly to pass, each horrifying event like the tick of a cosmic clock pounding out history with blind cruelty. And now the clock was beating out what was for him the most cruel tick of them all. There was so much he wanted to say, but if he said one thing, he would have to say the rest, and there was no time. No purpose. It would only confuse Kyle when the soldier needed to be most focused. It was Kyle who finally spoke, awed in the presence of John Connor.

"Did you know I'd be the one who'd volunteer?"

John surprisingly nodded, forcing a smile of encouragement. "I've always known. Sarah told me."

The young soldier's eyes went wide with astonishment. Kyle began to realize why his name was selected from the list over that of other, more experienced volunteers. Why when he first told John his name he had reacted so strangely. Kyle was somehow a part of a history that hadn't happened yet, and John had always known. Maybe that was why he was moved to John's unit. Why he was kept so close. And yet so distant.

Once, Kyle had found himself beside his commander during an ambush. Impulsively, it seemed, John had reached into his bloodstained field jacket and handed over the faded, wrinkled picture of his mother. Then, without a word, he had lurched up to rally his troops. Kyle remembered gaping at the small, stained picture of Sarah Connor. Although many men carried her picture into battle to inspire them, they were cheap copies. *This was the original.* It was quite an honor to be singled out for, and a strange gesture from his commander, who never seemed to single anyone out, unless it was to decorate them. Since that time, John had hardly spoken to him, except to issue orders. It was almost as if he were avoiding him, yet trying to keep him close. For what? This? It must be. A fierce pride and excitement surged through Kyle.

John asked, "They briefed you?"

"Yes, sir. I know what to do, but I'm not sure why."

John said, "You know what you need to accomplish the mission."

Kyle stiffened. "Yes, sir."

Then John did something that surprised Fuentes with its familiarity. He reached out, grabbing Kyle's shoulders in a firm, comradely grip. Kyle was all but overwhelmed.

John added, "And you will succeed." It was said with such a terrible certainty. John seemed to collect himself and continued in a more dutiful tone. "Provided you do not let your guard down one single moment."

"I won't, sir."

"Did you memorize what I told you to tell her?"

By the subtle shift in his commander's voice, Kyle understood this was very personal, and extremely important. He took a breath, and answered. "Every word, sir."

John closed his eyes and turned away. Kyle caught a profound look of sadness overwhelming his commander's smile. It wasn't a look he was meant to see. It troubled him, but then Winn approached and said, "Ready, Sergeant?"

Kyle nodded and was led past several makeshift

armored barriers that had been carried into the time-displacement generator's two enormous chrome rings, one inside the other, suspended over a circular hole in the center of the floor, freely floating on humming magnetic fields. Kyle hesitantly stepped onto the first ring. It bobbed slightly under his weight. Then he carefully shifted onto the inner ring and looked into the hole, suppressing a gasp. Below him lay a vast, echoing darkness. He looked back at John. His messiah was waiting for him to step into the bottomless pit.

John said, "Sometimes you have to put your faith in the machine."

Kyle would put his faith in only one thing: his commander. The nineteen-year-old warrior inhaled, then stepped into open space. Everyone tensed.

Astonished, Kyle looked down. He was walking on air, buoyed by an unseen field of force in the middle of the rings. Winn turned to the techs and ordered them to begin the time-displacement sequence. Several of them typed in coordinates on their portable terminals.

Slowly, the rings began to rotate around each other on different axes like some complex gyroscope. The humming of the force fields increased and their tones began overlapping, creating weird harmonies.

They all moved back as the floor opened like wedges in a pie that begin to pull back from the center. The rings spun faster, suspended in space in the middle of the receding floor wedges. Then, they began to descend, carrying Kyle with them. His eyes found John's again and locked on them as he lowered into an unbelievably vast circular space . . . the time-field generator. John approached the edge and watched him go, until Kyle was a tiny figure. The rings were spinning so rapidly now they almost disappeared, becoming a sphere of whirling steel. The humming harmonies rose several pitches, howling out an unintentional melody that raised the hackles. Small electrical sparks started spitting out from the generator walls. John leaned over the edge, seemingly mesmerized. With a stab of alarm, Fuentes reached for him before he lost his center of gravity and toppled into the time machine.

Lightning burst up from the generator and streaked across the room above the heads of the techs. Winn ducked, smelling the strong odor of ozone. A huge charge of energy was building up. Everyone fell back behind the makeshift barriers and hastily put on their safety gogglesd. This was going to be big. And Kyle Reese was right in the middle of it.

The chamber below had become a hell of energy with the young soldier at its center. The drone and crackle of the generator built to a pounding thunder. John's heart was racing as fast as the rings. There was a ripping scream, as if a god were being disemboweled. The room filled with hot-white light. Without the goggles, they would have been blinded.

When the glare faded, the floating rings were empty. They slowed to a stop, seared and smoking. In that endless instant of time displacement, Kyle Reese had vanished. Oddly, in its place was a sphere filled with whirling debris: crushed beer cans, faded yellow newspapers, dated 1984, and a slice of a dumpster, filled with garbage from that year.

Fuentes slowly lowered his goggles. *"Madre di Dios!"* Winn cautiously approached the edge and looked down. Sparks sputtered and then died out. The debris settled. "It works!" Winn said, excitedly, then continued, "That's space from 1984. It's been displaced, swapped with the space from now."

John stepped up, removing his goggles, his eyes still readjusting to the lack of light. Fuentes asked him, "Now what happens to Sergeant Reese, sir? I mean, what *did* happen?"

John's gaze seemed far away from this time and place.

"He accomplishes his mission and . . . dies."

Fuentes nodded. "He is a good soldier."

There was a dark, despairing expression in his eyes as John solemnly added, "And my father."

Fuentes stared in amazement. Now he knew what John had been dreading down here. And why John had not been able to fully appreciate their victory. The price was too high.

John turned from the smoking chamber, seeming years older as his features drained, sagging. He put a hand on Fuentes shoulder for support.

Fuentes realized this was the first time he had seen his commander lose strength. He'd seen him tired, lonely, and haunted before, but not like this. He shouted an order in Spanish to the sapper team behind him. "Set your charges. Let's blow this place back to hell."

John struggled to recover, shaking his head. "Not yet. There's one more thing we have to do." He turned to Winn. "What's your reading?"

Winn glanced down at a palm-sized power meter dangling off his belt. Looked up at John with a puzzled expression. "Just like you said."

John took a deep breath, feeling the wheels of destiny grinding near. Then, mustering his courage, he abruptly strode out of the room. Winn started to follow. Fuentes frowned in confusion and hurried after, grabbing the tech's arm. "What reading? What are you talking about?"

Winn indicated the meter. "This is the energy signal put out by the time displacement. I recorded two other identical pulses as we were fighting our way in here."

"Two?"

Winn impatiently continued walking. Fuentes stayed with him. "What are you talking about?"

"The first must have been the Terminator going through to 1984."

Fuentes was still confused. "Yeah?"

Winn careened into the corridor and quickened his pace to catch up to his commander. Fuentes dogged the tech. "What was the second?"

"Another terminator, probably."

John's footsteps clacked on the hard floor as he strode along the vaulted tunnel, followed by Fuentes and Winn. They passed numerous galleries filled with hulking machines, now cold and motionless; a vast library of strategic technology Skynet had designed and built. Even John's vaunted techs would need years to study it all. And once having deciphered the machines' functions, John would have to decide whether to destroy them, or trust that the new society rising up from the ashes could use them responsibly. He had no information to guide him in this, no memories of the past resonating with his future. On what happens after today, John didn't have a clue. But as he walked up to a massive steel door, the memories of the past flooded into his present. John knew he was looking at the door of fate. He knew that behind it he would find what he was looking for: the final answer to the question that had haunted him all his life. Was all of it true? Even to the last?

Winn approached the door and patched into a control plate with a small probe. He punched out the coded sequence he had recovered from a damaged HK's internal terminal, then hurriedly stepped away. Locking bolts were electronically slammed back and the door cracked open, accompanied by the hiss-whoosh of a vacuum being filled.

John stepped across the threshold, aimed his combat light at the far side of the room, then gaped. Fuentes and Winn came up behind him, adding their lights to his.

They were looking at a massive machine press that filled floor to ceiling. Still-warm feeder pipes emerged from the walls and centered on the steaming press, forming a hub, or a web. They walked underneath them to the place where the two twenty-ton plates met and shined their lights into the small gap, large enough for a man to step into. There was an indentation in the shape of a man. John squinted at something gleaming at the edge of a small round opening positioned where the neck would be. He reached out with the tip of his rifle. The gleaming drop of what looked like mercury flowed effortlessly onto the metal of the barrel and seemed to *soak in,* disappearing. John pulled the barrel out so the others could aim their lights on the end.

Fuentes scowled. "Where'd it go?"

Winn was studying the tip of John's gun as if he were a man about to see God. He could discern a subtle lump, maybe only two millimeters higher than the original surface of the barrel, circumnavigating the barrel's circumference.

"It's right there," Winn said.

"Where?"

"It appears to have bonded to the barrel metal and mimicked it almost flawlessly. Amazing . . . "

The last fragment of uncertainty in John's mind was blasted away. It was time to make the last move in the chess game he had been unwillingly playing with Skynet for fifteen long years. He knew a lot of what would happen, but past a certain point in his memory, he wasn't sure of the outcome. A knife embedded in a weathered picnic table with the words NO FATE carved in them was the dividing line between what he knew had happened and what might happen. His very existence could be erased. Or maybe everything would still turn out the same. Or . . . what? For the first time since he was a boy, John no longer had the answers. With growing apprehension, he handed the rifle to Winn, took the probe, and abruptly walked across the room to a heavy steel door covered with a thin sheet of melting ice. John punched out the code and waited. . . .

Ice shattered like glass as the door broke its seal and opened inward. He started to enter when Fuentes stepped in his way, rifle at the ready, and moved inside ahead of him, scanning the room for potential attack. His breath formed in front of him. They were in a cold-storage room. Fuentes gasped as his beam fell on a row of naked bodies, hanging on steel racks suspended from the ceiling.

John panned his light around. There were hundreds of men and women, in rows of ten. Within each row, the bodies were *absolutely identical.*

"Terminators," Fuentes whispered, his hand on his rifle butt, uneasy.

John quickly walked along the synthetic bodies to the end of a row and hesitated. He scanned the faces. No, not here. Then he gazed down the other row. All the same. Strange to him. Then . . . he turned to another row and stopped. It was filled with identical,

familiar faces. The broad, brutally handsome features
sent a shock of recognition through John.

It was he.

From so long ago and so far away, even before Judgment Day, when the world was halfway sane and
bright with color. John's eyes were burning with emotion. In a way it was almost as bad as with Kyle.

Fuentes stepped up, his gravelly voice snapping John
back to the Here and Now. "I'm gonna enjoy pushing
the button on this place." Then he noticed John's expression. "What is it?"

John faced the nearest familiar terminator. Its eyes
were closed. But it was not sleeping. It was waiting.
Then he turned to Fuentes with a cryptic answer spoken in a hoarse whisper, the words coming from a man
weary to the soul. "The only problem with time travel
is . . . it isn't over, even when it's over."

John hurried back to Winn, standing anxiously by
the doorway. Fuentes watched John point to one of the
racked terminators and chatter a lot of tech babble for
a few minutes, obviously agitated. None of this made
any sense. They'd won.

Hadn't they?

LIGHTSTORM

 ana Shorte had been fantasizing about his wife's younger sister. This was an extremely dangerous thing to do, not only because of where thoughts like that might lead, but because he was doing it while driving a big Kenworth semi-tractor-trailer on a treacherous downgrade in suddenly thickening fog. He was teasing himself with what he imagined Denise's breasts looked like when the red glare of a car's rear lights abruptly appeared out of the gathering mist. He slammed his foot against his brake pedal. The hydraulics squealed and hissed, locking up. The cab rapidly bounced along the road, the tires ripped off the asphalt by the unwieldy momentum made by thirty-eight tons of frozen squash in the refrigerated trailers. He ground metal downshifting the lumbering truck, wincing as the load shifted his way. In the explosion of adrenaline rush, he saw a clear vision of his truck jackknifing around like an angry scorpion, whipping the cab with tremendous force through the siderail and down the embankment of the 14 freeway to be dashed on the Vasquez Rocks below.

But tonight he was lucky. The tires hit a dry spot and grabbed once and for all. The truck shuddered and swerved, but held the road, backing off from the slow-moving car at the last moment.

Dana gripped the wheel, his breath coming in ragged jags. He decided that this had been a warning from God. Stop thinking adultery with your wife's eighteen-year-old sister or . . .

He sighed as he blearily spotted the Sierra Highway exit sign looming out of the fog like a welcome beacon. His foot gently touched the brake a few times, getting the monster vehicle to settle, then he drove down the ramp and into the parking lot of The Corral.

There were few spaces left in the all-night truck stop. The uncharacteristic summer fog had driven the nightly herd of truckers off the Antelope Freeway and into the worn, patched booths.

Dana rolled his rig up alongside another like his, then hopped down, bone-weary and butt-sore. He slammed the door and sauntered across the lot toward the garishly lit bar/restaurant, loosening his shirt, which was damp with perspiration. Jesus, he thought as he glanced at the bank of fog rolling across the highway, you'd think this stuff would cool things down. But it only made it more difficult to breathe. The muggy air seemed to grow heavier as he reached the entrance. It was suffocating and strangely charged, as if it were going to rain. Indeed, as he opened the door, he thought he saw a flash of lightning reflected in the glass. He looked up at the sky. All he could see was the mist, frontlit green and orange by the neon sign above the door. He shrugged and went inside.

If he had stayed a moment longer and looked back toward his truck instead of at the sky, he would have seen another flash of lightning, arcing between his rig and the one parked alongside. He might have thought it was Saint Elmo's fire. He would have been wrong.

The streetlights flickered and winked out. The fog began to flow back toward the trucks, forming a whirlpool of turbulence between them. Wild fingers of blue-white energy furiously danced in the steel canyon formed by the trailers, crackling like crumpled shrink-wrap. A dust-devil whirled up from the asphalt, sucking papers and cigarette butts into the churning air. A low hum rose to a howling peak, as if an invisible transistor radio were scanning static, searching for stations. Then it found one.

Here.

The strange lightning whirled into a roiling sphere of energy, shot through with racing currents. The side mirrors on both trucks bent outward and then shattered. A flash like a thousand Instamatic cameras going off. Then the static abruptly ended in a loud crack, like a muted cherry bomb. The light rapidly faded and a cloud of vapor blew away, revealing something standing there wher a moment before there had been nothing.

It was a naked man.

His massive body was covered with white ash that fell away like fine flour as he rose up and flexed his perfectly sculpted torso. His military-short hair was smoking. His face was devoid of emotion. His eyes cobalt-blue, alive yet dead, taking in but not giving out.

The arms were a study in powerful symmetry, the angry curve of the biceps narrowing with precision at the elbow, then expanding with mathematical balance into corded forearms that flowed into almost gracefully thin wrists.

The Promethean man inhaled, swelling the prodigious chest, tentatively tasting the atmosphere. He noted the high moisture content with no curiosity. It was a bald fact that had no meaning until it was joined with a dozen others, all of which gave a rapid overview of place and time.

Behind him, a curved slice had been cut out of the rear railer of a truck, the edges touched by the ball of time displacement still glowing from the charge. The arc continued to the asphalt, forming a circular crater under his feet. The man was standing in the middle of what had been an energy ball. He stepped from between the trucks to scan the parking lot, pausing to note three polished chopped Harley Davison motorcycles near the neon-lit entrance, precariously leaning on chrome kickstands, their extended front forks like metal sculptures of dogs stretching out their front paws. Muffled music from a jukebox thudded away. The man glanced through the windows. There were people inside, laughing and arguing and loudly ordering drinks and food. The man turned and strode toward the entrance. He knew he would find the owner of one of the cycles inside.

Dana had just settled into a booth. The place looked like hell, but at least the food was okay. Next to him two burly truckers were hunched over their chili-sizes, CAT hats pushed back on their heads. Three scruffy, jean-jacketed bikers played a game of pool in the back, their Miller empties lining the table's rail. The dive's owner, Lloyd, was a fat, aging bear in a soiled apron, who stood grumpily behind the bar. On the far side of the room, an impromptu card game was going on among a gaggle of truckers, waiting out the fog.

Dana glanced up as the waitress came over. He instantly scanned her features with interest. Too much makeup. Maybe five foot three or four. Probably twenty pounds overweight. But she wore most of it up front, and well.

Dana liked that. A lot. And she was chewing gum with that dazed, only half-conscious expression that indicated she probably watched a lot a TV sitcoms. Easy prey.

His kind of woman.

If he didn't already have a woman. Guilt welled up and he tried to suppress his growing lust with thoughts of his wife. Carla was a religious woman who took her marriage vows very seriously. Especially the part about being faithful. If she found out he had committed adultery, it would kill her. But he'd been married to Carla for over six years. He knew every nook and cranny of her body, and worse, every gesture and word she uttered in bed. Making love to Carla had become like watching an "I Love Lucy" rerun for the twentieth time. Comfortably boring. Lately the thought of new terrain obsessed him at every turn. He hadn't been this horny since he was in high school. He was painfully aware that half the human race was female. Strange females. Delightfully strange females. Like this waitress . . .

Her nameplate read Claudia. He said hello as she handed him the soiled menu. She returned his smile with a saucy wink and trundled off to the kitchen. Dana rested his eyes on her behind as it rolled and undulated away, rocking her apron ties as if they were a cradle. He sighed, letting his mind play with that image. And running alongside the sensual flow of his private porno film was the border of his conscience, straining to dam up the Machiavellian plots he was furiously hatching to hide the hoped-for adultery from Carla. He was so engrossed with the fruits of his mental labors that he didn't notice the front door open and the big naked guy stroll in.

Everyone else did, however, as the man calmly strode across the room, his emotionless gaze passing over the customers with seemingly little interest.

What the "man" saw was a forty-thousand bit digitized display of the room, overlaid with alpha-numeric readouts that changed faster than the human eye could follow. The faces of the gaping truckers, the wide-eyed owner, and the awestruck waitress, were electronically fragmented and each sector analyzed to interpret their emotional state and anticipate possible hostile behavior.

No one was moving, except one of the bikers. Robert Pantelli ate bad times for breakfast and spat out trouble for lunch. Most things in life didn't surprise him. What he was looking at now did. He stopped puffing on his foul-smelling cigar and slowly lowered it, a dark smile spreading across his wet lips.

The nude man saw a pulsing electronic outline forming around Robert's body. Thousands of estimated measurements rapidly flashed on and off in the man's internal visual scanner. The biker's clothing had been instantly analyzed and referenced with contemporary motorcycle riding gear. . . .

To Robert, this had taken perhaps two seconds. He showed his filthy teeth. A few in front were missing. His speech was slurred by alcohol. "This guy knows how to beat the heat."

Nervous laughter from his two friends.

The man showed no discernable reaction for a moment, then spoke in a bland, neutral tone that indicated no particular emotion. "I need your clothes, your boots, and your motorcycle."

Robert's eyes narrowed, then glanced at his buddies. They watched him expectantly. Robert decided to give them a show. He took a long draw on his stogie, getting the tip cherry-red hot, then turned back to the stranger. "You forgot to say please."

More laughter from Robert's friends, louder and more relaxed this time. They sensed this guy wouldn't fight. Despite his imposing physique, he stupidly just stood there, a blank look on his puss. He must have been some kind of looney.

Robert didn't like loonies. They reminded him of his asshole father. And besides, he wanted to get back to his game. So he lifted his cigar and ground it out on the stranger's chest. There was a soft sizzling, like bacon crackling on a griddle. Then a thick silence.

It shook Dana out of his reverie and he glanced over, registering the sight of the naked customer with a gasp. There was a smoking charred hole in the man's chest. And yet he was no showing the slightest indication of pain. What happened next went so fast, Dana almost didn't think it really happened. Almost.

The nude man calmly reached out and clutched Robert by his meaty upper arm in a powerful hydraulic grip. The biker felt the impossibly strong fingers crushing his flesh like steel pincers and screamed at the top of his lungs.

One of Robert's friend hefted his pool cue by the narrow end as if it were a Louisville Slugger. The heavy end whistled in a powerful swing and cracked in two across the back of the stranger's head.

Incredibly, the nude man seemed not to notice. Didn't even blink. Without releasing his grip on Robert, the stranger snapped his arm straight back and grabbed Pool Cue by the front of his jacket, then abruptly launched the heavyset biker through the nearest window. Glass erupted as he arced onto the pavement outside, hitting it like a rack of beef.

Next, the stranger lifted all of Robert's two hundred and thirty pounds clear over the bar, through the serving window, into the kitchen, where he landed on the big flat grill. Steam squealed up as the hot metal flash-seared his skin. Robert howled, flopping and jerking until he rolled to the floor in a smoking heap.

The third biker whipped out a knife with a six-inch blade and slashed at the big man's face. But the stranger clutched the slashing metal with his bare hand, and gripping it by the razor-sharp edge, jerked it from the biker's hand. He flipped it in a rapid blur, then snatched it out of the air by the handle. Whirling like a fan blade, the stranger slammed the biker facedown over the bar, then brought the knife whistling down, pinning the biker's shoulder to the bartop with his own steel.

Dana had blinked three times and it was over. Like the other customers, he was so stunned he simply sat there and watched as the naked man walked around the bar, pushed past Lloyd, and walked into the kitchen. It wasn't only that it happened so fast. Or that the perpetrator was obviously a lot more vicious than three obviously very vicious men. That was certainly enough to give everyone pause. But it was the man's *attitude* that made everyone keep their seats. There was no reasonable motive, no acceptable explanation, no frame of reference for the cool violence of the nude stranger. Which meant he was surely crazy. And someone that vicious and that crazy just wasn't meant to be fucked with.

The Mexican cook was thinking along the same lines

as he stumbled away from the stranger, who walked toward Robert, busy cursing in pain on the floor. The biker looked up as the shadow fell across him. Growling like a wounded animal, he struggled to get out his military issue Colt .45 auto pistol tucked under his charred leather jacket. But his deep-fried fingers couldn't pull the trigger. The stranger's arm lashed out and he grabbed the gun, like a man swatting a fly.

Terror flushed through Robert as he watched the man raise the weapon. But instead of pointing it at him, the naked man carefully examined the pistol.

For an electronically stretched instant, the man analyzed its caliber and operating condition. The idea of aiming at the biker on the floor didn't occur to the man as an option. The target was temporarily disabled. Shooting him would have been an unnecessary use of force. All the man wanted was what he had initially demanded. He turned his emotionless eyes on Robert.

The biker shuddered, all his brain cells taxed trying to decide what to do next. Further combat seemed out of the question. He didn't have the tools anymore. The crazy nudist had easily taken the gun. Robert had no choice now. He slowly reached into his pocket, wincing with the pain this caused his already swelling hand, and removed his motorcycle keys. He slid them across the floor to the looney's foot. Then, grunting from a shooting pain caused by a fractured rib, Robert started getting out of his jacket.

Dana was edging toward the front door when the stranger came out of the kitchen, now wearing the biker's black leather jacket, leather riding pants, and heavy cleated boots. He purposefully marched toward the crowd gathered around the moaning biker still pinned to the pool table. They hastily parted like the Red Sea as he walked up. Without slowing his stride, he jerked the knife out. The wild-eyed, bleeding man slumped to the floor as the stranger continued toward the door. Nobody dared to stand in his way. As he passed, Dana, trembling with fear, blurted, "Evening."

The man turned—no, more like swiveled—his head. His lifeless eyes focused on Dana for a microsecond that seemed to last a lifetime. Then he faced the door and pushed through, letting it slam as he went outside.

Dana shuddered and wiped his moist forehead with the back of his hand. *Christ, that was close!*

He shakily went to the window. Everyone else silently joined Dana, watching in fearful silence as the stranger crossed the lot to the parked Harleys. Everyone but Lloyd, who glanced outside, then down at the wounded biker on the floor. A growing pool of blood was staining the carpet. Lloyd threw his apron down and ran behind the bar, reaching for something in a hidden cubbyhole.

Outside, the stranger approached the three cycles. Slipping the .45 in his belt, he inserted the key in the first. It didn't fit. Without concern or hesitation, the man simply turned to the next. The key went in. He swung one leg over the massive Harley 1380 cc Fat Boy, with a customized saddle and cherry black paint-job. Any normal, knowledgeable motorcycle man would have gladly paid good money for a cycle like this one. The stranger was knowledgeable in the extreme. In fact, he could recall in an instant a complete technical rundown on every component in the motorcycle. But...he was not a normal man. He picked this kind of vehicle for its potential reliability, flexibility, and speed; all vital requirements for the mission he was about to undertake.

He slipped the dagger in his boot and kicked once, powerfully. The engine instantly caught with a throaty rumble that vibrated the cycle's metal frame. The stranger glanced around, penetrating the rapidly thinning fog, then slammed the heavy iron into gear with a klunk.

Before he could release the clutch handle, Lloyd appeared at the door with a sawed-off 10-gauge Winchester lever-action shotgun. He fired into the air, the blast echoing over the Harley's thunder, and jacked another round in fast, aiming at the stranger's back.

"I can't let you take the man's bike, son. Now get off or I'll blow you off!"

The man turned and considered Lloyd coldly. A second later, he eased the shifter up into neutral. Rocked the cycle onto its kickstand. Swung his leg over and walked calmly toward the owner. Lloyd stood his ground, fury and fear warring for supremacy, as the man walked right up to him, staring straight into the shotgun's muzzle. Lloyd blinked sweat out of his eyes, trying to decide if he was going to kill a man in cold blood over a piece of machinery that wasn't even his. Of course, he couldn't let this guy get away with terrorizing his customers and stealing their property. This was his place. And he needed the loyalty of every one who came through his door. If this nutcake got away with this, he'd lose business. On the other hand—

The stranger's hand blurred out like a striking cobra and suddenly he was holding the shotgun. One smooth, efficient motion, and the muzzle was now inches from Lloyd's face.

Lloyd gaped, slack-jawed. He was just beginning to think about what it would feel like to have his head exploded at close range by a shotgun when the man held the weapon rock steady in one hand and reached out with the other, fingers stretching . . .

Oh shit . . .

But the stranger merely slipped a large pair of sunglasses out of Lloyd's shirt pocket, put them on, then abruptly turned and walked back to the Harley. He shoved the gauge across the handlebars, through the clutch and brake cables, and roared off in a shower of gravel.

Lloyd slumped against the door frame, so happy to still be alive.

Dana watched the motorcycle disappear into the fog and considered how twice in one night he had come close to death. It had to be an omen. He swore to himself then and there that he would never again fantasize about adultery.

Carla was only the first of many innocents whose life would be inadvertently and irrevocably changed by the coming of the second terminator.

The Terminator roared down the freeway, merging south into the 5 Freeway, heading toward Los Angeles. The cold green-white overhead lights intermittently streaked across the chrome of the roaring cycle and flowed over the cyborg's wraparound sunglasses like the tracks of tracer rounds.

THE TWO AUSTINS

In the deep shadows under the Sixth Street Bridge, amid the creative clutter of graffiti, someone had carefully spray-painted in small, precise letters: "History is Dead." This was an extraordinary piece of clairvoyance, considering what was already beginning to happen to the fabric of reality. The words had been spray-painted in a few other locales around the city. Mostly in the East L.A. barrio, near Dodger Stadium, and on a wall outside Griffith Observatory atop the Hollywood Hills.

Nobody noticed.

L.A. was brimful of seers who predicted various scenarios of mass destruction, natural and man-made. It was part of the scenery, along with smog and palm trees. But whoever had painted those three words throughout the city knew. Maybe they didn't know that they knew, but . . .

They knew.

Officer Joe "Lucky" Austin, cruising under the bridge at ten miles an hour, patrolling the empty street, certainly didn't notice or know or care. His attention was on the shifting shapes his spotlight was making as it splayed through the rusting chain-link fence in front of the graffiti-decorated building. He hated working this section alone. But his partner had gotten food poisoning during roll call and there wasn't enough time to get a replacement. There had recently been a surge of White Fence gang activity. A thirteen-year-old girl and her four-year-old brother had been wounded in a drive-by yesterday morning, and everyone was on the alert for several known suspects. They were, of course, more well-armed than the police, and none too eager to be incarcerated. So Austin was not in a particularly philosophical mood tonight.

He was scared shitless.

He couldn't possibly guess how misplaced his fear was. It wasn't going to be a coked-up MAC-10-wielding homeboy he would face. What he was going to run into this morning was not born of woman. It would be birthed in a storm of light, arcing into existence and ejected by the convulsing of two time zones that were swapping places in the continuum. . . .

A flash of blue-white light suddenly spilled out between the buildings a hundred yards ahead. Austin sped up. But he would arrive too late to see the nacreous ball of light hovering a few feet off the ground. Strands of energy whirled out from the surface to rake up and down the sides of the framing buildings, as if it were a drunk steadying itself. Loose debris and papers spiraled up, capering like two-dimensional ghouls in and out of the jagged bolts of light. A fire-escape ladder and landing glowed a dull red, sucking up the rapid heat thrown off by the lightstorm. There was a crackling sound that rapidly rose in pitch. Then a bright flash. Austin cursed and slammed on the brakes, just outside the range of electro-magnetic disruption. Had he driven the car a few feet further, the headlights would have flickered out, and the engine would have died. But the cop was mesmerized by strange lights dancing on the walls around him. They rapidly faded away.

As he started to get out of the car, it was quiet except for the distant sound of a stray dog howling. He took a breath. Ozone.

Austin's heart thudded in his chest. He felt like he had just jogged a mile. No way in hell did he want to go into that alley alone. On the other hand, he was wearing a uniform. He was a skilled professional. And he was armed with a Beretta 9mm auto, with fifteen bullets nestled in the grip. What if it were just a transformer shorting out? Could start a fire. Austin sighed and, muttering curses, cautiously moved into the shadows between the two buildings.

The cop glanced around, seeking forms in darkness and failing miserably. There was no streetlight here. It had been blown out or shorted out by . . . whatever had just happened. The vast concrete arches of the Sixth Street Bridge loomed overhead. He was under it now, heading toward a dead end formed by a chain-link fence. Beyond there were only railroad tracks and beyond that, the concrete canals of the L.A. River. There was something odd about that fence. The officer furrowed his brow as his flashlight fell on a perfectly symmetrical hole cut in the wire. He stepped closer and noticed that the edges were smoking, still glowing from heat. Instinctively, Austin's free hand unsnaped his holster and rested on the grip of his weapon. The cop looked down There was a smoothly cut spherical crater on the far side of the fence. It appeared as if something had simply scooped a section of the asphalt away. Austin tried desperately to supress the urge to run. It was too bad he was so successful. He might have lived longer.

Someone glided out of the night behind the office. Just a weird blur, gleaming somehow. It caught Austin's eye and he started to turn, sensing a presence. There was a sudden flash, as if someone had cut a single white frame out of his stream of his consciousness. His mind skipped a beat and he was dimly aware of being flat on his face. A dull pain welled from his left cheekbone, which had been fractured when he hit the cold pavement.

Hands were gliding over his uniform. Something wet was flowing from his nose. Nothing felt right. His neck seemed to grate as if it were pivoting on sand. As his sense of self began to detach, he wondered idly why a member of the White Fence would want his uniform. Whatever the reason, it couldn't have been good. But, that was somebody else's concern now. He had other things to do . . .

Like die.

A cat wandered into the alley and looked at the far end. It saw a naked man kneeling over the body of the policeman touching the uniform. The animal's pea-sized brain could not possibly comprehend what was happening, but its eyes saw nonetheless. The naked man's body began to change, turning dark blue. A silver badge emerged from the chest.

Uneasy, the feline darted away.

A few minutes later, the assailant strode up to the police car, wearing Austin's uniform and badge. The man slipped behind the wheel of the black and white. He scanned the cruiser's interior, the instruments and controls. They were all familiar, deep in his memory, although he had never actually seen them before. An Electro-Com MDT-870 computer terminal linked to the police network was mounted on the passenger side of the dash, its screen dark. He pondered it. It was the first time he'd laid eyes on it, but he remembered every millimeter of the generic model's circuits. He reached out and tapped on a key. The screen jumped to an on-line menu. Satisfied, the man turned the ignition, then looked in the rearview mirror. It was a handsome face, with strong features framed by military-short brown hair. His gray-blue eyes were furrowed with deep concentration, confident.

The "new" Officer Austin, badge number 473, put the car in gear and drove into the night. It was only appropriate that he had assumed this particular identity. After all, he *was* here to protect and serve.

THE GENERAL

RESEDA, CALIFORNIA
Saturday—10:58 A.M.

he Ramones' "I Wanna Be Sedated" blasted
from a boom box in an open garage in a slightly
run-down suburban neighborhood. Front lawns
were being watered. Children were riding bikes
in complex patterns, weaving around people washing
their cars in their soapy driveways. The sky was a rare
blue, the light wind coming in through the pass pushing the smog all the way back to San Bernadino. Inside
the garage, half listening to the thudding distortion
masquerading as music, John Connor expertly adjusted the carburetor on his Honda 125 dirt bike. His
long stringy hair framed a sullen mouth and eyes that
revealed a surprising intelligence for a ten-year-old.
Yet, from a distance, dressed as he was in a cutoff Public Enemy T-shirt and soiled, artfully ripped Levi's, no
one could have guessed this ten-year-old was much different from Tim, his equally scruffy friend standing
nearby, idly tossing a flathead screwdriver into the air
and catching it one-handed. But if you stepped closer
and bothered to look, you would see a slight, dazed expression in Tim's eyes. In John's, you would see knowl-

edge and memories far too complex and severe for one so young.

A thirty-three-year-old woman appeared in the doorway of the garage. Janelle Voight used to be cute. She'd always had dates her senior year in high school. But she was never considered particularly smart. Unarmed with a savvy comprehension of the continual downpour of trivial day-to-day disappointments, her natural ebullience had been eroded with a harsh recognition that life wasn't going to get any better than it had always been, which had been mildly disappointing. She had no idea why this had to be, and it disturbed her. Janelle had become increasingly irritable over the years until now her fuse was woefully short. In the process, her cuteness had melted away, leaving a firm, cruel set to her mouth, and a dullness to her eyes that sometimes reminded John of a cow absently feeding on the side of a hill.

One of her disappointments had been her inability to bear children. That was why she had signed up for the foster parent program. That was why she was now John's guardian. And that was why she was standing there with a graceless scowl and frazzled hair. John Connor had seemed at first a vulnerable, shy youth desperate for some basic affection. While that may have been true, he was also spirited, moody, independent to a fault, and mostly, a brat.

In the last few months, Janelle's patience had already worn thin. This morning it was tearing. The problem was however much she wanted a child, she was emotionally ill-equipped to raise one. And, of course, she had no idea who the boy now prematurely aging her really was, or would be: the general of a vast multinational army, comprised of people much like herself. But that was Faraway and Not Yet.

She had to shout over the music. "John! Get in here right now and clean up that pigsty of yours!"

Tim heard, but John acted as if he hadn't.

"John?" Janelle screamed, using THE VOICE, sharp with ultimate authority, primed with all kinds of unspoken threats only an adult knows how to unleash.

But John replied by turning up the volume on the boom box. Tim hid a grin behind his hand.

"I know you can hear me! Turn that music off and get in here!"

But John racked the Honda's throttle, racing the engine.

Janelle caught Tim's expression and narrowed her eyes. "What are *you* laughing at?"

Tim leaned closer to John, ducking out of sight behind the bike's gas tank.

Janelle angrily gave up with a slam of the house's front door.

Tim waited until he was sure she was really gone, then said, "She must be on the rag today."

John seemed to have no overt reaction, as if he had funneled his concern, if he had any, into a convenient storage compartment in his brain, ready to be taken out later for objective perusal. "Gimme that screwdriver," was all he said.

Tim instinctively handed it to him. Although he was two years older than John, he was the follower. John had a tone of voice, a look in his eyes, and a knowledge of things that made him a natural leader, no matter how much he resisted it.

Janelle stormed into the living room. Todd Voight, her husband, was sprawled on the couch, quietly watching a baseball game on TV. His pale, thin face was puffy with sleep, his hair disheveled. He looked world-weary and defeated. And it wasn't even noon. He wanted so much to have a peaceful moment to digest his breakfast. But that fragile hope evaporated.

"I swear I've had it with that goddamn kid. He won't even answer me."

Todd couldn't really blame John. At first he didn't answer her either. Janelle had an irritating habit of marching into your business and announcing her frustrations as if everyone were merely pretending to do something interesting while actually waiting with baited breath to hear her latest complaint. Jesus, he thought, eyes still glued to the set. The Mets were trailing by one, and Howard "HoJo" Johnson was coming up to the plate and he looked like he was gonna kill the ball.

"Todd? Are you gonna sit there on your butt or are you gonna do something?"

Todd held off answering as long as he could, then, before she could get uglier, he sighed. "What do you want him to do?"

"He hasn't cleaned his room in a month!"

"Well, that's an emergency," he muttered.

Todd glanced around the unkempt living room and added, under his breath, "especially around here." Luckily, Janelle didn't hear the last. She had her hands on her hips. Once he'd loved kissing those hips. The fun sure drained out of this marriage fast, he thought. And when John came into their lives, the downward slope of their union had seemed to steepen. He threw down the TV remote and headed for the garage.

John heard the door close. He rapidly finished tightening a screw and tossed the screwdriver into the open toolbox. Todd walked into view just as John was kicking the toolbox (*his* toolbox) across the stained concrete floor.

"Look at all this oil! I told you not to work on that thing in here."

"Get my bag," John barked to Tim. The boy slipped onto the bike behind John, grabbing a nylon knapsack. John brought the engine up to redline. Over the screaming mechanical whine, Todd yelled, "John, get your ass inside right now and do what your mother says!"

John pinned Todd with a defiant glare. "She's not my mother, *Todd*!"

The boy released the clutch and peeled out of the garage, almost flipping Tim off the back. Todd dodged as they raced past him down the driveway.

"Stay off the street with that thing until you get a license!" he shouted as they accelerated away, making a couple of college students on ten-speeds scramble out of the way.

Todd felt like a fool standing there. The little prick loved to humiliate him in front of his friend. But in a way he felt relieved. John was gone now, and therefore any further confrontation was delayed until he returned later that night. Until then Todd could watch TV. And maybe get in a quick nap. If Janelle would only zip her lip.

John was a natural on the dirt bike, leaning comfortably into corners, alert for the child or car that might suddenly lurch into view, yet willing to take calculated risks for the sheer exhilaration of it. He wheeled down the quiet streets and veered into a vacant lot to a trail that ran beside a fenced-in drainage canal. He gunned the bike through a hole in the mesh, *accelerating* rather than slowing. Tim reflexively tucked his knees as they roared past the edges. That was only John pushing it to the absolute edge. Tim was determined not to let his concern for self-preservation show. But he couldn't help his eyes going wide when John roared down the concrete embankment as if they would never stop.

They zigzagged along the drainage canal, which John used as his private road to avoid being tagged by cops, veering to within inches of the straight-up, thirteen-foot-high concrete walls, throwing up a roostertail of muddy water. Tim whooped, pretending he didn't just see his life flash before his eyes. He slapped John on the back.

"Major moves, man!"

They hit a small puddle and the Honda slid sideways, threatening to go down, but John casually jammed his foot down and immediately righted the motorbike. Tim gulped and then tried a laugh. It came out a croak. To cover, he yelled a question. "Hey, where's your real mom, anyway?"

When John didn't answer, going into one of his somber moods, Tim pressed harder, a little irritated. "Well . . . she dead or something?"

"She might as well be," he said, so quietly Tim wasn't sure he'd said anything. Sometimes the kid got real rigid, like steel, and nothing could break through. Tim was about to say something else when John suddenly twisted the throttle all the way and they lunged forward.

Tim shut up and held on.

PATIENT 82

ou couldn't see it from the main road. You could drive all the way through the small bedroom community on up the scenic drive of Happy Camp Road, past a recreational vehicle park and still not see it. You'd have to be looking for it hard before you would come across the small paved road that wound around a domelike hill dotted with twisted oak trees. Behind the hill you would finally come upon a sign that read PESCADERO STATE HOSPITAL FOR THE CRIMINALLY DISORDERED.

It was clamped to a chain-link fence topped with concertina wire. An armed guard sat in a guard shack on the far side of the heavy iron gate. Beyond it squatted a dozen large buildings. All the windows were barred. Private security cars patrolled the overmanicured grounds. The place looked about as inviting as KGB headquarters.

Inside the building, it was worse. The place was a surgically sanitary prison for the mind. Antiseptically white walls. Attendants in white linen uniforms pushed the all-female patients along the oppressively unembroidered hallways; the usual extent of their exercise. Wheelchair alley, it was called.

Down the hall to the left was a shorter sally-port corridor with electronic doors at either end. The first one was like a jail-cell door. The one at the far end was a solid steel firedoor. Two burly attendants sat in front of the latter, idly chatting and glancing at a bank of video monitors on the console before them. They could see what was on the other side of the door.

The isolation wing.

Here the most unpredictable and potentially lethal patients were kept under constant lock and key. They were too savage to be allowed to intermingle with each other, so each patient had his or her own gray cell. It was as stark and depressing as solitary confinement in any federal penitentiary. And the food was just as bad, too.

Dr. Peter Silberman was leading a dutiful group of young interns down the corridor outside the cells, followed laconically by three husky attendants, each looking like a recent retiree from professional football. Silberman was moving with a slight limp. Each step caused the bandage around his knee to stretch the swollen, sensitive skin. He tried to compartmentalize the pain, concentrating on the task at hand. It wasn't too hard. He was comfortably in his element, waxing eloquently about a subject in which he felt expert. It was difficult not to suppress a tendency to flaunt his superior intellect to these callow young men and women, but most of the time he managed it. This was not one of those times.

"The next cell," he was saying in a low, drawling voice suitable for a radio psychologist, "is occupied by patient number eighty-two, a twenty-nine-year-old female diagnosed as acute schizo-affective disorder. She has shown the usual indicators . . . depression, anxiety, violent acting-out, delusions of persecution."

Most of the interns hung on his every word. Silberman's precise and dryly composed papers on various identity disorders had won him a certain reputation in his field. Not quite at the top, but a solid specialist in the hard-to-reach cases, although his cure rate was not particularly high. To a few of the more savvy interns, it was clear that Silberman had a woefully lackluster bedside manner. But he was not a stupid man. He had been a consultant to the Los Angeles Police Department for years and had conducted complex studies of dozens of the most extremely psychotic criminals, including some recent, infamous mass murderers. Perhaps his largest failing was that he was a little too clever for his own good.

"Here we are." He stopped outside a cell door. It was soundproof, communication being carried out through a grilled two-way speaker mounted beneath the tiny Plexiglas window. The door seemed somehow simultaneously medieval and high-tech. He peered in.

Sunlight glared through a grimy window, creating a barred slash on the bare institutional wall. The room was empty of all furnishings save a stainless steel sink, toilet, and a polished metal mirror.

The latter had been dented.

The bed has been stripped of the mattress and leaned upright against the wall, legs facing outward. Sweaty hands gripped one leg and the tendons knotted and released as the inmate did slow pull-ups, blowing long hair that was tangled and matted with perspiration out of almond-shaped, mahogany-hued eyes. The young woman was wearing a tank top and hospital pants as she hung from the top leg of the vertical bedframe, her lithe body rigid and straight as a steel ruler. Her knees were bent so the feet cleared the floor. Her lean, muscular arms pulled up, lowered, pulled up, lowered. Absolutely no change in rhythm.

Like a machine.

He stepped aside so they could all look in and see.

The woman was faced away from the door and so far acted as if she didn't know she was being observed. That was not the case.

She knew.

She had caught the movement of faces at the small window in the reflection of the dented mirror. But she was not going to acknowledge the indignity of being gaped at like a lab rat. She kept doing the pull-ups, her arms shuddering as the muscles finally began to tire.

When the interns had finished peering in, Silberman took their place and, manufacturing an unconvincingly cheerful smile, flipped the intercom switch. "Morning, Sarah."

Sarah Jeanette Connor turned from the bedframe and glared at Silberman. The years in hiding had severely marked her. Her expression was defiant and intense, but her eyes skittered around looking for escape at the same time. She seemed perpetually on the verge of fight or flight. Her once softly curved cheeks were now hard and sculpted. She still looked beautiful, fiercely so, but also haunted, trapped, anguished. . . .

And very much like she belonged where she was.

She spoke in a low, chilling monotone. It reminded Silberman of an animal softly growling. "Good morning, Dr. Silberman. How's the knee?"

Silberman's smug composure dropped a second. He arched an eyebrow. "Fine, Sarah." He switched off the intercom and turned to the students. "She, uh . . . stabbed me in the kneecap with a screwdriver a few weeks ago."

There were quickly stifled smiles. Silberman continued, seeking solace in the familiar, comfortable labels. Sarah was a curious and powerful force of nature he had boxed in, literally, and now figuratively, with soothing jargon.

"The delusional architecture is interesting. She believes a machine called a "Terminator," which looks human, of course, was sent back through time to kill her. And also that the father of her child was a soldier, sent to protect her . . . he was from the future, too. . . . " He could not keep himself from smiling. "The year 2029, if I remember correctly."

The interns took their cue and chuckled.

"The delusion seems to have begun with the boyfriend and then been adopted by the patient. A fascinating case of ideational transference. But not so rare as you might expect. We've been seeing more and more of this new syndrome. A kind of acute phobic reaction to increasingly complex technology. It's perhaps an attempt to defend against the dehumanization of relationships in a modern society. If the patient's tremendous energy could be channeled into therapy rather than stubbornly maintaining the elaborate delusion, she'd have been released by now."

Silberman paused, remembering the first time he had met Sarah, years ago in a police station interrogation room. She had been involved with a violent paranoic who later escaped with her and was eventually killed. She had vanished for a few years, and, ironically, came back into his custody after attempting to blow up the local offices of some computer corporation. Since then, she had been his most uncooperative patient. She should have gotten better by now. It disturbed him slightly that he had not been able to motivate her cure. Struggling to regain control, he abruptly said, "Let's move on, shall we."

The interns glanced uneasily at one another, then walked to the next cell. Silberman stayed behind and turned to the head attendant. Douglas was six feet four, two hundred fifty pounds, and warmhearted as a rattlesnake. Silberman spoke so the students couldn't hear. "I don't like the patients disrupting their rooms like this. See that she takes her Thorazine, would you, Douglas?"

Douglas nodded and gestured for the other two attendants to stay with him. Silberman then turned and followed the interns out of the wing.

Sarah looked up as the cell door opened. Douglas walked in slow, idly tapping his wooden nightstick against the door in an ominous rhythm. The other two orderlies eased in behind him. One of them carried something that looked like a sawed-off cattle prod. Sarah knew from experience this was a stun baton that delivered a nasty jolt. The other had a tray with cups of red liquid. Thorazine.

"Time to take your meds, Connor," Douglas said.

Sarah faced him, weight centered, her feral eyes darting from one to the other. She could feel the fury and fear intermingling and rising to a jagged peak.

"You take it," she answered.

Douglas grinned, casual as can be. But that stick of

his still went tap-tap-tap. . . . " Now you know you got to be good 'cause you up for review this afternoon. . . . "

"I'm not taking it. Now I don't want any trouble. . . . "

"Ain't no trouble at all—" He whipped the baton in a whistling backhand that took her square in the stomach. She doubled over and dropped to her knees, unable to breathe.

Douglas kicked the bed and it slammed down with a crash, inches from her head. She rolled away, hissing through the pain, "Do that again and I'll kill you, you fucker!"

He frowned, then took the stun baton from the other attendant and stepped closer to Sarah.

She knew what was coming. "Get away from me you psychotic son of a—AAAHHH!"

The baton hit her between the shoulder blades as she tried to rise. It drove her back to the floor, pinning her like a bug. Little electric arcs crackled as the baton made her convulse. Douglas grabbed her by the hair and jerked her up to her knees, then brought the cup of Thorazine in front of her lips.

"Last call, sugar," he cooed.

Gasping, Sarah tried to break loose, but despite her customized workouts, Douglas was still too strong for her. She couldn't afford to allow herself any more physical damage. She would need all her strength if she were to find a way out of this hellhole.

Wincing, she reluctantly choked the zombie juice down.

Soon, she would be dreamwalking. Already Sarah felt the first wave of induced lethargy rolling through her body. Then they could do anything they wanted to her. She would be locked far away from the world.

And then anything could happen to her son.

Her son . . .

THE POLAROID

John was furtively hunched before a Fed-Teller machine at the rear of the Federal Security Bank while Tim stood nervous lookout. John slipped a stolen ATM card into the machine's slot. A ribbon-wire was soldered onto the rear of the card, trailing into a small Radio Shack chassis in John's knapsack, which in turn was connected to a laptop keyboard lying next to it.

"Hurry it up!" Tim urged.

John did not hurry. He had been taught to remain cool under pressure. Hurrying led to mistakes, which took time to correct. He only wanted to do this once. So he calmly entered a few commands and the tiny LCD displayed the card's PIN number. He then typed it on the Fed-Teller's keypad and punched in a request for three hundred dollars. The machine hesitated. John knew that among other things it was doing, the still-video camera behind the panel atop the machine was clicking off a shot of whoever was standing in front of it. But John had already misted it with a squirt from a can of Arrid Extra Dry deodorant. Once dried to pow-

56

der, the spray would block the lens. It would get no exposure.

Tim noticed a station wagon pull up in the parking lot nearby and a plump woman get out, groping in her purse. "Someone's coming!"

John reflexively grabbed Tim's shirttail. "Stay right where you are."

Tim hesitated, watching the woman move toward them, head down, eyes still on her purse. A moment later the Fed-Teller whirred, dispensing fifteen crisp twenty-dollar bills. "Easy money," John said.

Tim looked back over his shoulder, amazed. "Jeez! Where'd you learn all this stuff?"

John reached up and wiped off the deodorant powder with his sleeve, then began scooping the twenties into his bag as the machine kicked them out. "From my mom. My real mom, I mean. Come on, baby. . . ."

Tim glanced at the approaching woman. She was looking at them now, but still too far away to see exactly what they were up to—he hoped. "Let's go!"

They sprinted around the corner to an alley where the Honda was parked and huddled behind it as John counted out Tim's share. Five twenties. Tim was slack-jawed. This was unbelievable. Every day John had something else up his sleeve. But this . . .

When John opened his knapsack to put in his money, Tim noticed a picture in a plastic sleeve. "Who's this?"

John glanced down at the soiled, worn Polaroid of a young woman sitting behind the wheel of a Jeep. A German shepherd sat next to her. She wore a sad, sweet expression. John wondered what she had been smiling at. He could see the top of her stomach, gently swelling with . . .

Him.

It always weirded him out to think about that. "It's my mom."

"So she's pretty cool, huh?" Tim grunted.

John frowned. A confusing mixture of emotions welled up, as they always did when he looked at her face. He couldn't begin to explain them to Tim, who was loyal but not too swift, so he simply said, "Actually, no, she's a complete psycho. That's why she's at Pescadero. She tried to blow up a computer factory, but she got shot and arrested."

This sounded to Tim like a real load of beef bull, but you never knew . . . "No shit?"

"Yeah, she's a total loser. C'mon."

John had tried to sound macho casual, and by Tim's becoming-bored expression, he had probably succeeded. He slapped Tim on the shoulder and they jumped onto the Honda. John fired it up and they whined off down the alley.

But his mother's face swam into view, her eyes on him, watching, judging. Like always.

Screw her, John thought.

But then, why do you still keep the photo she gave you? a little voice asked. Screw you, too, John answered silently, slipping on shades and accelerating onto the boulevard.

THE SEEKERS

The cruiser's police computer was displaying a Juvenile Division file. Subject: John Connor. Below his arrest record were his vital stats. Mother: Sarah Connor. Legal Guardians: Todd and Janelle Voight. And below their names, an address: 19828 S. Almond. Reseda, Ca. The car was parked out front. It had been there for several minutes while Officer Austin took in the details of the neighborhood. It wasn't just his eyes he was seeing with. His entire body registered the environment in a dozen subtle ways that nevertheless were noted and filed for future strategic reference.

Austin stared at the driveway of the shabby-around-the-edges three-bedroom home. Noted doors and windows. Then decided to move.

As he got out of the car and walked up the driveway, he continued to scan the street, filling in the details, sensing no immediate danger. Except . . .

He heard the sharp staccato bursts of a dog barking, coming from the backyard. Estimating the creature to be a medium-sized breed, Austin added that factor in and continued walking to the door.

Todd Voight staggered off the couch at the three

solid knocks, blearily gaping at the TV. The game was already in the third inning. He must have dozed off during the second. And why was the dog raising hell? It sounded as if a whole army of strangers were invading its territory.

Another three, measured knocks. Somebody else at the door. Todd grumbled to himself, muttering curses. Why wouldn't the world leave him alone on Saturdays? So far it had been one goddam thing after another. He thudded down the hall to the front door and angrily whipped it open on . . .

. . . the unsmiling face of a uniformed police officer, his blank expression somehow chilling, beyond the screen door.

Todd swallowed his anger, and said in a voice low and hoarse with sleep, "Yeah?"

"Are you the legal guardian of John Connor?"

A cloud crossed Todd's mind and he sighed. "That's right, officer. What's he done now?"

Austin said nothing for a moment, his eyes casually scanning the living room beyond Todd. He saw the shepherd-mix through a sliding glass door. It was locked inside a section of the backyard that had been fenced off. And it was agitatedly running back and forth in the confined space, barking incessantly.

Janelle came out of the bathroom, a *People* magazine dangling from one hand, and stepped up behind Todd, concerned. The cop studied her briefly, then said, "Could I speak with him, please?"

Todd shrugged. "Well, you could if he was here. But he took off on his bike this morning. Could be anywhere."

"Do you have a photograph of him?"

"Get the album, Janelle."

Janelle hesitated, frowning, then said, "Just a minute." As she went to the fireplace mantle, Todd turned back to the officer. "You gonna tell me what this is about?"

"I just need to ask him a few questions."

Janelle came back with a photo album. She slipped out one of the few photos she had of John, a standard-issue school picture showing a scowling boy about as happy to be photographed as being force-fed spinach.

The cop took the picture and glanced down at it casually. There was a moment when his eyes eerily locked on John's features. But Todd and Janelle didn't see that. "Nice-looking boy," the cop said. "Do you mind if I keep this picture?"

Janelle nodded absently, remembering something. "There was a guy here this morning asking about him, too."

Todd grumbled with irritation, remembering the guy distinctly because he made him miss a great pitch by Gooden. "Yeah, he was a big guy. On a cycle. That got something to do with it?"

Todd noticed the cop hesitate for a fraction of a second. Then he smiled reassuringly. "I wouldn't worry about *him*."

The Terminator rode the Harley in a mechanical crisscross pattern, digitizing and recording for reference the streets of the Valley, as the cyborg scanned the area in a slow sharklike manner for John Connor. In the last half-hour, the Terminator had become thoroughly familiar with the city in a seven-kilometer radius, riding with expert efficiency, getting accustomed to the ebb and flow of traffic. The cyborg knew such knowledge might be strategically useful. He also knew where the boy lived and where he recreated. It would only be a matter of time before their paths crossed. He gunned the cycle and turned down a street toward the drainage canal several blocks away.

If the cyborg had pulled to the side of the road and simply waited another thirty seconds, he would have seen John and Tim flash by on the Honda a block away.

But sometimes even terminators can be subject to the whims of Fate.

VISITING HOURS

S lashes of sunlight fell across Sarah's bruised face. She was sitting on the bed, her back against the wall, drifting. Her cheek twitched and her eyes darted under the lids. She was breathing raggedly, exhausted, yet trying to stay conscious, to fight her way out of the drug-induced coma. She was beginning to lose, slowly falling back into herself and the sad, lonely coldness of meaningless oblivion when a hand gently stroked her cheek. The fingers brushed her skin lightly and the lethargy seemed to shatter like plate glass. "Sarah, wake up," a familiar voice whispered.

Sarah opened her eyes and looked up at the man sitting on the edge of her bed. He had scruffy blond hair and wore a long, soiled raincoat. His eyes were soft, young, adoring, although his face was scarred, weathered by a brutal childhood. A tingle went up the back of her neck and she stopped breathing.

It was Kyle Reese.

Hot tears painfully welled. The vision of him wavered. She wanted to see him clearly, but was afraid to blink, lest he disappear.

"Kyle?" she whispered. He didn't answer at first, but he was no ghost. She could feel the heat of his hand against her cheek. And there was so much love in his expression . . .

Love for her . . .

Love that inspired him to give his life for her. His life—

The impossibility of the situation hit like a hammerblow to her temple. "You can't be here. You're dead." She sighed.

He nodded and answered in that high, soft voice that reminded her how really young this battle-scarred veteran had been. "I know. This is a dream, Sarah."

"Yeah. I thought so. The Thorazine. They shouldn't make me take—"

They gazed longingly into each other's eyes. And for a moment, all the horror and pain and death Sarah had carried with her since he'd died was set aside, so that she could feel the love for him underneath, pure and strong as the moment they had made love. She wanted to reach out and touch him, but her arms felt like lead weights. "Hold me," she whispered.

Kyle pulled her into an embrace and gently rocked her. Now the tears came, rolling down her cheeks against the smooth, warm skin of his chest.

He spoke again, tenderly. "I love you. I always will."

"Oh, God . . . Kyle. I need you so much."

He lifted her chin and kissed her on the mouth, his lips lightly brushing hers at first, then pressing harder as their passion built. Oh God, she thought, I can taste him. The powerful ache in her stomach melted away, replaced by a stirring below as the solid feel of him seemed to bring her back to life.

She pressed her face into his shoulder, weeping uncontrollably, losing the edge she had been so carefully building the last ten years, feeling it sandblasted back by the intense love she felt for this dead man.

This time when he spoke, his voice was strangely cold. "Where's John, Sarah?"

Suddenly there was empty space where he had been. Gasping, she opened her eyes.

Kyle was now standing across the room, pinning her with an accusing gaze. She had never seen that expression on his face before. It sent a shudder of black guilt through her body.

"They took him away from me," she said quietly.

"It's John who's the target now. You have to protect him. He's wide open."

"I know!" Frustrated, Sarah tried to rise, to reach out for him, but somehow her body wouldn't work.

"Don't quit, Sarah. Our son needs you."

She struggled to stop crying, but it was like holding back a tidal wave. She hadn't cried for a long time. But here, in front of Kyle, she couldn't stop. "I know he needs me, but I'm not as strong as I'm supposed to be. Nobody believes me. Not even him. I've lost him. *I'm screwing up the mission!*"

"On your feet, soldier," he said, lifting her up off the bed. "Remember the message, Sarah . . . the future is not set. There is no fate but what we make for ourselves." He was reminding her of the message the adult John Connor had told Kyle to give her when he first arrived. It had stirred in her a sense of her own destiny, as it was intended to do. She often thought of that phrase over the years. But in the last few months she had forgotten it. In the overwhelming animalistic drive to escape this place, she had forgotten a lot. Too much.

Kyle turned toward the door.

Her heart slammed against her ribcage. "Kyle don't go!"

He slowly faced her, a reprimand in his voice. "There's not much time left in the world, Sarah."

Then he opened the door and walked out. Sarah strained to move her legs, but they were like lifeless tubes. She looked up at the open door, frantic. With a sudden surge of adrenaline, she staggered across the room. She yanked on the closing door and slipped out into the corridor. She looked one way. Empty.

"Kyle," she shouted, panicked.

She turned the other way. Impossibly, he was already a hundred feet away, striding away down the dim corridor, silhouetted in raincoat, disappearing around a corner.

Sarah ran after him, her bare feet slapping the cold linoleum, her hospital gown floating out behind her. It seemed as if the corridor were tilting upward, as if on a gigantic treadmill. The corner seemed to stretch away from her endlessly. With a surge of energy, she finally reached the corner and slid around it.

Reese was just ahead, turning another corner.

She came after him, hesitating at the intersection. Kyle stood at the end of the hall before a double door. He opened it and stepped through, emerging into a beautiful, sunlit morning. Sarah ran along the corridor and burst out onto green grass. She looked around.

It was a playground, filled with giggling children, sliding down slides, clambering through a jungle gym, arcing high in swings. Reese was gone.

An overwhelming sense of dread rose like screaming lava. She was about to see the worst thing in the world.

She opened her mouth to howl a protest but no sound came out. It was too late. There was nothing she could do but watch as a second sunrise blossomed on the horizon. The sky was suddenly bled of all color. Then everything exploded, followed by a searing shock-wave of intense heat. Sarah could see it rolling across the horizon, blackening everything it touched, shriveling trees, houses, and roads into steaming slag. Then it reached the playground . . .

In the unholy glare, hotter than a thousand suns, the children ignited like match heads. Sarah, too, was burning, still trying to scream as she watched their flesh being blasted off to reveal gleaming white bone. There was no sound, no escape from the indescribably obscene images.

And there was too much light. More light than was ever meant to be, mercilessly illuminating the death-agonies of the children as they writhed like charred worms on the heat-rippled ground. She reached out, gripping the smoking fence, her hands flaming.

The blast-wave whipped across the seared horizon like a near-solid wall of compressed air, followed by the awesome force of two hundred and fifty miles-per-hour winds.

The children, charcoal statues now frozen in positions of play, exploded and swirled away.

The shockwave slammed into her, instantly tearing the carbonized flesh from her ribcage. She was sucked right into the whirling maw of the radioactive mushroom cloud itself, into the heart of the nuclear blast, where the fused matter glowed like hell yawning open to receive her soul. . . .

Sarah turned her head away from the hot sunlight blasting in through the window, blinking back tears, gasping. Her whole body was shaking, her muscles rigid. Her hospital gown was soaked with perspiration.

She opened her eyes and looked down. She was on the floor by the overturned bed.

The Thorazine had unlocked the Stygian nightmare again, the nightmare that was soon to become reality. Sarah knew only too well the war was coming. She had died in it a thousand nights. You would think each time it would become more ethereal and ineffective, as normal dreams do. But this was a vision of what was to be, and each time it got worse, as if the forces of Fate that set it in motion where driving it closer with each beat of her heart.

But Kyle never came to her in these dreams. What did that mean? Nothing? Or was she finally cracking, going insane, desperately seeking escape from reality in the arms of a corpse? But no, he had said something important. Her scrambled brain struggled to remember the dream-words. . . .

It was about John. He was the target now. And the world didn't have much time left. It had been her worry, from her own subconscious, but never had they been put into the mouth of Kyle Reese.

Sarah felt the hairs on the back of her neck rise as a wave of dread rolled through her.

Something was about to happen.

And she was completely unable to stop it from here.

She brushed back her matted hair and pulled herself to her feet. One way or the other, she would have to get out of here.

Tonight.

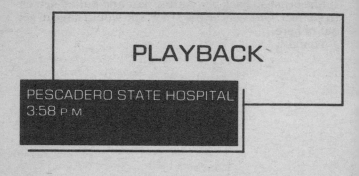

PLAYBACK

arah was standing in a small bare room; only a cubicle really. She was puffing on a Marlboro she had convinced one of the attendants to give her, arms crossed, listening to her own voice, sounding tinny and distant. She turned to the video monitor that sat on a roll-around cart across from her and saw herself in it, talking softly into the camera, eyes struggling to focus against the lulling pull of the drugs they had given her. The tape had been made shortly after she'd been committed. Sarah was amazed at how much fight she had back then. Her former self was saying, "... it's ... like a giant strobe light, burning right through my eyes ... but somehow I can still see. Look, you know the dream's the same every night, why do I have to—"

Silberman's patronizing voice spoke on the tape now. He couldn't be seen as he was off to the side, out of camera range. "Please continue ..."

The real Silberman was seated nearby, watching Sarah watch herself. There were two attendants standing near the door, idly watching the video with vague interest, ready to act should Sarah lose control.

On the monitor, Sarah reluctantly went on, scowling

68

with resentment at the unseen Silberman. "The children look like burnt paper . . . black, not moving. Then the blast-wave hits them and they just fly apart like leaves. . . ."

The video Sarah couldn't go on. She was shaking her head, crying. The real Sarah studied the woman on the monitor with a cold expression, her eyes red-rimmed, but dry.

Silberman spoke up on the tape, his voice maddeningly soothing. "Dreams about cataclysm, or the end of the world, are very common, Sarah—"

"It's not just a dream. It's real, you moron! I know the exact date it happens!"

"I'm sure it feels very real to you—"

"On August 29, 1997, it's going to feel pretty fucking real to you, too! Anybody not wearing number two million sunblock is gonna have a real bad day, *get it*?"

"Relax now, Sarah—"

But of course, the Sarah on the monitor could not relax. She furiously writhed, burning with the righteous tone of a mad seer.

"You think you're alive and safe, but you're already dead. Everybody . . . *you're all fucking dead*!"

She was rising out of her chair. An attendant rushed into camera range and slammed her back down. It had no immediate effect except to turn up the volume of Sarah's shrieking. "You're the one living in a dream, Silberman, not me! Because I know it happens. *It happens!*"

The real Silberman raised a remote control and paused the tape, freezing on Sarah's insanely contorted face.

Patient 82 turned away from the screen, her expression stony. She knew Silberman was waiting for an answer. She gathered up whatever sanity was left and presented it to the supercilious bastard, working up a smile that almost made her puke. She managed at last to say, "I was afraid . . . and confused. I feel much better, now. Clearer."

Silberman nodded, mulling it over with a condescending smile, toying with his foundtain pen. "Yes, you're much improved lately." Sarah noted with small satisfaction that Silberman absently slipped his pen into his jacket.

The next thing she did was perhaps the hardest she ever had to do. Be civil to Silberman. It helps me a lot to have a goal, something to look forward to."

"And what is that?" Silberman asked, surprised again.

Sarah hesitated. She glanced at what she guessed was a one-way mirror. She sensed that on the other side was another observation room where the interns from the earlier rounds and a couple of staff psychologists were smugly smoking and making occasional notes.

If she could only grab a chair and ram it through the glass and their arrogant faces—

She stopped herself. This was the most important day of the rest of her life. She had to do anything to get out of here. Crawl on her belly to these fools. Play their stupid games. They were judging her every move, noting every facial tick, measuring her sanity from their hidden rooms. If she just said the right words, like magic they might let her go.

She turned back to Silberman and strained to give him a steady, even smile. "You said I could be transferred to the minimum security wing and have visitors if I showed improvement in six months. Well, it's been six months, and I was looking forward to seeing my son."

Silberman slightly rocked back his chair, balancing for a moment, pondering, then said, "I see. Let's go back to what you were saying about these terminator machines. Now you think they don't exist?"

The smile started to crack, but Sarah scrambled to shore it up. "They don't exist. I see that now," she said as convincingly as she could.

Silberman nodded again and scribbled something in a file, then looked at Sarah again, eyes boring into hers. "But you've told me on many occasions about how you crushed one in a hydraulic press."

"If I had, there would have been some evidence. They would have found something at the factory."

"I see. So you don't believe anymore that the company covered it up?"

The crucial moment. Silberman's pen lightly tapped on the page, beating out the seconds before Sarah responded. "No. Why would they?"

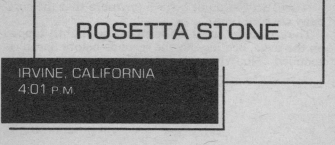

ROSETTA STONE

Miles Dyson stood at the window on the top floor of the Monolith, a three-story black basalt and glass building that was the sprawling headquarters and labs of Cyberdyne Systems, and watched the sun gleam off the tops of cars in the parking lot below. He yearned to return to his lab and the work waiting for him. The third floor was the administration building, where the marketing and corporate executives worked. Dyson knew little of what they did and cared even less. He was a practical, pragmatic man, intent on dissecting his little corner of the universe with his wits and his quarterly budget. The latter was up for review by the Cyberdyne executive board, and this was causing the former grave strain. Dyson was never much good with people outside his field of expertise, but lately he'd had to come out of his pure research shell to deal with bureaucratic concerns. It was an intrusion he very much resented, however necessary.

Miles Dyson was perhaps the most important man on the planet, perhaps even in history, although no one, not even Dyson, would ever guess such a thing. He was Special Projects Division supervisor at Cyberdyne, a brilliant microphysicist and chemist. But all he'd originally wanted to do was play basketball.

The six-foot-two, rail-thin youth had graduated from an inner-city high school in Detroit hoping to win a sports scholarship to a university in the West. But he wasn't a good enough player. Uncertain of what to do next, he talked to a guidance counselor who sensed hidden talents. She had him retake his SATs.

He scored so high on math he won a special federally funded scholarship to CalTech in Pasadena. This was a time when the United States was hungering for brilliant mathematicians to eventually compete with the Japanese. They bent over backwards to get anyone who showed any math talent into higher education.

Dyson had been extremely dubious at first. Sure, he was comfortable with algebra, but it didn't juice him like a good game of hoops could. But after his first year at CalTech, he had realized a tremendous affinity for equations and formulae.

At first his professors had viewed him with skepticism. His social background, mediocre SAT scores in English and biology, and his still colorful inner-city colloquialisms branded him as a freak, an idiot savant. Perhaps there had been a touch of rascism. At that time, Dyson walked, talked, and looked like the black youth from Detroit that he was.

But later, as Dyson's facility expanded with his fascination for science, he became accepted into the inner circle of young geniuses on campus. He was wooed out of graduate school by Cyberdyne recruiters and put to work as a lowly lab tech, but on a remarkable and very secret project. Only two years later he had shunted aside all his competitors and risen to project coordinator. And now Cyberdyne had grown from a small, aggressive microchip firm to a megamillion dollar corporation on the verge of a major breakthrough in artificial intelligence.

Right now, Dyson just wanted to get back to work.

The owner and CEO of Cyberdyne strode into the large glass-and-steel office. Greg Simmons had not aged gracefully in the ten years since he'd founded the company. Beating off competitors and struggling to maintain control over the other board members, who were merely investors, had driven a couple of nails into his coffin. He was only fifty-one, but he looked a decade older. His once-thick shock of dark hair had turned thin and gray. Liver spots dotted his pale skin, and he walked with a slight limp from arthritis in his hip. He would live a lot longer, and become a lot wealthier before he died, but you wouldn't know it to look at him. Cancer patients looked healthier.

The major blow to Simmons's peace of mind had happened five years ago when his partner, a squirrelly but brilliant young man named Jack Kroll had died from a brain tumor. Kroll had been the real driving force behind the company's original success and was on the verge of developing a completely new form of microchip called a wafer-circuit. It would revolutionize the computer industry and make Simmons a billionaire. But the poor kid died before he could complete his research. It had taken years to find the right replacement. Now Simmons thought he had it in the man who stood by the window. Dyson still looked like he was in his twenties, although he was thirty-three. Despite his blue-collar appearance, Dyson had finally deciphered Kroll's last complicated notes and was now carrying the research forward into new areas on his own intellectual steam. Instead of discovering the workings of individual circuits, Dyson was developing an understanding of the whole device.

The only problem was the man was a sieve with money. He wanted more and more staff members, and Cyberdyne had to pay top dollar to steal them away from the other top R and D firms. And the more people on the staff, the more difficult it was to maintain security. Dyson was well known for being casual in this regard. Many times Simmons had him on the carpet for security infractions. It was like scolding a child. A child who held all the aces. For Dyson knew by now that Simmons was more salesman and money-raiser than scientist. Although he could comprehend the end uses for the products his company was developing, he had little knowledge of how they were actually made. He was not a scientist. He was not even particularly smart. Oh, he'd been a draftsman and design tech for various little electronics firms, but his success was built on one thing only . . .

. . . a peculiar stroke of fate.

Ten years ago, Simmons had been working at Kleinhaus Electronics outside of Los Angeles, doing preliminary design charts on computer. One morning, he'd come into work and had to wait outside the building while the police scraped up a body from the factory floor. Evidently there'd been an explosion the night before. Two people, a man and a woman, had broken in for some reason and set something off. The man was killed and the woman supposedly went nuts.

Once he was let in, Jack, who had been his assistant back then, brought him a strange piece of microcircuitry. His curiosity had driven him to sneak across the police line and grab some of the more interesting pieces of debris from the explosion.

It was like no technology either Simmons or Kroll had ever seen. Rather than turn it over to Kleinhaus, they quit their jobs, borrowed up to their eyeballs, and opened their own company. They called it Cyberdyne.

The first two years they had nearly starved, just trying to figure out what they had found. Eventually, Jack Kroll had begun to decipher the workings of one tiny circuit loop, which, like an electronic rosetta stone, pointed the way to other minor but profitable discoveries. The company succesfully marketed a new accelerator chip. They were in healthy profit the third and fourth years. And then Kroll got the tumor. He worked feverishly, scribbling notes in a drug-induced daze, but died before he could reach the next breakthrough.

Now there was Dyson. Also on the verge.

But eating the company's profits as if they were popcorn.

Simmons cleared his throat and Dyson nervously faced him.

"Sorry it took so long," Simmons said, "but the other

members of the board were confused about some of the line items on your budget."

Before Dyson could make a fuss, Simmons held up his hand. "Don't worry. I wiped away some of the fog."

An idle bluff, thought Dyson. He knew the old man didn't know what his own R and D was really up to. But Simmons could smelling a killing a mile off, and Dyson warily waited for him close in.

Simmons offered him a drink of Scotch. Dyson politely declined.

He had to wait while Simmons gulped down his. Finally, the old man grinned. "Well, you got your budget for the next quarter. I had a hell of a time justifying it to the others. They want results we can market by the end of the year. I assured them you would validate my confidence in you. So do me a favor and don't spend it all in one spot."

The laughter between them was forced. They weren't friends. You have to have a basic understanding of one another to be friends. And these two men were far apart in almost all aspects. Except the Special Projects Division. And even then, they each had different objectives in mind. Dyson wasn't above enjoying his high salary, but he wasn't in it for the money. He just wanted to *know*. And if in the process of knowing he could make the world work a little better for his children, then fine.

Simmons just wanted more of what he already had.

In a way, they were both obsessed men.

Dyson *thought* he was the happier man.

He shook Simmons's hand and promised to personally keep him posted on his division's progress.

As quickly as he could, Dyson left and hurried into the elevator. Alone in the carpeted cubicle, he made a triumphant leap. He'd been certain most of his requests would be turned down. Obviously he'd underrated Simmons's passion for Special Division and their current project. Now he'd gotten everything he wanted to complete the work. It wouldn't be long before they would leap the final hurdle and know all there was to know about Lot Two.

The doors whispered open on the second floor. Dyson

walked across the maroon foyer to a solid security door. A chrome sign above it read: SPECIAL PROJECTS DIVISION: AUTHORIZED PERSONNEL ONLY. He zipped his electronic key card through the scanner. The door unlocked with a klunk.

He entered the A.I. (Artificial Intelligence) lab. The place was filled with banks of processors, disk drives, test bays, and prototype assembly areas. Everywhere thick cables snaked across the floor. A layman wandering through the clean but cluttered lab might think it was a slightly sloppy phone company switching station.

Dyson strode to the center of the room and turned to the eager faces. "Greetings, troops. You're getting your raises!"

Jokingly, his colleagues saluted and cheered. There was not a lab coat in sight. This was a strictly jeans and sneakers crowd. All young and bright like Dyson. They sat at their consoles drinking Pepsis, eating lunches out of fast food bags, and changing technology as the world knew it. And now they clapped their boss on his back and shook his hand. Dyson settled everyone down and told them to punch out early. There was a general groan. Nobody ever punched out early. The competition among the techs and assistants was fierce. The man who left his desk first was considered a pariah. Not only did some of the research staff work six-day weeks, they often worked late on Saturdays. These people were not looking to get laid or take the family to a movie. They wanted what Dyson wanted: the answer to fascinating questions. And the power to change the world.

Bryant, one of the more brash young lab assistants, rushed over to Dyson. "Mr. Dyson? The materials team wants to run another test on Lot Two before they wrap up."

"Yup. Come on. I'll get it."

Bryant had to hustle to keep up as Dyson quickly crossed the lab. "Listen, Mr. Dyson, I know I haven't been here that long, but I was wondering if you could tell me . . . I mean, if you know . . . "

"Know what?"

"Well . . . where it came from."

"I asked that question once. Know what I was told? Don't ask."

Dyson waved to the guard outside the vault-room door. He followed Dyson and Bryant into the small room and stood with them before what looked like a high-tech bank vault. Like the launch controls in a nuclear silo, it required two keys to open. The guard and Dyson inserted their keys and turned them simultaneously. Dyson then typed in a passcode on a keypad mounted in the wall. A moment later, the vault unlocked itself with a sequence of sharp snicks. The door swung open and Dyson went inside.

Bryant stayed outside with the guard, who noted Dyson's name and the time on a clipboard.

Alone in the vault, Dyson walked to a stainless steel cabinet and opened it. Inside was a small artifact in a sealed container of inert gas. Marked Lot Two, in it was a ceramic rectangle, about the size of a domino, the color of liver. It had been shattered, painstakingly reconstructed, and mounted on a metal frame. In that spec of technology was a mystery that had already netted Cyberdyne millions of dollars. And there was more. The circuit design and materials used were totally alien to any known to Dyson. The Other Question nagged at him again, brought up by Bryant, and in the past by himself.

Where, indeed, had it come from?

Who had originally built the circuit?

The Russians? Unlikely. The designs were too delicate.

The Japanese? A possibility, but why hadn't there been similar technology developed overseas in the last few years?

No, this was a one-of-a-kind thing. Dyson couldn't believe it came from the mind of the old man. And Jack Kroll took the secret with him when he died. There was no evidence of where the strange circuit chip originated in his notes. But, Dyson had other, more answerable questions to deal with. That was his life, now.

He reached in and removed the chip, still in its inert-gas flask, and set it on a specially designed cart, handling it like the Turin Shroud. As he closed the cabinet, his eyes fell on the adjacent one. It was labeled Lot One.

If Bryant and the others only knew what was behind *that* door. Only three people did. One was dead. The other was the owner of the company. The third was Dyson. He impulsively unlocked the cabinet and glanced inside at a larger object . . . a mechanically intricate metal hand and forearm.

At the elbow, the metal was twisted and crushed. But the forearm and hand were intact, although the chromed surface was slightly scorched and discolored. It stood upright in its vacuum flask, as if saluting. Dyson stared at it, lost in thought.

Who the hell made *this*?

Don't ask.

A moment of dread passed through him like indigestion. Lot One and Two could have been stolen. He didn't trust Greg Simmons. What if . . . ? But then the rational part of his mind balked. The doubt was reduced to its component parts and locked in a compartment for later contemplation. Maybe they were stolen, maybe they were created under a secret government contract. Once he had opened up the final secret of Lot Two, he thought he might know. Until then . . .

Reluctantly, he closed the cabinet and locked it up tight.

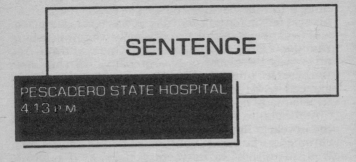

SENTENCE

PESCADERO STATE HOSPITAL
4:13 P M

he stillness in the the interview room was deafening. Sarah could hear her own breathing, and the distant drone of the insects, hypnotically thrumming. The attendants by the door stared at Sarah as if she were one of them.

Behind the mirror, the doctors and Silberman were comparing notes on her. She sensed their objective eyes still on her. Knew they were deciding her fate. She'd been so strategically inept. She had told them too much. And the truth had not made her free.

But she'd been carrying the secret with her for so long. When they first caught her, they were so damned understanding. She trusted them. Trusted they knew their jobs and could tell she wasn't crazy. She had been wrong.

They were doctors, whose world view was filtered through a psychologist's eye. The only "handles" they had on reality came from study of abstracted human behavior. They couldn't accept that she was a perfectly sane woman in an insane world.

Even though she was in a mental hospital, Sarah knew the razor-sharp dividing line between reality and fantasy, between dream and prophesy, between imagination and experience.

While at Pescadero, she had crossed that line many times. But she always knew where she was. Silberman could never understand that. He saw everything from one perspective. His. And he had science and philosophy on his side. And this was his territory. The hospital was filled with women with messianic complexes. She realized she fit the profile perfectly. After all, her son's name was John Connor. J.C. Jesus Christ. And he was fathered by a phantom from the future. Her son's birth was as close as you get to an "immaculate conception." And his sacrifice would save the world. Oh, yes, she had broken laws. Destroyed property. It was clear to her that from Silberman's point of view, she *was* crazy.

Who wouldn't be, knowing what she did? Knowing that civilization was about to slip over into the abyss. That millions of innocent people would die horrible deaths. And even if she could get out and keep protecting John until he rose up out of the ashes with his rebel army, there would still be mass death and destruction incomprehensible even to the most ruthless warrior.

Win or lose the war, the children would still die.

And if she was kept inside these walls, and John was somehow killed, it would be the end of mankind.

Of course she was insane.

But she knew what she was doing.

Silberman came back into the room, wearing his reptilian smile, and sat opposite her at the table. He scratched his nose, then absently stroked her file cover. Finally, he said, "You see, Sarah . . . here's the problem. I know how smart you are and I think you're just telling me what I want to hear. I don't think you really believe what you've been telling me today."

Sarah knew she had always been a shitty liar. Playing him hadn't worked. There was nothing else to do but beg. She leaned forward, channeling the frustration and pain into a single, plaintive sentence. "Let me see my son."

Silberman turned away. Sarah's eyes followed him. Was he considering it? No, she realized, he was stifling a yawn. She reached out one more time.

"Silberman, please. It's very important. He's in danger. At least let me call him—"

"I'm afraid not. Not for a while. I don't see any choice but to recommend to the review board that you stay here another six months."

She'd reasoned with him, tried to trick him, cooperated in every way, fought him, pleaded with him, told him everything he'd wanted to know about every intimate detail of her life, bared her very soul, and none of it had mattered. Silberman's mind had been made up a long time ago.

He was as immovable as blind fate.

And Sarah knew she'd lost.

The barely suppressed hostility erupted into animal fury and she abruptly leaped across the table and grabbed Silberman by the throat, screaming, "YOU SON OF A BITCH!"

Silberman fell back, batting at her ineffectually, and the iron grip of her fingers began to close off his windpipe. But a second later, the two attendants ripped her away, slamming her against the wall. Stunned, she fell on her rear, but then rolled out from under their reach. She was going for Silberman again, and would have gotten him if the larger attendant hadn't been a linebacker in his college days. He tackled her low and they both slammed to the floor, he on top, nearly cracking her ribcage with his weight. The breath was knocked out of Sarah, yet still she writhed and twisted like a cornered bobcat.

Silberman groped in his coat pocket and whipped out a syringe. Gingerly, ducking Sarah's flailing arms, he jabbed it into her.

"Goddammit. Let me go! Silberman! You don't know what you're doing! You fuck! *You're dead! YOU HEAR ME!*"

Silberman had no trouble at all hearing her. His ears rang with her Banshee howls. He quickly signaled, and the attendants mercifully dragged her out. The door slammed behind them and it was suddenly quiet.

Flushed, Silberman brushed a few strands of hair out of his eyes, gasping for breath, then stiffened, remembering he was still being observed by the others behind the mirror.

He cranked up his smile and faced them, shrugging. "Model citizen."

Sarah was dragged to her cell. She fought all the way. But she couldn't break free. The attendants shoved her inside. She backed against the wall as Douglas appeared in the doorway. He grinned and raised two plastic cups.

"I can tell. You really need your meds." He started for her.

Sarah played her last, desperate hand. "Douglas, wait. Listen. I'll do anything to get out of here. Do you understand? *Anything*!"

Douglas stopped a few feet away. Seemed to be thinking it over. Then he said, "How about taking your pill?"

The other two attendants moved in closer. One of them was carrying the electric prod. Douglas added, "I'm a married man. What kind of slime do you think I am?"

And then he offered the cups.

Numbly, she reached for it. Her eyes dulling over, she mechanically swallowed the pill from one cup, and water from the other, then handed them back. Douglas nodded, handing them to one of his assistants.

"Open up," he commanded Sarah.

She obeyed, and he ran his finger around the inside of her mouth, searching for the pill. It was difficult for Sarah not to bite down with all her might.

Douglas withdrew, winking at her. "See, I'll bet you're feeling better already." Then he led the others out. Sarah waited until the face disappeared from the little window, then hurried to the toilet. She stuck her finger down her throat and forced herself to throw up the pill. She quickly flushed it away.

She took a deep breath, trying to center all her energies, and went over to the bed. She flipped it up against the wall and began to pull herself up by her arms. One, two, three, four. Mindless mechanical movement. A place for the frustration and fury. Into her muscles. Making her stronger. One day strong enough to fight them off.

She wasn't going to give up.

Not ever.

TARGET ACQUISITION

The two ten-year-old girls stood in front of the Subway sandwich shop and shyly studied the photo the policeman had offered them. He was leaning out the cruiser window with a broad smile that would have been warm had it not been so forced. One of the girls looked away from his strange expression, instinctively uneasy. The other, not noticing, said, "Yeah, he was here about fifteen minutes ago. I think he said he was going to the Galleria."

"The what?" Officer Austin asked.

She pointed toward a massive concrete complex visible above the houses several blocks away.

Austin turned and stared intently. Abruptly, he snatched the photo back and screeched out of the parking lot toward the Galleria, startling the girls.

Several blocks away, the Terminator cruised slowly on the Harley, eyes roving back and forth across his field of vision with the blind perseverance of a security camera.

A matter of time.

And the Terminator had all the time in the world. There was enough energy stored in the power cells buried deep in his hardened inner chassis to keep him going for at least a hundred years without stopping. With conservation modes, the time could be extended indefinitely. Patience was not a virtue with the man/machine. It was a strategic advantage.

Sooner than later, the cyborg would acquire its target.

He rumbled across an overpass above a drainage canal. The Terminator was scanning not only with its eyes, which of course saw an extended range of visible frequencies, but also with its ears, one of which recorded the full, unequalized range of external sounds, while the other automatically filtered all wind and traffic noises until it narrowed the range down to one auditory signature: a 1990 Honda 125 dirt bike. The command to listen and watch for this particular vehicle was locked in priority memory under target profile.

Sooner than later.

In the last three hours it had locked onto two possibilities. One was ridden by a teenaged girl, the other by a middle-aged man, neither of which fit the profile.

Then it happened again.

The Terminator's head suddenly swiveled. It had heard the signature again. His eyes darted in a shotgun pattern, quickly pinpointing the source of the sound.

Two kids on a 125 down in the canal below.

The zoom servo behind the false-front eyes rotated, snap-magnifying the image by fifteen times, then digitally froze on the driver's face. IDENT POS flashed next to the blurry image of John Connor.

The Terminator wheeled the big Harley around, cutting onto a street that ran parallel to the canal. The target was racing along in the concrete canyon. Terminator had to accelerate to keep it in sight. One eye pointed directly forward, artificially creating depth perception by creating a computer-generated off-angle ghost image. The other eye locked on the target, running ref-checks on the passenger, which came up blank (there was no memory data, perhaps an oversight), and making instantaneous kinetic studies of trajectories, concluding that the target was too far away, and moving too fast for an attempt at contact.

He would have to head him off.

The Terminator hunkered down and increased speed, the Harley's tires hanging onto the gravel-strewn dirt path running alongside the canal by micrometers.

Then he came to another street and had to slow, repositioning its other eye for emergency backup, and using its hyperreal sense of motion and mass to shoot around an oncoming station wagon, missing it by a heartbeat. When Terminator tried to reestablish visual contact with the target, it had disappeared.

Rapidly rescanning the canal below, he came up with zero.

But he could hear the dirt bike's high-pitched squeal. Instantly, he rapid-scanned the area down to the moving quarry.

The dirt bike had driven up a ramp out of the canal back onto the street a half block away, and was wheeling into the parking garage of the Galleria, a vast, four-tiered shopping mall.

The Terminator smoothly leaned the cycle around several slower cars and closed in.

ATTACK RUN

John pushed through the crowded video arcade. It was a riot of cheap electronic sound-effects and glowing monitors depicting mass destruction in video miniature. Tim peeled off by an "Aliens" game where he saw two of his friends. John nodded to a few familiar faces from school, then angled in behind a teenager he didn't know, getting all his "Desert War" F-14s wasted by missiles. John studied the attack patterns.

He was good at that.

When the last aircraft exploded in a shower of digitized debris, and GAME OVER flashed on the screen, John took over the controls and dropped in a token. He pulled back on the stick and the "ground" rapidly fell away. John's brow furrowed and his whole being focused in on the screen. The first missile launch caught him by surprise, but he reacted instantly, evading it by diving low. Then another arced out. John fired his wing cannon and vaporized it.

This game was easy.

In the parking garage, the Terminator's idling Harley rumbled as he stopped at a row of bikes near the escalators. John's little Honda sat proudly with the big

88

street-bikes. The Terminator parked his cycle and shut off the engine.

Officer Austin moved through the flow of people. The place was clogged with Saturday shoppers of all ages. The cop looked from one young male face to the next, anxiously seeking the familiar one. He approached a few kids near Perry's Pizza on the second floor, then showed them the photograph. They could only shrug. He glanced over at a security guard who was eyeing him curiously. Austin considered the possible alternatives and a second later walked up to the man and showed him the photo, asking him to look out for the boy.

In the arcade, John was now lost in an intense battle, going for a new high score at "Missile Command." He deftly parried as the enemy ICBMs deployed their MIRVs . . . the warheads streamed down . . . three, four, no, five, at once. John flicked the controls as rapidly as he could, but it was more than he could deal with. The world erupted in a white hot mushroom cloud.

Game over.

His score appeared. It was in the upper third percentile range, but he had lost the war. Bored, he slouched away from the game, looking for another.

Outside the window, Officer Austin passed. His eyes rested on the spot John had occupied. . .

. . . just as he left it and blended into the crowd.

The cop moved on, down the concourse, out of sight.

John stopped by an "Afterburner" simulator game. Checked his pocket of tokens. Plenty more. He slipped into the cockpit.

The Terminator strode through the shoppers like Paul Bunyon through the forest, incredibly carrying a box of long-stem roses, like some hopeful guy with a hot date. He moved with methodical purpose, knowing the target was close. Face after face was rapid-scanned. No internal bells were sounded.

Sooner than later . . .

Austin had reached the end of the walkway. He had given a cursory check of the stores on all the floors. No

John Connor. He turned to reassess his path, glancing at the storefronts: hot dog stand, shoe store, gift shop, pizza parlor, taco stand, bookstore, video arcade, seafood restaurant—

Austin turned back to the video arcade. A dozen kids posed outside the entrance, each vainly trying to impress the other. More were going in and out all the time. Austin decided to start with a more detailed search of the arcade.

He walked into the maze of chattering, bustling youths.

Across the room, John was shooting down MiGs at Mach 2. Tim slid up next to him, tapping him on the shoulder, trying to play it cool but only partly succeeding. There was controlled panic in his voice. "Some cop is scoping for you, dude."

"Right," John said, shrugging him off.

"Really, man, look!"

John knew this was bullshit, but glanced around the corner of the "Afterburner" ride anyway. A tall, lean uniformed cop was showing a picture to a group of kids nearby. They were gaping at it, frowning. One of them pointed his way.

Adrenaline kickstarted John's heart and he ducked just as the cop glanced over. John scrambled out the other side and headed for the back of the arcade, instinctively retreating.

One early lesson his mother had taught him was that cops were bad news.

Austin approached the ride and caught a glimpse of John moving down a row of arcade machines. Austin lunged after.

John glanced over his shoulder and saw his worst fears take shape as the cop began pushing through the crowd. The boy increased his pace, darting around a short, fat teenager.

The cop was closing in, slamming the fat kid to the floor. An eddy of outrage began to build behind him as he started running right for John.

John needed no more incentive. He broke into a dead-run.

So did the cop.

Kids scattered like ten-pins as Austin charged through them. John sprinted through the arcade's back office and storerooms, dodging the assistant manager, and burst out a firedoor into the service corridor. The long, underlit tunnel led directly to the parking garage and escape. If only he could make it. Heart hammering, John burst into a flat-out dash for the far door.

He was halfway there when the Terminator stepped into view.

In an instant, John recognized the face. He had seen it many times in the newspaper clippings his mother had shown him as he was growing up. It was that guy. The crazy dude who shot up that police station. The one his mother thought was a terminator. He was standing here now, plain as the nose on his face. John desperately tried to brake to a stop before he collided with the stranger.

The target was acquired.

The cold black steel of his shotgun emerged as the box fell open, the roses spilling to the floor. The Terminator's boot crushed the flowers as it moved forward, raising the gauge's barrel.

John, transfixed by terror, was trapped in the narrow featureless shooting gallery of the corridor, a proto-plasmic version of a video target. For an instant time seemed to grind to a halt, and in his hyped state, the boy realized that the crazy dude was going to try to kill him.

The Terminator expressionlessly jacked a round into the chamber, moving slowly and fluidly, as if he'd done it a million times. The *ker-chack* was thunderous in the corridor.

Time began to rev back up to speed as John skidded to a stop and whirled to run the other way.

But the cop was sprinting toward him in a fast, as-sured lope, pulling his Beretta pistol as he came, and aiming right at him!

John looked back at the stranger. He was staring into the black muzzle of the gauge, leveled at his head. John had never felt so desolate in his life. The cold, bloody visions of mindless violence that had plagued his nights for years were now becoming real, with him in the center.

John couldn't do one thing about it.

Then something crazy happened . . .

The man with the shotgun suddenly said, "Get down," in a bland, casual voice.

John liked the sound of that so much he obeyed instantly, throwing himself to the floor.

The shotgun blast over his head nearly deafened him.

John looked back to see the cop catch the shell square in the chest just as he fired his pistol. His bullet ricocheted harmlessly off the ceiling. Before he could reaim, the stranger pumped another round into him.

Then another.

Advancing a step each time he fired, he emptied the shotgun into the cop, blowing him backward down the corridor, the shock of each hit making the man's body buck. John saw no blood, just flashes of chrome as each shell struck the cop. The sounds of each explosion ran together into a harsh, ringing echo.

Then hollow silence.

John sat up, eyes wide, not breathing, just gaping at the dead man at the other end of the hall.

The cop was on his back, unmoving.

A shadow fell across John and he looked up at the stranger looming right over him. But he wasn't looking at John, he was watching the far end of the corridor. John turned back.

The cop slowly sat up.

John frowned, thinking he was back in the nightmare.

The officer rose to his feet as if he'd just tripped instead of been shot with five 10-gauge rounds. It didn't make any sense to John.

It did to the Terminator. He grabbed John roughly by his jacket and clutched the kid to his chest, then spun around as the cop opened fire with the Beretta. He coolly pulled the trigger so fast it almost seemed like a machine-pistol. The 9mm slugs slammed into the Terminator's back, punching bloody holes in the motorcycle jacket.

A startled man emerged from a restroom and stepped right into the line of fire. He was instantly cut down by the fusillade. Then the Beretta clacked on empty.

John looked down, shaking, and realized with relief he wasn't hit. The crazy dude's body had taken all the impacts. But he seemed to show no pain whatsoever. John gaped at the bleeding wounds as the man lifted him with one hand and then shoved him into an electrical utility room. He dropped the empty shotgun and started walking toward the officer.

The cop dropped his spent magazine. It clattered to the floor. He rapidly, but calmly, inserted another one and in a continuous motion, snapped back the slide.

The Terminator still had twenty feet to go. He didn't break his purposeful stride. The cop opened fire. Bullets raked the cyborg's chest, raising miniature red geysers of blood and tissue as they impacted. The Terminator didn't even flinch. Ten feet to go. *BLAM BLAM BLAM BLAM!*

Neither the cop nor the Terminator showed the slightest change in expression as the gun ripped the Terminator's jacket to shreds. The pistol emptied again. The Terminator stopped two feet in front of the cop. They appraised each other for a second. The cyborg towered over his lean, uniformed opponent. It looked as if the former could snap the latter in two like a matchstick.

The Terminator did multiscans and knew instantly what he was up against. But there was little detailed technical information other than nomenclature and basic operational strengths and weaknesses. The programming for this information had been hastily made by a man who had only memory to go on. The cyborg began racing through tactical probabilities, a dozen a second, and none of them was coming up positive.

One thing the cyborg concluded quickly was it was

better to be on the offensive. It lashed out an arm, grabbing the cop in its massive hands, but Austin snapped back with a surprisingly powerful countergrip.

John peered around the door and gawked at the two combatants as they slammed each other into the walls on both sides of the corridor. The thin plaster was smashed in. The smaller man lifted the Terminator into the air as if he were a toy and flung him through the wall, then leaped in after.

John sat on his haunches, frozen with shock. His mind could not form a frame of reference for what had just happened. And then another adrenaline rush kicked in and he staggered to his feet, remembering to run. His legs felt like limp rubber and he almost tripped, but the muted thuds of the two men thrashing around on the far side of the wall stiffened them. John picked up speed as he ran down the hallway, rammed the door, and burst through into the parking garage.

The security guard was on the first floor of the mall promenade, still scanning the crowd for someone who looked like the suspect the cop had shown him when he heard a loud crash high above him. It came from the third floor. A shower of plate glass was raining down. People were screaming. The guard danced back as the shards pincushioned a large planter, shredding the topiary tree in it, and reached for his .38 revolver, fumbling with the holster snap. When he glanced up again, a man crashed through the third floor metal-and-glass railing and arced out in an ungraceful backflip, as if he had been flung like a ragdoll. He hit like a sack of wet cement amid the screaming crowd.

Officer Austin appeared at the railing, swatting aside a store mannequin that had gotten entangled around his leg, and glanced down. The security guard lowered the gun, uncertain, as he saw the cop abruptly turn and walk out of sight.

Stunned patrons scrambled to create a path for the grim-looking policeman as he headed back through the shattered clothing store window, accelerating slowly into a loping, predatory run. He was vectoring the target's possible escape trajectories in what would have felt like a fluid rush of meaningless digital codes to a human mind. Because, of course, "Austin" was as far from human as you could get.

Within six seconds, it had careened back into the service corridor and was running down it like a humanoid locomotive on a downgrade to destruction. As it ran, the thing reloaded the Beretta, almost as an afterthought.

On the first floor, the Terminator lay totally still amid glass shards. A man who had been snapping off pictures of his girlfriend near one of the planters whirled and cautiously stepped forward, jaw dropped, and impulsively took a picture of the body. Then the dead man's eyes suddenly snapped open.

The man blinked and backed away as the Terminator sat up and looked around. His internal sensors indicated he had had a consciousness discontinuity for approximately four seconds, brought about by massive simultaneous shock to the complete system. But immediate damage assessment indicated all systems were back on-line. All servos were within operational parameters. He rose smoothly to his feet. The amazed man's camera whirred as the motor-drive ran on by itself, taking shot after shot, the owner unknowingly depressing the shutter, his eyes on the large corpse pushing through the confused crowd. The Terminator ran toward the escalator, racing up them in a blur.

Fearing the usual endless delay of the elevators, John had run all the way down the stairs to the garage level where his bike was parked. All the while his mind labored under the heavy load of unreality. Why had the cop tried to kill him. Who the hell was that other guy? And most importantly, how come neither one of them was dead? As John raced up to his Honda, lungs heaving, a spark of a thought sputtered. About men who would not die easily. Something his mom had told him. But no, that was really crazy.

Wasn't it?

John frantically pumped the kick-starter. Nothing.

The engine refused to turn over. His hands were shaking so badly he couldn't find the choke. The sound of rapid footfalls made him look up to see—

The cop running out of the stairwell toward him.

John's body went into overdrive, and a strange, vibrating calm came over him. If he didn't set the choke properly, he would die. Willing his fingers not to tremble so violently, he made the adjustment. This time, when he kicked the starter, the bike screamed to life. Which was good because the cop was almost on him.

John slammed the bike into gear and spun it out into the main aisle of the garage. John saw the man coming after him in the rearview mirror, legs blurring at an impossible rate. He twisted the throttle and gunned the bike up to forty miles an hour, which was asking for trouble in the confined space John had to maneuver in.

Incredibly, the officer was gaining! John went into a radical lean and brodied around the rear of a parked car, then raced out the exit ramp, flying right into the street and the busy traffic.

John had to lean hard to avoid a wall of metal looming up in his lane. The huge Kenworth tow truck was designed to haul out-of-commission semis, and its massive wheels bore down on the boy on the dirt bike, locking at the last moment and going into a skid.

The driver swore and hit his air horn. Goddamn crazy punk, he was grumbling as he watched the dirt bike weave dangerously around the slower-moving traffic ahead. Kid should get his head bounced against the pavement once or twice to teach him some road manners.

But ruder things were about to happen. There was a loud thump as something slammed against the driver's door. He glanced over and saw a cop clinging to the open window. Suddenly, he ripped the door open and in one powerful movement, gripped the amazed driver by the throat and pulled him right out of the still-moving truck, tossing him onto the street as if he were a paper cup. It was the driver's head that bounced on the pavement several times, as he rolled into the opposite lane. Brakes squealed and cars fishtailed all around him. He wound up in a sitting position, dazed, and watched the cop leap onto the seat and accelerate away without missing a beat.

Some fucking police emergency, the driver thought, as he reached for his throbbing head. As he tried to crawl out of the street, people were getting out of their cars to help him. He looked up as one ran toward him.

"I'm all right," the driver said, hoping he was. Then all the onlookers scattered and the driver saw a man on a huge motorcycle racing toward him. He wasn't slowing down. In fact, he was picking up speed. The driver struggled to get to his feet, but his legs wouldn't work right. The cycle was practically on him, the man driving impossibly fast into the now nearly stopped traffic, weaving crazily away in the direction of the stolen truck.

John had seen the truck driver tossed onto the pavement by the crazed cop in his mirror. He angled around a braking Jeep and glanced back again.

The cop was now behind the wheel of the huge tow truck, and gaining on him by smashing through traffic like a drunken dinosaur, slamming into one car and driving it onto the sidewalk into a small tree, sideswiping another, bouncing it into oncoming traffic. The cop upshifted and roared on.

The truck was now only two car-lengths away from the dirt bike. John saw an intersection coming up and suddenly heeled over, arcing in front of a station wagon and darting down a side street.

John didn't have to look back to know the cop was following. He could hear the screech of brakes and the crunch of metal grinding on metal. But there *was* an out. A place where this nightmare couldn't follow, especially in that truck. John's private little road.

He downshifted and brodied his bike down the service ramp to the drainage canal faster than he'd ever done it before. Feeling the tires beneath him losing traction, he slammed his foot down to prevent a slideout. Then he leaned over the handlebars and opened the throttle all the way.

The little Honda shot off the ramp onto the damp bottom of the canal, and raced into a narrower tributary that has vertical sides. Now no one could see him from the road. And he was on a direct route back to his house. If the cop hadn't gotten his license plate, maybe he was home-free.

Holding his breath, John slowed and dared to look back.

No sign of pursuit.

Except . . .

No, no no, John thought as he saw the sun blocked out by a great shadow. The tow truck, big as a house, all chrome and roaring diesel engine, crashed through the overpass berm, blasting concrete bricks in all directions, and launched itself right into the center of the canal.

It looked for a moment as if it would fly, but then gravity reclaimed its dominance and the truck came crashing down in a shower of debris. It hit nose-first and bounced up, still going about fifty. For a moment, the wheels were crossed up, and it smashed into the concrete wall with a hideous grinding of metal. But it ricocheted back, bellowing like a gutshot stegosaurus, and just kept on plowing forward, gathering speed.

Right for John.

The boy twisted the throttle, milking every last bit of power the 125cc engine had. The Kenworth was all muscle, tearing along the canal like a train in a tunnel. Its big tires sent up huge sheets of muddy spray, backlit in the setting sun. It looked like some kind of demon, hungry for his soul. John could feel it creeping up, see in his mirror the canal behind him cut off by the looming truck. It looked as though he could reach back and touch the tow truck's grill. But the throttle would not turn any farther. The Honda's rpm gauge was nearing redline. The bike was going sixty-four miles an hour, blasting through pockets of water and slashing through small mounds of debris.

And still the tow truck was gaining.

John was too busy trying to stay ahead of the truck to notice, but above them on the service road running parallel, a Harley was roaring along not far behind. It was the Terminator, fighting to overtake them.

The cyborg saw John and the Tow Truck from Hell, now only about twenty feet behind him, closing the gap. The Terminator pulled the shotgun he had retrieved from the service corridor from inside his leather coat. Aimed one-handed and fired.

The shot punctured the chrome exhaust-pipe near the driver's side. The cop didn't turn, his eyes only on the small target just ahead of it in the canal.

John hit a pool of water and slewed momentarily, losing speed. The massive push-plate on the front of the truck slammed into his back fender. The rear wheel almost broke loose. The truck's diesel engine was howling in his ears, and the push-plate began to close in on the Honda's rear wheel again.

The Terminator retargeted and fired again, but the uneven gravel and dirt surface caused his aim to deflect half a millimeter, which was enough to throw the shot so far off it took a chunk out of the concrete wall behind the truck. The cyborg concluded it could not complete its mission under these conditions. So it altered the conditions.

The Terminator cut the bike suddenly hard to the side, leaving the road and hitting an earth embankment just right. The cycle vaulted into the air, flying over the fence bordering the canal. The big Harley was the least aerodynamic vehicle possible, but the cyborg made rapid shifts in his position relative to the gravity vectors to force the cycle to stay upright as the seven-hundred pound machine sailed out into space and plummeted fifteen feet into the canal. It hit hard, bottoming out, an explosion of sparks shooting out from under the frame. Only the ultra-fast reflexes of a machine could have kept it from sliding out. The Terminator fought for control.

And won.

The cyborg gunned the throttle and the powerful motorcycle shot between the tow truck and the wall, inches from either, then blasted through and roared up beside John's tiny Honda.

John glanced over and saw the Harley match his speed. A big hand reached out and swept him off his bike. For a second, he dangled by one of the man's enormous arms. The pavement blurring by below, the Honda still moving, still upright from the momentum, the truck edging closer . . .

The Terminator swung John onto the Harley, in front of him. The Honda weaved and fell back, smashed instantly under the Kenworth's thundering tires.

The Harley's powerful engine was fed maximum throttle and it surged ahead, reaching eighty in three seconds. The tow truck began to fall back, unable to match the speed.

Ahead was an overpass, and supporting it an abutment that bisected the canal into two channels. The Harley thundered into one channel, essentially a short tunnel.

Officer Austin rapidly calculated that the truck couldn't fit on either side. Neither would its mass and speed allow it to stop in time. However, the damage to itself could be minimalized. Tires locked and slid on the muddy concrete and plowed into the concreted abutment at sixty-five miles an hour.

Concrete and steel kissed and in their passionate embrace came an earth-shattering orgasm of rent matter. The cab of the truck rode up the abutment for a few feet before the rest of the mass crumpled it like a cardboard box. Gasoline spurted out from the ruptured tank. A loosened battery cable dropped into a pool of it and . . .

The Harley emerged from the tunnel, looking back to see a fireball blasting through behind them as the truck's side-mounted gas tanks exploded.

The Terminator went into a slide and stopped the cycle. John peered around his body to see the destruction. It was a blast furnace in the tunnel. Yet something was moving in it. And it was coming their way.

The stranger reached into his jacket and started to pull out the shotgun. Then hesitated.

A burning wheel wobbled out of the tunnel and flopped comically in the mud. John saw the hungry flames engulf the truck and send black smoke into the air. There was no way anything could have walked away from that hell.

The Terminator revved the bike and they sped away down the canal, disappearing around a bend.

Flame boiled from the tunnel as if a living thing reaching after them. Then it did become "living" as a figure moved in the blaze.

Just an outline. Walking slowly . . . calmly.

The humanoid figure emerged from the tunnel, its smooth, chromelike surfaces reflecting the conflagration behind it. It looked like liquid mercury poured into a human mold. Its joints didn't bend or fold, they flowed around angles. It was not a servomechanism like the Terminator was underneath, with its complex hydraulics and cables. Its face was simple, unformed, devoid of features.

Unruffled by the thousand-degree heat, it walked out of the tunnel. With each step detail began to return. First the shapes and lines of its clothing emerged from the liquid chrome surface, then finer details . . . buttons, badge, facial features, ears. . . . But it was all still metal. Like mercury. The mercury man.

With its last step, the color returned to everything. It was Officer Austin again. Handsome young face, cold eyes. Those eyes focused on the drainage canal ahead. Where the target had gone.

It didn't have a wafer-circuit brain to think with. It was something on a completely new level of artificial intelligence. The molecular brain acted like the rest of the thing, a liquid. And now it bubbled with possibilities.

All of them lethal.

The distant sound of approaching sirens reached its auditory sensors, which could have been formed anywhere on its body (since every molecule had the "genetic" blueprints for all needed parts programmed into them), but were now in the shape of human ears. It climbed out of the canal in the cover of the suffocating smoke as several patrol cars arrived. Policeman jumped out and pushed the gathering crowd of amazed onlookers back, keeping a path open for the first of the fire engines that were racing to the scene. One of the cops who pushed back the crowd had a handsome young face and cold eyes. There are always cops at disasters and scenes of violence. The mercury man's choice of protective mimicry was, of course, perfect. Perfect because it was here to protect and to serve.

To protect and serve Skynet.

As a fire engine screeched up and the firemen leaped off, trailing hoses, "Officer Austin" walked among the other cops unnoticed, and got into one of the squad cars. No one paid attention.

It started the engine and drove off to complete its mission.

REVELATION

Terminator, with John in front of him on the Harley, roared down an empty suburban street, having taken one of the circuitous routes Terminator had mapped out earlier. John was still shaking from the experience of what had just happened. In that moment he was completely an adolescent kid. But he was also more than that.

He was John Connor.

With the genetic structure and the social smarts to finally begin to put this nightmare into perspective, as no other child could have. Which was not to say it was easy. Because it meant accepting something so wild that it made his skin crawl. But John respected facts. And he was riding with one now. About as solid a fact as you could get.

John craned his neck around to get a look at the person/thing he was riding with and said, "Whoa . . . time out. Stop the bike!"

Terminator immediately complied, leaning the bike into a turn. They headed into a nearby alley and came to a stop. John slid off the gas tank, his legs still weak. Terminator impassively stared at him. John checked him out. There were bloody bullet holes all over his back.

Wild. But it had to be.

"Now don't take this the wrong way, but you are a terminator, right?"

The "man" answered in a tight, neutral tone. "Yes. Cyberdyne Systems, Model 101. Series 800."

"No way!" John blurted out, but he was already convinced. Still, John touched Terminator's skin. It felt warm, but somehow . . . different. Then the blood on his jacket. It looked very real. And now he let the realization sink in, and his mind overloaded as the reality of it hit him.

"Holy shit . . . you're really real! I mean . . . whoa! You're, uh . . . like a machine underneath, right . . . but sort of alive outside?"

The cyborg answered as if reading a technical manual. "I'm a cybernetic organism. Living tissue over a metal endoskeleton."

"This is intense. Get a grip, John. Okay, uh . . . you're not here to kill me . . . I figured that part out for myself. So what's the deal?"

"My mission is to protect you."

"Yeah?" Really wild. But John was a practiced paranoic. He put it to use and asked, "Who sent you?" If he answered that one right, it was shorts-eating time.

"You did. Thirty-five years from now you reprogrammed me to be your protector here, in this time."

John swallowed his shorts. "This is deep."

Terminator glanced around and determined that they had stayed in one spot too long. He suggested that they keep moving. John was too blown away to do anything but numbly hop on.

A few minutes later, they were weaving through the side streets again, blending into the evening traffic. In the gathering darkness, Terminator's wounds were not readily visible. John craned his head up and back.

"So this other guy? He's a terminator, too, right, like you?"

"Not like me. A T-1000. Advanced prototype. A mimetic polyalloy."

"What's that mean?"

"Liquid metal."

"Radical," John said.

"You are targeted for termination. The T-1000 will not stop until it completes its mission. Ever."

That sounded wonderful. And familiar. But John couldn't let himself think about that yet. They were turning onto Ventura Boulevard, and traffic was thickening as dates sought the many restaurants on the street. "Where we going?"

"We must leave the city immediately. And avoid the authorities."

"Can I stop by my house?"

"Negative. The T-1000 will definitely try to reacquire you there."

"You sure?"

Terminator looked down at the boy through the dark sunglasses, his expression unreadable, and said, "I would."

John realized something with a shock and shouted, "We got to get to a pay phone!"

Terminator saw one a block ahead and accelerated to it. John leaped off the cycle and ran to the battered booth. He quickly went through his pockets for change, pulling out a huge wad of twenties, but no coins. "Shit!" He turned back to Terminator. "Look, Todd and Janelle are dicks but I gotta warn them. You got a quarter?"

Terminator dismounted and walked up, reaching past John to smash the coverplate off the phone's cash box with the heel of his hand. A shower of change tumbled out. Terminator handed a quarter to John.

"Thanks," John said and started dialing.

About seven miles across the Valley, Janelle Voight picked up the kitchen phone and cradled it with her shoulder while she continued to chop vegetables with a large knife. "Hello?" she said sweetly.

"Janelle? It's me," came through the receiver. In the backyard the German shepherd was going bonkers, barking viciously at something.

"John? Where are you, honey? It's late. You should come home, dear. I'm making a casserole."

John could barely hear her over the noise of the dog. Even so, he knew she didn't sound right. He covered the phone's mouthpiece and whispered to Terminator, "Something's wrong. She's never this nice."

Todd came into the kitchen from the hallway, sleepy-eyed. He'd been asleep in the back bedroom, totally out of it until the dog's barks had yanked him back to consciousness. He passed Janelle, ignoring her as usual, and fished around in the fridge.

"Shit, outta beer," he said to nobody in particular. There was a half-filled carton of milk. Reluctantly, he took a sip, and turned toward the backyard. The dog was running back and forth behind its fence, hardly taking a breath between yaps. "What the hell's the goddamn dog barking at? SHUT UP, YOU MUTT!"

Todd started to walk out of the kitchen behind her. Janelle calmly switched the phone to her other hand and reached out. Her arm started to melt into liquid metal, then harden into a gleaming spike. Todd looked down at it incomprehendingly. He was about to smile, thinking this was some kind of impossibly screwy joke when the cold metal shaft penetrated the milk carton in his hand and on through to his throat and the back of his brain with a sharp sluicing sound.

At the pay phone, John cupped the phone again, turning to Terminator. "The dog's really barking. My mom used to say that dogs could spot terminators. Maybe it's already there. What should I do?"

Terminator took the phone from John's hand and listened. Janelle was saying, "John? John, are you there?"

Terminator answered in a perfect imitation of John's voice.

"I'm right here. I'm fine." Then he turned to John and whispered, "What is the dog's name?"

"Max."

Terminator nodded and spoke into the phone. "Hey, Janelle, what's wrong with Wolfy? I can hear him barking. Is he okay?"

The answer came back without hesitation. "Wolfy's fine, honey. Where are you?"

Terminator unceremoniously hung up the phone. John frowned expectantly. The cyborg said it like a weather report: "Your foster parents are dead. Let's go."

Terminator headed for the bike. John, shocked, stared after him.

In the Voight kitchen, Janelle hung up. Her expression was neutral and calm, even though she was looking at her husband pinned to the kitchen cabinet by the spike at the end of her metal arm. His eyes were glassy and lifeless. She rapidly withdrew the spike and Todd stood there a second before slumping to the floor amid a pool of blood-streaked milk.

The spike smoothly changed shape and color, transforming back into a hand. The rest of Janelle followed suit, melting into the T-1000's version of Officer Austin. It had more work to do here. It needed a little more time. But the dog would create too much attention.

The T-1000 approached the dog, which slunk away from it, barking in fear now. The cop opened the gate and stepped inside the dog run. The animal backed into a shadowed corner, trembling, unable to comprehend what this thing standing before it was.

In a sudden blur too rapid for the German shepherd to detect, the T-1000 leaned down and rapidly formed a finger spike. It perfunctorily rammed it into the animal's neck. The cop rose, examining the bloody dog collar. It read the word MAX on the side. Realizing it had been fooled, it dropped the collar and headed back toward the house.

The parking lot behind the gas station was off a quiet street. The Harley sat well back from the pool of yellow cast by an overhead sodium-vapor streetlight. Terminator had determined they could stop for strategic communications for only a few minutes. The cyborg stood near the motorcycle blankly watching John pace before him. John's brain was calling time-out. "I need a minute here, okay? You're telling me it can imitate anything it touches?"

"Anything it samples by physical contact," was the toneless reply.

John thought about that, trying to grasp their opponent's parameters.

"Like it could disguise itself as anything . . . a pack of cigarettes?"

"No. Only an object of equal mass."

This bit of information didn't help. John was still reeling from meeting one terminator, which now seemed downright conventional next to the exotic new model. "Well, why didn't it just become a bomb or something to get me?"

Terminator spoke without emotion, yet it seemed by the words it chose there was just the slightest trace of professional jealously. "It can't form complex machines. Guns and explosives have chemicals, moving parts. It doesn't work that way. But it can form solid metal shapes."

The T-1000 walked down the dark hall, passing the bathroom. The real Janelle's legs were through the half-open door. The shower was running. Her blood mixed with water on the white tile floor.

The cop strode into John's bedroom and began searching methodically in the dark. It didn't need lights. It could sense the molecular structure of things by touch. Calmly and dispassionately it ran its finger across the surfaces of things in the room. As it touched a desk, the fingers fleetingly turned dark brown, then as they passed over a sheaf of papers, white. Whatever the fingers stroked, they momentarily began to mimic its molecular structure. The T-1000 hesitated over the small Tandy home computer, letting the digitized information on the discs nearby flow into its hand. Names. Dates. Video games. Schoolwork. It could read magnetically encoded plus-minus information directly, if it chose. There was nothing that the T-1000 found useful. But it was all filed anyway in the liquid memory.

It was only when it ran its hand over a Public Enemy poster on the wall that it stopped. But it wasn't what was on the flag. It was what was beneath it. The cop ripped the poster down and saw a small hole that had been crudely carved into the wallboard. In it was a battered shoebox filled with stacks of audio cassettes.

It visually scanned the labels. They were marked "Messages from Mom," and numbered. There was also an envelope with three folded letters, and a dozen snapshots. It began looking through the latter.

Sarah in olive cammos with an RPG grenade launcher, teaching John how to aim.

Sarah with a group of military-clad Guatemalan men, standing next to cases of stinger missiles.

John and Sarah in a Contra camp, deep in the mountains.

They were images that had no emotional impact on the T-1000, since its construction was even less likely to produce feelings than a computer. But to John or Sarah Connor, they were the emotional touchstone of their relationship during the years when they were on the run, in hiding.

Fifteen miles away, John was sitting on a rusting car, lost in stunned thought. Terminator stood above him, watching the street like a hyperalert Doberman. He glanced down at John as the boy continued to talk, uncertain if the words had any tactical relevance, but listening just in case they did.

"We spent a lot of time in Nicaragua . . . places like that. For a while she was with this crazy ex-Green Beret guy, running guns. Then there were some other guys." The rest he said with an undertone of bitterness. "She'd shack up with anybody she could learn from. So then she could teach me how to be this great military leader. Then she gets busted and it's like . . . sorry kid, your mom's a psycho. Didn't you know? Oh, you thought all mothers acted like that? Well, yeah, what did I know?

It's like . . . everything I'd been brought up to believe was just made-up bullshit, right?"

Then John felt the anger rushing up from where he usually managed to keep it confined, deep in his chest, behind his heart. "I hated her for that," he said softly. Then he looked up at the towering "man" beside him and the anger melted into shame and John said, "But everything she said was true."

There were hot tears waiting to be cried, but they didn't have time. John had allowed the final realization of the day's events to wash over him. And now his whole world had flipped upside down again. His mother wasn't crazy—the world was. The proof was next to him, scanning for the enemy. And now John realized that not only was the world wrong about Sarah Connor, but he had been, too. *She was right.*

Right.

There was no time to think about it, to feel about it, anymore. If everything his mother had told him was right . . .

John rose to his feet, and if someone human were standing next to him, they would have seen that spark of purposeful command that would one day make him a leader of men. "We gotta get her out of there."

The cyborg did not hesitate. "Negative. The T-1000's highest probability for success now would be to copy Sarah Connor and wait for you to make contact with her."

"Oh, great. And what happens to her?"

Terminator's reply was typically matter-of-fact. "Usually, the subject being copied is terminated."

"TERMINATED? Shit! Why didn't you tell me? We gotta go right now!"

"Negative. She is not a mission priority."

"Yeah, well fuck you! She's a priority to me!"

John turned and strode away. Terminator went after him and grabbed his arm. John struggled uselessly against the cyborg's powerful grip. "Hey, goddammit! What's your problem?" he screamed, furious.

Terminator started dragging John back to the bike.

The boy spotted two college-age slab-o-meat jockstraps across the street and started yelling to them.

"Help! HELP! I'm being kidnapped! Get this psycho off of me!"

The two glanced at each other, then smiled. "Goddamn molester. Let's go get him." They started crossing the street, eager to be heroes.

John yelled at the top of his lungs at Terminator, "Let go of me!"

To his surprise, Terminator's hand opened so fast John fell on his butt. Startled, the boy looked up at the open hand. "Oww! Why'd you do that?"

"You told me to," the cyborg answered evenly.

John stared at him in amazement as he realized . . . "You have to do what I say?"

"That is one of the mission parameters."

"Prove it. . . . Stand on one foot."

Terminator expressionlessly lifted one leg. John grinned, thinking I'm the first on my block to own . . . The thought was so outrageous, he had to say it out loud. "Cool! My own terminator. This is *great!*"

The two jocks walked up and looked at the big guy in black leather and dark glasses standing there calmly with one leg up in the air. A whacko.

One of them turned to John. "Hey, kid. You okay?"

John realized he no longer needed to be rescued. "Take a hike, Bozo."

Fucking gratitude, the jock thought. "Yeah? Fuck you, you little dipshit."

"Dipshit? Did you say dipshit?!" John howled. Then he turned to the cyborg and said, "Grab this guy."

Terminator complied instantly, hoisting him one-handed by the hair. The guy's legs were pinwheeling in air.

"Now who's a dipshit, you jock douchebag?"

Immediately, things got out of hand. The guy's friend jumped behind Terminator and tried to grab him in a full nelson, but the cyborg threw him across across the hood of the car, whipping out his .45 in a quick blur, aiming the muzzle at the guy's forehead.

With a yelp, John instinctively grabbed the cyborg's arm as he pulled the trigger. John's weight was barely enough to deflect the gun a few inches.

The guy flinched, stunned by the *K-BOOM* next to his ear. He gaped, shocked so bad he wasn't aware that he had wet his shorts. John screamed at Terminator. "Put the gun down! NOW!"

Taking the command literally, Terminator set the .45 on the sidewalk. John scooped it up fast, then turned to the stunned civilians, who couldn't believe what had just happened. "Walk away," the boy said.

They did.

Fast.

John grabbed Terminator by the arm and tugged him toward the bike. John still held the gun, reluctant to give it back.

"Jesus . . . you were gonna kill that guy!"

"Of course. I'm a terminator."

John gaped at the impassive face. Having your own terminator just became a little bit less fun. "Listen to me very carefully, okay? You're not a terminator anymore. All right? You got that? You can't just go around killing people!"

"Why?"

"Whattaya mean, why? 'Cause you can't!"

"Why?"

"You just can't, okay. Trust me on this."

Terminator did not understand the concept. It had been given a programming command. Destroy anything or any entity that threatened the life of John Connor. It had also a priority hierarchical command that would not allow him to let an attack against itself go unanswered. And yet, he also had an order to obey the commands of John Connor. So he tried to comply, but he was having trouble with the concept of trust. He had read the definition off its internal lexicon, but even in this contextual situation, it seemed a paradox. Machines, even ones with artificial intelligence closely approximating the complexity and depth of a human being's, did not like paradoxes.

John was looking at the huge cyborg and suddenly

realized the weight of responsibility that came with power. The thing was like his personal sidearm, and he now had to watch what he said. And yet, if he were to go get his mother before anything else could get to her, he would need that weapon. On the other hand, he had no time to discuss the matter. He handed the .45 back to Terminator, who put it away.

"Look, I'm gonna go get my mom. I order you to come with me."

John started to walk away.

Terminator stuck his .45 in his waistband and followed the boy over to the Harley. He had no choice but to obey.

At the Voight house, in John's bedroom, the T-1000 was reading the last of the letters from Sarah. It scanned the return address on the envelope, PNT-82, ISOLATION WARD, PESCADERO STATE HOSPITAL, and the date, (only two weeks ago), and quickly concluded that the primary target may go there. In a matter of moments it was moving down the street, away from the city, and toward its secondary target.

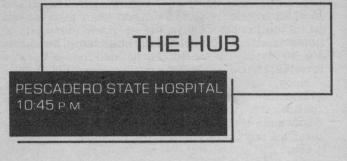

THE HUB

The black-and-white photograh was a nightmare image from the past: a surveillance camera still-frame that showed blurry forms of cops frozen in the emergency lights of a burning corridor. A black-clad figure stood at the end of the corridor. He had short-cropped hair and dark glasses. An AR-180 assault rifle in one hand, and a 12-gauge in the other, holding them both like toy pistols. Another photo was slapped on top of the first: the same angle, a moment later, showing the figure standing very near the surveillance camera.

Detective Weatherby pondered the images with weary eyes. It was a bitch of an unsolved case. An entire night shift of cops killed or injured, by one gunman. They had never found him. Weatherby had lost a friend that night. But he wasn't on this case for personal reasons. He was out to stop a cop killer. And he had to rely on this poor woman's obviously fragile memory to help him do it. He looked up at Sarah Connor and said, "These were taken at the Rampart Division West Highland police station back in 1984. You were there."

They were in the examination room Sarah had been dragged out of hours ago. She looked at the stack of

114

photos Weatherby had tossed on the table in front of her. She looked up at the detective. It was not a kind face, but it was not particularly cruel either. He was just doing his job. His partner Detective Mossberg, an unassuming man with ill-fitting clothes and bad teeth, sat across from her. Sitting beside them all was a watchful Dr. Silberman, trying unsuccessfully to sublimate his irritation.

Two uniformed cops stood by the door, flanking Douglas, who didn't even try to disguise his irritation. Sarah stared listlessly at the top photo. She looked like the day she'd been having.

"He killed seventeen police officers that night. Recognize him?"

Weatherby slapped another black-and-white eight-by-ten on the table: A close-up of a bloody terminator rising up from a pile of glass, surrounded by an astonished crowd. Of course, it wore the same face. "This one was taken in a mall in the valley. Today."

Sarah said and did nothing. She just looked down at the photograph and breathed. From the outside she looked like a typical, drugged, high-security basket case. From the inside she was straining to maintain control in the face of an enormous desire to flip over the table, smash it into Silberman's face, then crash through Douglas and the cops at the door, then race down the hall and burst through the security doors and out into the parking lot and hot-wire a car—

But it couldn't happen that way, so she just sat there, hoping it would happen the other way, the way she was now piecing together as she looked down at something next to the photos.

Weatherby broke the moment of silence. "Ms. Connor, your son's missing. His foster parents have been murdered, and we know this guy's involved."

Sarah looked up at him. A cold and empty expression. And said nothing.

Weatherby scowled and said, "Talk to us."

She had been in a few junior-high-school plays. Her drama teacher Mrs. Kolb would have been delighted by her performance here.

"Don't you care?"

Evidently not, by the wall of indifference she showed him. Weatherby glanced at Silberman, then his partner, and shrugged. "Guess this wasn't such a good idea. Come on, we're wasting our time."

One of the uniformed cops opened the door and Mossberg strode into the hall. Weatherby and the two uniforms followed him out, with Silberman right behind. That supercilious tone had returned to his voice as he said, "Sorry, gentleman . . . "

Sarah slumped under the bright overhead light. She knew Douglas was watching her. So she moved her hand almost as slowly as the minute hand on a clock, creeping along the edge of the table toward the stack of photos. She slipped off the paper clip binding the stills together and hid it between her fingers, just as Douglas jerked her up by the arm and led her out.

In her cell, Douglas cinched up the last of Sarah's restraints, then leaned over her, studying her. Even wrecked as she was, there was still beauty in her face. He smiled slightly, then bent down, licking his lips. She felt his hot breath on her face. Willed herself not to react.

He opened his mouth and ran his tongue across her face like a dog would. She didn't even blink. Her dull eyes seemed to see through him.

Douglas grunted. Not much sport messing with a brain-dead loser. Even a pretty one.

She didn't blink an eye. Douglas hesitated a moment longer. Then he laughed and went out. The cell was shut and the lock snapped closed. Sarah could hear the sound of his nightstick tapping its way down the corridor, growing fainter.

Sarah's eyes snapped into an alert intensity. She spat the paper clip out onto her chest, then groped for it, awkwardly spreading it open into a straight piece of wire. With slow, painful concentration she moved it toward the lock of the restraints that bound her wrists to the bed. This is not an easy thing to do. But Sarah had taught herself a lot of things in her years of hiding. This was one of them. Handy for getting out of police cuffs, she never thought she'd have to break out of asylum restraints.

With a final, agonizing twist, she managed to open the lock. She rapidly worked on the other wrist, all the while eyeing the cell window just in case Douglas or the night-watch should stroll by. Thirty-eight seconds later, Sarah sat up and released the Velcro straps on her ankles. She rolled off the bed and hit the floor a new person, almost feral in her movements.

At the main gate, in the clean, blank confines of the pristine guard-shack, the bored security guard glanced up. An LAPD black-and-white pulled up, its headlights blazing. He activated the barricade motor and nodded at the officer as he drove through onto the grounds.

The cruiser pulled into a parking space next to Mossberg's unmarked car. The T-1000 got out, scanning the lot, and instantly determined the tactical possibilities with a surge of liquid awareness. This was the hub of the energies it was seeking. Here it would find the center of its existence.

The termination of its target.

It moved toward the main entrance of the hospital.

Sarah was still in her cell, using the paper clip on the door lock. She wasn't moving in a panic now. She was calm, focused, intent on the lock. An echoing tapping sound distracted her. It was getting louder, coming her way. She went back to work on the lock, moving more quickly, but still with a steady hand.

Douglas was tapping his stick along the wall, strolling down the dimly lit corridor. He carried a little maglight that he shined in the cell windows as he passed, barely slowing. There was no reason to make a more thorough check. All the patients were deep in Thorazine stupors, weakened, disoriented, near-vegetables. Even Ms. Hardcase was tame tonight, Douglas thought, bemused.

He rounded the corner, his footsteps echoing in the dark hallway. The tip of the stick hit the wall. Tap, tap, tap . . . He reached patient eighty-two's cell and stopped, about to shine his light in. But his eye had caught something across the hall. A utility-closet door was half open. Maintenance getting sloppy again.

Douglas sighed and went to shut it, absently flicking his light into the dark closet. There was something strange among the buckets and cleaning supplies. A mop lay on the floor, its handle snapped off about halfway up. The other half was missing.

Douglas pondered that for half a second, then heard a door open behind him and spun around. Sarah's cell door hung open. Before that thought could register fully, the missing two feet of mop-handle filled his vision as it cracked viciously across the bridge of his nose.

Sarah watched with great satisfaction as the two hundred and fifty pounds of doughy attendant hit the floor with a resounding thud. She then expertly slammed the makeshift baton down across the back of his head, bouncing him off the linoleum. For Douglas, the world suddenly fell away for a while. He was in his own stupor now.

Sarah dragged the limp body into her cell and locked him in with his own keys. Then she grabbed his heavy nightstick, hefting it like she knew how to use it better than the mop handle, laid back along her forearm, police-style. She moved down the dark corridor, cat-stepping in her bare feet, definitely armed and dangerous.

Past the main entrance doors there was a long corridor that ended at a reception area, which was closed, and beyond that a night receiving desk, which was behind a glass window where they could buzz you in through an adjacent heavy door. The night nurse, an ordinary-looking woman named Gwen, typed at a desk nearby. She looked up at the sound of footsteps and saw the young cop walking toward her. Compared to the others already inside, she thought this one was very nice-looking. She worked up her best smile. It had little effect on most men. The T-1000 wasn't very interested either. It spoke with a soft, pleasant voice designed to modulate the listener's subconscious-resistance to strangers. "You have a Sarah Connor here?"

"Running late, aren't you? The others have been here some time."

She turned to the inner door to buzz him in, but saw Silberman and the cops coming toward the door from the other side.

"Your friends are on their way out now," she said, turning back to the officer. But he was no longer standing there. Puzzled, she went to the counter and leaned out to see if he was at the drinking fountain. No Reception was empty. And so was the long corridor beyond. She frowned, remembering the stories her cousin used to tell her about her policeman husband. Maybe all cops were that weird.

Silberman came through the solenoid-operated door with Weatherby, Mossberg, the two uniformed cops, and a hospital security guard. As the latter retrieved his Browning 9mm pistol from a lock-out box behind the night desk, Silberman faced him. "Lewis, see these gentlemen out and then lock up for the night."

Lewis nodded deferentially and said, "Yes, sir." Silberman walked back through the door into the secure area of the hospital while the cops walked down the long corridor to the entrance. Weatherby was mumbling, "That was productive." Mossberg added, "Yeah, I just love staying up all night."

Lewis locked the entrance doors behind, then slowly walked back. The light at the night desk far ahead was like a sanctuary. His footsteps rang hollowly on the tile floor. His keys jingled. He was thinking of nothing in particular, idly noting the black-and-white checkerboard pattern of the floor tiling.

As he passed one spot, it began to shiver and bulge upward like a liquid mass, still retaining the two-tone checkerboard of the tile. It hunched up silently into a quivering shadow in the darkness behind the guard.

The night nurse had her back to her typewriter, working diligently on a report. The guard stopped at the coffee machine. Punched out a selection. Turned to the nurse. "Hey, Gwen, want some coffee?"

"How 'bout a beer," she kidded.

Lewis laughed and took his coffee cup from the

machine. It was covered with drawings of playing cards, each with a different number. Some kind of game. He squinted at the bottom of the cup, spilling the hot fluid, trying to read the game rules. "Hey, maybe it's my lucky day."

Behind him the fluid mass had reached six feet of height and began to resolve rapidly into a human figure. It lost the color and texture of the tile and turned to the gray of the guard's uniform.

The T-1000's mass had been spread out a quarter of an inch thick over several square yards of floor. When Lewis walked over it, his structure had been sampled in that instant. Now it was drawing in and pulling up to form a mirror image of the unwitting guard.

The feet were the last of the "liquid floor" pulling in to form shiny black guard shoes that detached with a faint sucking sound from the real floor as the T-1000/guard took its first step.

The real guard whirled at the sound of footsteps to see . . .

. . . himself.

Not only someone who looked just like him, but someone wearing his uniform, complete with his nametag.

He had one deeply disturbing moment to consider the ramifications of seeing oneself while working in the loon farm.

Like maybe insanity was catching.

Before he could even begin to clutch desperately at flimsy rationalizations to beat back the obvious impossibility standing before him, it raised its hand and pointed the right index finger directly at Lewis's face, only a too-close foot away. In a split second, the finger speared out, elongating into a thin steel rod that snapped out like a stiletto, slashing into the guard's eye. It punched past the eyeball, a little like a transorbital lobotomy tool, and emerged from the back of the guard's skull.

Life quietly drained from Lewis's face. He went from living being to meat in a matter of seconds. The rod/finger suddenly retracted—*SSSNICK*. As the guard slumped, the T-1000 took his weight easily with one hand and walked him, as if carrying a suit on a hanger, back toward the night desk. The wounds were so tiny, no blood dripped onto the floor.

The nurse glanced up as the T-1000/guard walked past, casually dragging something that she couldn't see because it was below the countertop.

"Whatcha got, Lewis?"

"Just some trash," he answered cheerfully.

She nodded absently, disinterested. As she went back to typing, the T-1000 moved past, dragging the limp guard toward a closet door a few yards from the night receiving station. It removed the Browning 9mm pistol and the keys from the guard's belt, then stuffed the body into the utility closet.

The T-1000 came back and glanced at the nurse. "All set," he said with a smile. She glanced up and saw the pistol in his holster.

"Gotta to check the gun first, remember."

"Yeah, sorry."

The T-1000 opened the locker and blocked it from her view with its body, then mimed putting the gun inside. Actually, it was inserting the pistol into its own chest, where the gun disappeared inside as if dropped into a pot of hot fudge. As T-1000 withdrew its hand, the chest was once again a surface that looked like cloth, buttons, and nametag. T-1000 slammed the locker door and waited as the nurse hit the button unlocking the door with a *BUZZ-CLACK*. The T-1000 went through. It moved through the halls, looking for the isolation ward.

A few minutes later, it reached the isolation ward security checkpoint. The two bored attendants barely looked up as the T-1000/guard approached them. It glanced at a chart near the door that indicated PNT-82 was in cell number 19. The T-1000/guard went into the isolation ward through the two doors, which locked behind it.

The T-1000 passed the nurses' station, which looked like a cage, walled-in by heavy metal mesh. Silberman, leaning in the open doorway, was talking to an attendant inside. He didn't even glance twice as "Lewis" passed by.

Sarah, moving like a ghost in the darkened corridor, heard footsteps coming and quietly but quickly unlocked a cell next to hers with Douglas's master key. She slipped inside and waited as the footsteps passed. She glanced at the far side of the room. A wild-eyed female inmate, strapped tightly to the bed, watched her with birdlike eyes and quivering lips. Was she about to scream? Sarah hesitated, heart pounding, then grasped at a straw. She put a finger to her lips and said, "SSHHH."

The inmate slowly nodded with a knowing expression. Sarah sighed with relief, then peered out the cell window, seeing the back of the security guard as it turned a corner. She waited until she couldn't hear the footsteps, then she moved.

Silberman was yawning as he reviewed the medication allotments with the night attendant. It had been a long Saturday. He was contemplating sleeping-in late Sunday. Then he remembered that damn symposium on female violence he had promised to lecture at. He was glancing at his watch, trying to remember when he was supposed to be there, when he saw movement out of the corner of his eye.

Sarah Connor slammed into him, hurling him through the door into the cage and following him in. The orderly jumped up, going for his stunner baton, but she nailed him first with Douglas's nightstick. His legs folded and he did a great imitation of an inanimate object.

Silberman lunged for the alarm button, but she cracked down hard on his arm. He cried out and grabbed his wrist. Sarah grabbed him by the hair and shoved him facedown on the desk, smacking him behind the knees expertly with the baton. His legs buckled and he dropped to his knees with his chin on the desk. She pinned him with one hand. His expression was all outraged disbelief. "You broke my arm!"

Sarah's voice was chilling to hear. "There's two

hundred and fifteen bones in the human body, mother-fucker. *That's one.* Now don't move!"

Moving rapidly, she whipped open a medication drawer and grabbed a syringe. She jammed it into the stunned attendant's butt and fired the whole shot. Still holding the empty syringe, she saw what she needed next. They kept the toxic cleaning supplies in the cage so the inmates wouldn't try drinking the Drāno. She grabbed a plastic jug of Liquid-Plumr and slammed it down on the desk inches from Silberman's eyes.

She jabbed the empty syringe into the plastic jug and drew back the plunger. His horrified eyes racked toward the fifteen cc's of blue death filling the cylinder. "What are you going to do?" he gasped. She removed the needle and jammed it into Silberman's neck. Her thumb hovered over the plunger.

Jerking him to his feet by the collar, she got a tight grip on him, then hauled him through the door.

The T-1000 stopped outside cell number nineteen and looked in the window. Douglas, his face a bloody mess, yelled to be heard through the soundproofed door. The T-1000 didn't have to hear. It could read lips.

"Open the door! The goddamn bitch is loose in the halls!" Douglas was shouting. To his amazement, the guard impassively turned and walked away, leaving him inside, face pressed to the glass, furious.

Outside, Terminator and John were approaching the guard gate on the Harley. The cycle pulled over and stopped nearby. The noise of the big engine idling caused the guard to look up.

John said, "Now remember, you're not gonna kill anyone, right?"

Just the slightest hesitation before the cyborg answered, "Right."

John was not convinced. "Swear."

"What?"

"Just say 'I swear I won't kill anyone.'"

John held his hand up, like he was being sworn in. Terminator stared at John a moment, running all the possibilities through his wafer-circuit brain. There was nothing in there that covered this human gesture. Uncertain of its usefulness, Terminator mimicked the gesture, then said, "I swear I will not kill anybody."

Then Terminator slid off the cycle and walked toward the gate.

The guard, sensing trouble, had his gun drawn as he came out of the shack. Terminator continued toward him, his scanners rapidly checking all the lethal strike zones in the human anatomy and excluding them as target factors, then extrapolating where the non-lethal ones were. He smoothly drew his .45 and shot the guard with surgical accuracy twice in the knees. The guy dropped, screaming and clutching his legs.

John couldn't believe his eyes. "What the hell are you doing?"

Terminator kicked the guard's gun away, then smashed the phone in the shack with his fist. He pushed the button to raise the gate and walked back to the Harley. He read consternation on John's face and said, "He'll live."

Terminator climbed on the cycle and released the clutch. They moved through the gate and headed down an ambulance ramp into an underground emergency receiving area. John turned back and yelled at the groaning guard, "Sorry, mister."

On the isolation floor, the attendants at the security checkpoint looked up at the monitor as someone entered the corridor. They saw Sarah, holding Silberman at syringe-point.

Sarah spoke to them through an intercom on the wall. "Open it or he'll be dead before he hits the floor."

The attendants' adrenaline levels started going off the scale. The first attendant adamantly shook his head no. The second attendant keyed the intercom mike. "There's no way, Eighty-two. Let him go."

Silberman's face was the color of suet, but he managed, "It won't work, Sarah. You're no killer. I don't believe you'd do it."

Her voice was a deadly cold hiss. "You're already dead, Silberman. Everybody here dies. You know I believe that. So don't fuck with me!" She punctuated the last by jabbing the needle deeper into his skin.

"Open the goddamn door!" he screamed, wincing.

The attendants looked with uncertainty at one another. One finally hit the solenoid button. The far door unlocked with a metallic clang.

Sarah pushed Silberman ahead of her into the lock-out corridor. The nearer, barred door had to be unlocked manually. One of the attendants cautiously approached and nervously unlocked it.

"Step back!" Sarah ordered.

He wasted no time moving back.

She faced both of them. "Down on the floor! Now!"

They hesitated. She gave them a feral expression and jammed the needle in all the way. Silberman grunted in agony as a trickle of blood began to flow. . . .

They quickly hit the floor with their stomachs.

Sarah came through with Silberman, giving them a wide berth. She backed down the hall away from them, still holding her hostage. It suddenly occurred to her in the middle of her own adrenaline rush that she was actually going to pull this off.

But that was because she couldn't see the third orderly waiting just around the corner. He was poised, ready to jump her when she came abreast of him.

Sarah backed toward him. Like a tango dancer in a violent dip, he lunged, grabbing her syringe-hand. Sarah immediately spun on the orderly and caught him across the throat with the nightstick. He quickly lost all interest in her, dropping to his knees and gagging for air. Silberman pulled away, screaming at the top of his lungs. "Get her!"

They scrambled up as Sarah took off like a shot around the corner. One of them hit the panic button and alarms began to sound.

In the isolation ward, the T-1000 was looking in at a very stoned attendant inside the nurses' station when the alarms shrieked through the halls, making the attendant startle to his feet, wide-eyed. He gaped in astonishment as he saw what looked like Lewis reach into its chest and pull out a pistol, then move on to the security entrance.

In another corridor in the maze of the vast hospital, Sarah ran like an animal, her bare feet slapping on the cold tiles. The orderlies were charging after, not far behind her. She turned a corner, caroming off the wall, and sprinted on without slowing, slamming into a steel door.

Locked.

Footsteps pounded behind her.

She fumbled with Douglas's keys, breathing hard. Jammed the master in. The orderlies were bearing down on her at full tilt, rapidly closing the gap.

Sarah got the door open and dove through, slamming it and turning the deadbolt knob just as the first orderly grabbed the latch on the other side.

He was one second too late.

Sarah saw them through the little window, fumbling with their keys. Gasping from exhaustion, she turned. She was in another sally-port corridor. A jail-cell-type barred door was between her and the corridors of the ward beyond.

She sprinted to the wall of bars, jabbed the key into the door, unlocking and pulling it open just as she heard the latch of the one she'd just come through being turned.

Sarah flung herself frantically through the barred door as the first orderly came through behind her. She yanked the bars shut. *CLANG.* With a stab of despair, she saw the keys were dangling from the lock on the other side from her. The orderly was racing at her, white-lipped with rage.

She reached back through the bars, turned the key, and purposefully snapped it off in the lock. An instant later the big orderly slid into the door, grabbing through the bars for her as she danced back.

Just out of reach.

He lunged against the steel bars, enraged.

Sarah had no time for any sense of personal triumph. She was on a commit run to find her son. Before the second terminator did. So she simply spun and sprinted away.

The frustrated attendants shouted at each other,

struggling to fit their keys into a lock already occupied by the broken-off key tip.

Silberman stumbled up behind them, holding his throbbing neck, took in their confusion, and screamed at them. "Go around, goddammit! Go around!"

The orderlies ran past Silberman, back the way they came, and careened into an intersection to another set of doors.

Sarah rounded a corner and saw the elevators ahead. Home-free.

At a full-tilt dash, she had nearly reached it when the elevator doors parted.

And then she saw the worst nightmare come alive and step out into the hall, complete with bloodstained leather jacket, sunglasses, and shotgun. The horrifyingly familiar face of the Terminator swiveled to hers.

Sarah tried to stop, but her momentum was carrying her right into the killer cyborg. Her bare feet slipped on the slick tile and she hit the floor, gaping up at the leather-clad figure.

Sarah lost all semblance of courage and a sizable chunk of her sanity. She was not even aware that she was screaming as she scrambled back along the floor like a crab, spinning and clawing her way to her feet along the wall.

She felt as if she were whirling in the nuclear winds of her vision. If she looked back she would have seen John step warily out of the corridor behind Terminator. John saw his fleeing mother and realized instantly what had happened.

"Mom! Wait!"

Sarah couldn't hear over the sound of her own wail. She kept going, a cornered rat, desperate for an opening in the hellish maze of the hospital.

Terminator and John ran after her.

She pelted down the long corridor, back the way she'd come. As she reached an intersection with a cross corridor, a white-clad figure emerged in a blur. The attendant hit her in a flying tackle. She skidded across the floor, shrieking and struggling. The other two orderlies leaped into the fray.

"No! It's coming now! It's gonna kill us all!" she shouted, pleading, trying to get them to understand what was only a few steps away. Heedless, they grabbed her thrashing limbs. They didn't even look where the out-of-control woman was pointing . . . back along the corridor. They pinned her to the cold tiles, a ring of furious faces above her. A female attendant appeared, holding a syringe with a full load of trank.

Sarah craned her neck and saw the dark silhouette of Terminator coming up behind them. It was maddeningly identical to the first terminator. And it was here now, years later. Skynet's walking weapon, punching through time and distance, to kill her. She screamed in utter hopelessness.

But Terminator did something very strange, and very different from her expectation. Holding the shotgun in one hand, the cyborg reached down and grabbed one of the orderlies with his other hand, hurling the two-hundred-pound man all the way across the corridor against the far wall. *SMACK!* He dropped to the floor, trying to breathe around two cracked ribs and not liking how it felt one bit.

The other two orderlies reacted instantly, leaping onto the intruder. Terminator seemed to disappear for a moment under the two big guys. Then there was an explosion of white, as the orderlies were flung outward as if they had stepped on a land mine.

One crashed through a safety-glass window and was saved from worse injuries by the outer steel security bars. But he wasn't conscious long enough at that moment to be thankful. The other plowed through an office door, splintering it into kindling and rolling up against a desk leg. He looked up and decided the acoustical tiles on the ceiling were extremely fascinating subjects for study, considering that he was going to have to look at them from that stunned position for some time.

The female attendant, who could easily benchpress ninety pounds, backhanded the intruder's face with all her strength. The man recoiled slightly, his sunglasses flying off. Her hand throbbed, as if she had slammed it against a cement wall. He slowly turned back to her and put a palm on her chest. She grabbed his thumb and tried to pry it back with a force that should have broken it. Instead, he simply shoved her away. It was hardly more than a tap, but executed with such kinetic energy that the woman was thrown backwards several yards and slammed onto the hard floor. She skidded to a stop, not particularly interested in getting up for a while.

During all this, Silberman was flattened against the wall, a forgotten cigarette dangling from his lips. He watched the utterly expressionless face of the intruder as he strode back to Sarah. His confusion about the motive of this man suddenly became awesomely clear.

Sarah was right . . . this guy wasn't human.

Not even close.

And if she was right about this humanoid thing, he realized that she was probably right about all the other things.

The unimaginably tragic things . . .

He felt the fabric of his reality start to tear.

Sarah blinked, staring up at the looming figure of death. Her eyes shifted to an impossible sight: her son, kneeling next to her.

"Mom, are you okay?"

She looked from the Terminator to John and then back to the Terminator.

Here she was, on the floor, amid several bodies, staring up at the worst and best thing in her world. She had no way to react to this except madness, or laughter. . . . She decided which way to go when John leaned in and grabbed her shoulders, shaking her hard.

"Mom!"

She felt his grip, smelled his breath, and in an instant of massive shock, realized . . .

. . . this was real.

Surviving that knowledge was the easy part, because what happened next was just too silly to be sane. Terminator politely reached its hand down to her, palm up.

Evidently, it wanted to help her up.

Sarah started to laugh, the convulsion wracking her like a deep orgasm. But it was choked off in her throat by what the cyborg tonelessly said. "Come with me if you want to live."

Sarah glanced around. The orderlies were stirring back to pained consciousness. The alarms were still blaring. Soon, more people would arrive. Her son started tugging at her arm. "It's all right, Mom. He's here to help."

In a quite understandable daze, Sarah took the huge hand in her shaking fingers. Terminator lifted her to her feet in one easy movement.

Almost like a dance.

John turned to go and saw a policeman standing thirty feet away, on the other side of the wall of bars. John realized with a start who it was.

It was him.

Terminator followed John's horrified gaze.

The T-1000 had his pistol in his hand, at his side.

Terminator pushed John and Sarah behind him. They all started backing up.

Sarah saw what they saw and was unable to react, her soul on overload.

The T-1000 walked forward. Because of the man's obesity, it had been stressing its ability to expand molecularly by remaining in the Lewis form, so it had defaulted back to the more energy-efficient Officer Austin. It reached the bars. But it did not stop.

Its body began to divide like Jell-O around the metal bars. As it squeezed itself through like PlayDoh, its surface reformed perfectly.

The cigarette in Silberman's mouth fell out as his jaw dropped. A faint snapping sound went off in his head, and he started to shrink inside his body.

Now Sarah could react. She gasped. All frames of reference had been shattered. But the sight of the viscous paste reforming into a policeman, and three thoughts hit simultaneously:

It wasn't a policeman.

It was from the future.

It was probably going to try to kill her son.

Her rage began to blast up from her center again, and her muscles went taut.

For her, it seemed the reality of the nightmare would never end.

There was a *CLINK*. The guard's gun had caught against the bars ... the only solid object. The T-1000 simply turned its wrist and tried again, slipping the gun endwise through the gap.

Terminator grabbed John by the seat of his pants and hooked him up onto his back. John clutched him around the neck. Terminator raised the shotgun and continued backing away. He turned to Sarah. "Run!"

Good idea, Sarah thought, then turned and ran after them.

The T-1000 lunged toward them. Its boot slammed down on Terminator's fallen sunglasses, crushing them. It opened fire with the Browning Hi-Power. But Terminator straight-armed the 10-gauge like a pistol and fired. The stunned orderlies flopped facedown on the floor as the corridor was filled with high-velocity lead and acrid smoke. Terminator was hammered by several slugs. The T-1000 was in turn cratered by several slugs. It staggered, but kept coming on. It was measuring the velocity and angle of each hit, and actually opening itself up slightly to cushion the shock of the entry wounds. Bright mercury formed in the craters as they closed and resealed, disappearing in a second.

Bullets could only slow it down.

Terminator made it around the corner and broke into a thundering run. Ahead, Sarah was already at the elevator. Terminator and John piled in and John slapped the "Garage Level" button. The doors started to close. The T-1000 cleared the corner with odd grace, fluidly shifting the center of its gravity in ways no human could.

Terminator slammed John and Sarah back against the side walls as the T-1000 charged them, rapid-firing the Browning.

The rounds hit the doors as they closed. Inside, Sarah

saw the metal being punched in from the far side in a perfect grouping that would have taken her head off had there been nothing between her and the bullets.

The Browning locked open, empty. The T-1000 dropped it without a glance back. The doors closed with a soft clump. Then they were rocked in their foundation as the T-1000 hit them a split-second later.

The elevator hadn't moved yet. A swordlike blade rammed in between the doors, then impossibly melted and then rehardened into hooks. They locked onto the doors and began to force them open.

Terminator seemed to hesitate, while Sarah watched with horror as the safety of their temporary sanctuary was being ripped open.

But terminators do not hesitate.

It had been calmly waiting, time a mere calculation of the passing of events, until the gap widened enough for him to jam his shotgun through. The muzzle slammed right *into* the T-1000's face, sinking a few inches into the "flesh." An instant later, Sarah and John jerked as the report from the shotgun battered their eardrums in the confined space. Through the slit, they watched the T-1000's head blown apart by the blast. It was hurled back by the tremendous release of energy. The elevator doors were now allowed to close. The car jerked slightly, then began its descent. John looked up at his mother. She was staring dazedly at the elevator doors, shaking. "What the fuck was that?" she muttered hoarsely.

In the corridor, the T-1000's head was lying in two mutilated masses on its shoulders. The concept of pain had never factored into the sensory sphere of the liquid machine. Pain was an indicator of damage to a part of the organism. But this "organism" didn't have parts, except on the molecular level. And its molecules were each primitive, miniaturized versions of the total machine. If any section were parted, the separated halves would revert to metal poly-alloy. The only default command it had in molecular memory was to find the main mass again and rejoin it. Each molecule had a range of fourteen kilometers. And the blasted apart sections of the T-1000 were much closer than that. So, after a moment of hesitation caused by ballistic shock, it rapidly reformed into a healthy human face, with absolutely no trace of "injury."

It turned to the closed doors and jammed its hands between them, the fingertips becoming pry-bars that were easily able to pull the doors apart. Without hesitating, the T-1000 leaped into the open shaft.

It plummeted two floors, as aerodynamic as a brick.

In the elevator, all three looked up at the loud thump on the roof. Terminator rapidly finished reloading the shotgun and jacked a round into the chamber.

Sarah grabbed the .45 from his waistband and aimed it at the ceiling. Nothing was going to kill her son.

No thing.

John took a short, sharp breath, then . . .

CLANG! A razor-sharp, chromed spike punched through the ceiling and speared down four feet into the elevator car.

Inches from Sarah's face.

Reflexively she opened fire, *BAM-BAM-BAM,* the bullets punching right through the roof. Lightning-fast the spike withdrew and thrust down again, slashing Terminator's jacket, and missing John by inches.

The blast from Terminator's 10-gauge opened a hole in the ceiling. The first of many as Terminator rocked out in a fury of firing/cocking/firing as the metal shaft slashed down again and again, as if a crazed man were jabbing a can with a surgically sharp icepick. Sarah yelled in agony as one of the strikes sliced open her shoulder blade.

A polite bell went off. The indicator over the door flashed "Garage Level." The doors slid open and Sarah pulled John out as soon as the gap was wide enough.

They emerged into the basement. The Harley was parked nearby, useless now that there were three people. Terminator scanned the area for an appropriate escape vehicle.

In the elevator, the T-1000 had bashed a hole in the ceiling big enough to pour itself through. A massive blob of mercurylike alloy liquefied and extruded through the opening, then dropped to the floor, rising into the form of Officer Austin. As all its sensors repositioned, it hesitated a second, reorienting after the molecular taffy-pull with itself.

In the garage, a blue-and-white hospital-security car roared up to the entrance and screeched toward them. Without breaking stride, Sarah ran right at the car, which skidded to a shrieking halt. She aimed the .45 in the guard's face, holding it firmly with both hands. "Out of the car!"

The guard took a moment to figure out that this gun-toting patient was probably very insane. Too insane to reason with.

It was a moment too long for Sarah. She put a round through the glass next to his head to hurry him up. "RIGHT NOW!"

The door was immediately opened and the guard lurched out with his hands up. The cyborg ran up and almost absently flung the man out of the way as he slid behind the wheel. Sarah shoved John into the backseat and dove into the front passenger side. Terminator yanked the car in reverse and punched the accelerator, spinning the tires on the slick ramp.

Terminator handed the shotgun over his shoulder to John and said, "Reload." John pulled some shells from the pocket of his army jacket and started feeding them in.

Sarah held on as Terminator powered backward up the ramp, scraping along one wall, barely in control, because . . .

. . . the T-1000 was running at them from the elevator. It was completely unharmed, shifting from all-chrome-mode back to the cop-form as it rapidly increased speed up the ramp.

Terminator handed Sarah another magazine for the .45. She dropped the expended one out and slapped in the full one. Cocked the slide.

The car backed out of the garage and along the service driveway toward the security gate.

John finished reloading and handed the shotgun

back to Terminator. He leaned out the window and took aim at the pursuer. The T-1000's face was right in the headlights.

Terminator fired, blowing a hole in its shoulder. Shiny liquid-metal formed in the hole, closing it, then turning into the uniform.

Sarah, half out the passenger window, pulled the trigger of the .45. The first two shots went wide, but the third centerpunched the forehead. It only made the T-1000 break stride for a moment. She fired again and again. Bullet strikes cratered the thing in the chest and head. Instead of channeling power to reform, the T-1000 put all its energy into forward momentum, rapidly gaining on the car. It crashed through the main gate barricade.

"Hold on," the cyborg-driver calmly said as he cut the wheel hard. The car slewed into a reverse one-eighty-degree turn, swapping ends with a screech.

The T-1000 was almost on them.

Terminator's hand blurred over the shifter and his foot pushed the accelerator all the way to the floor. The car surged forward.

The T-1000 jumped into the air, landing on the trunk. Its hand became a metal spike and it slammed down through the lid. A moment later, it formed into a gleaming chrome hook. Feet dragging on the pavement, the T-1000 slammed its other hand down, punching another hook into the back of the car, pulling itself up.

Terminator turned to Sarah and said, "Drive."

She grabbed the wheel as he heaved himself half out of the driver's window. Sarah slapped her foot down on the throttle, keeping the car moving at seventy miles an hour.

John was looking back through the rear window as the T-1000, fully on the car now, held on with one hook-hand while it raised the other to strike. The boy ducked just as it shoved the other hook-hand through the back window, exploding the glass and missing him by inches.

It drew back for another swing, lunging forward as

Terminator whipped the shotgun down over the roof of the car and fired.

The T-1000's arm was hit just above the "hand" anchoring it to the car. The 102-gauge blew the "wrist" apart, severing the hook-hand.

Officer Austin tumbled backward off the accelerating car. John rose and looked out the shattered window, eyes wide. The T-1000 hit the pavement hard but, in a single movement, rolled back to its feet and continued running after them.

But now he was dropping way behind. Sarah had the pedal floored and the liquid-metal killer had its limitations. It couldn't catch them on foot.

John saw the "crowbar hand," still stuck into the trunk right in front of him. John gingerly reached out and pried the metal loose, tossing it onto the street. It stretched to an ovoid by the forward momentum, then fell back into a quivering blob.

The car sped off into the night.

A moment later, the T-1000, slowing to a walk, watched the taillights recede. The target's escape meant nothing to it. The delay could only be a measurement of time. Although terminators had internal chronometers, the T-1000 did not. It was part of Skynet's new design. Knowledge of time had its uses, but in most cases of pursuit, it was an unnecessary element. Time did not matter when the thing after you could not be killed, could not be stopped, and would never tire.

The T-1000, blissfully unaware of anything except the target's projected escape route, glanced down. The liquid metal blob on the asphalt began to shudder, then elongate, stretching like a liquid finger until it touched Officer Austin's "shoe," flowing into it, rejoining the main mass.

Time was only a temporary respite from inevitable.

HIGHTAILING

The hospital-security car blasted across the lonely stretch of moonlit highway, headlights off, a ghost car punching a hole in the wind.

Air blasted in the shattered window as Terminator drove, easily staying aligned with the dotted dividing line. John could see the cyborg's eyes glow faintly red in the rearview mirror.

"Can you even see anything?"

Terminator's real eyes behind the prop human ones were on night-vision mode, probing the view ahead, drinking in the reduced photons to form a monochrome image of the highway that was bright as noon on a sunny day. Various readouts flashed by, giving Terminator a holistic sense of motion and mass that made him the safest autopilot in creation.

Terminator replied in a matter-of-fact tone that would have sounded like bragging if Sarah and John didn't know their companion was a machine. "Everything."

"Cool," John said, somewhat comforted.

Sarah was studying Terminator, still not quite believing this was happening. The Sarah who was always a few minutes late to her waitress job at Big Buns so many years ago needed to spend only another second or two dealing with the unbelievable. Then she turned to the most vital priority of her life. She faced John in the backseat. "You okay?"

He nodded.

She reached out for him. John's heart raced in his chest. His mother had never taken much time to show affection. There'd been too many other priorities. But now she was actually pulling him into an embrace. Maybe she'd changed. Maybe now she really cared about him, not his stupid mission in the future. Happily, he flung his arms around her. But instead of hugging him, she rubbed her hands over him, checking for injuries. To John it seemed very clinical, the way a vet checks a dog for broken bones. There was concern.

But not real love.

He angrily pulled away from her. And this was no act. He hated her always checking him, treating him like he might break, like some piece of rare china. "I *said* I was okay."

Sarah looked at him, exasperated and stern. "It was stupid of you to go there."

John could not believe her. Usually, you expect your mother to razz on you for doing something wrong, but now he was getting yelled at for saving her goddamn life! Before he could respond with his own consternation, the fires of her anger flared. "Goddammit, John, you have to be smarter than that! You're too important! You can't risk yourself, *not even for me*, do you understand? I can take care of myself. I was doing fine. Jesus, John. You almost got yourself killed!"

His chin quivered. The old feelings were coming back now. She was putting up this image of some kind of superman and trying to shove him into it. It was way too big, but she didn't seem to notice or care. She never did. And, as usual, anything he did was inadequate. To stop the hot, shameful tears, he blurted, "I . . . had to get you out of that place . . . I'm sorry, I . . . "

John thought there seemed to be more compassion in the cyborg's empty eyes than in hers. The force of the tears wanting to come surprised him and his face crumpled. He turned away, not wanting her to see him weaken. But she saw his body starting to rack with the sobs he could not stop. She spoke more softly this time, more a plea . . .

"Stop it! Right now! You can't cry, John. Other kids can afford to cry. You can't."

Terminator took one eye off the road, compensating with phantom depth perception, and looked at John hurriedly wiping at his eyes. Fluid was leaking out. Terminator searched in its memory for references. Found nothing. Was this an injury? "What is wrong with your eyes?"

"Nothing," John sharply said, wiping his nose on a sleeve.

Sarah took a breath, realizing how keyed-up she was. Her whole body was vibrating. Her mind was fragmented, the images and ideas of her life exploded, all the pieces now drifting back to mental ground level where she was hurriedly trying to push them all back together. In there somewhere was a dim awareness of having done something wrong with her son . . . again. It was hard enough raising a child as a single mother, but impossible when the child was to become the hub of destiny, a great leader of men, a man who would literally save humanity. . . . She had to harden herself to learn survival skills, to kill the part of herself that loved tenderly. Once she had done so, everything became much simpler. But there was a price to pay. She and her son had been robbed of a normal life. All they knew was preparation for global war. And it had cost them. Sarah was doing her best, and defensive as hell about how she was going about it. She loved her son deeply. But if she showed it, might she not weaken the boy? He needed strength, wisdom and skill with weapons, not love. But the hate in his eyes now . . .

It *had* cost a lot.

In the meantime, she was going on automatic reflexes. In a way, like a machine.

She turned to Terminator, giving him another wary once-over.

"So," she said, "what's your story?"

DESTINY'S JESTER

Black-and-whites were everywhere on the lawn, their Christmas lights whirling. Amid the flashing red and blue colors, it looked like a convention of flatfoots. Ambulances were shouldering their way through the throngs of confused staff and some wandering patients. Dr. Silberman muttered as the attendants dragged him toward an ambulance. His words ran together into an excited babble, but it wouldn't have made any sense to anybody even if slowed down to normal. He was saying, "... it was all true and we're all going to die and the guy changed, I saw him change, right before my eyes, he walked right through the bars like they weren't there, you have to believe me, I'm not having a psychotic episode, I'm a doctor and I know these things, and I'm telling you ..."

His ramble was muffled as he was strapped onto a gurney and they closed the doors on him. His days as a psychiatrist were over.

Leonard Silberman, one of the lucky few to survive the first terminator's assault years ago, was now the inadvertent victim of the second.

Fate does love a jest.

140

* * *

The T-1000 strode toward the main gate and the milling cops. A motorcycle cop going in the other direction slowed when he saw Officer Austin. "You okay?"

The T-1000 spent fourteen microseconds pondering the man's motorcycle. Then he said, "Gee, that's a nice bike."

The twenty-eight police officers and detectives on the grounds did not see the T-1000 drive away on the motorcycle. They wouldn't find the real policeman's body until a few hours later, stuffed unceremoniously into a trash dumpster. No one would ever suspect Officer Austin had anything to do with it. That "he" was the most dangerous thing on the planet, assigned by something that didn't exist yet, to close the account book on humanity with one well-placed blow.

They were too busy taking down the names of possible witnesses.

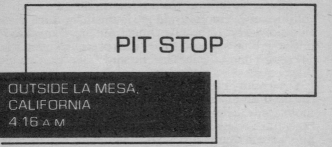

PIT STOP

Terminator drove tirelessly, at a steady rate, a human-shaped cruise control. Sarah was still puzzling out what she'd just heard, calmer now, focused, the strategic Sarah kicking in one hundred percent. "This T-1000 . . . what happens when you shoot it?"

"Ballistic penetration hydrostatically shocks it, but only for a few seconds. Based on recent observation, it can liquefy its molecular structure to allow bullets to pass through. Or to alter its appearance."

"Can it be destroyed?"

"Unknown. However there is a high probability that when the T-1000 hardens its structure to make weapons, or to enter into combat, its molecular structure becomes brittle. It would be most vulnerable then to a concussive shock wave."

They rode along in silence for a few moments, then Sarah saw something up ahead: lonely neon in the blackness.

"Pull in here. We have to ditch this car."

Terminator drove into a rundown Benthic Petroleum gas station with a buzzing neon sign and no one around. They slowly cruised past the empty office. A sign in the

142

window read: CLOSED SUNDAY. They continued around the building to the garage's back door.

Terminator got out, and in an abrupt gesture, broke the lock on the roll-up door and lifted it. Sarah slid over and steered the security car in out of sight. Terminator rolled the door down behind them.

For a moment, they were as close to safe as they could be.

Sarah switched on an overhead droplight. She and Terminator looked at one another. He was shot-up and bleeding. She had a vicious slash on her right shoulder, and her tanktop was soaked with blood.

"You look like handmade shit," she said.

Terminator projected the words onto a screen and ran through the file for contextual definitions of the colloquial vernacular. A list appeared:

Fuck you, Jack.

Kiss my ass.

You're no beauty yourself.

I'm okay, you're okay.

In a microsecond, Terminator selected the last entry, and it said aloud, "So do you."

Sarah almost smiled.

Almost.

A few minutes later, they had broken out the first-aid kit from the office, some not-too-oily rags, a bottle of rubbing alcohol, and a few small tools. John watched Terminator set down a bloody rag and handed him a clean one.

Sarah was sitting on an empty crate beside the cyborg. He was suturing her wound with some fine wire they had taken from the winding of an alternator. It was glowing a dull red from the makeshift sterilizing process; Terminator had held it in front of a butane cutting-torch for a few minutes before beginning. She remembered what Kyle had told her long ago, that pain could be controlled, compartmentalized, subdued, so you could go on with your mission. Kyle's face began to form in her memory, bringing with it the old emotional ache, and that might incapacitate her mind when she most needed it. She slammed a door on the face and kept hold of the concept of controlling pain as she turned back to her arm. Using a pair of needlenose pliers, Terminator threaded the wire through her pale skin with machine precision.

She had a little trouble finding compartments for all the pain.

Terminator picked up the slightest wince in her face and mechanically adjusted what he was doing to alleviate her discomfort. She felt the pain lessen, but even if she knew what the cyborg had done, she wouldn't have thanked him.

He said something intended to reduce her stress and lower her heart rate, thereby reducing the loss of blood. "I have detailed files on human anatomy."

It didn't quite work. Sarah stared into his face, inches away, her pulse still raging with barely suppresed hostility. She didn't like him being this close to her to begin with, let alone carving on her. "I'll bet. Makes you a more efficient killer, right?"

Terminator said, "Correct," as he continued to stitch.

John was watching, grateful to Terminator for tending to his mother, but wondering why she could see only the dark side of the cyborg. After all, it was just a tool, wasn't it, programmed by himself in the future to protect them now. Terminators weren't inherently evil. They just were. It was how you used them. Sorta like a gun. He wanted to explain this to Sarah, but she didn't seem anywhere near in the mood.

A few minutes later it was the cyborg's turn. The leather jacket was riddled with bullet holes. Sarah and John pulled it off, revealing Terminator's broad, muscled back beneath, marred with a dozen oozing holes. There were other wounds on the backs of his arms and legs. Fortunately they were all 9mm. The entry wounds were small and the damage only cosmetic.

"Does it hurt?" John asked.

"I sense the injuries. The data could be called pain."

Sarah started washing out the bullet holes in his back with the alcohol, flashing on a cold night in a drainage culvert when she'd clumsily dressed the wound of a young man. It had been her first field dressing. He had complimented her. And—

That face again, finding other doorways to her heart. She slammed them all. It was much worse agony to do that than the throbbing in her now-bandaged arm, but it was necessary. She fumbled for words to help her back to the grim Here and Now. "Will these heal up?"

"Yes."

"Glad to hear it. Because if you can't pass for human, you won't be much good to us."

She reached into the bloody wounds with pliers and found the copper-jacketed bullets, flattened against his armored endoskeleton, and pulled them out. They clinked one by one into a glass.

John was now realizing just what they were dealing with. A man/machine, who could take point-blank bullet hits and walk around to tell about it, was essentially like, well, immortal. He asked, "How long do you live. I mean last?"

"A hundred and twenty years on my existing power cell, under normal conditions."

Sarah pulled out the last few slugs. The glass was nearly full of flattened bullets. Then she started to sew the holes closed with the wire sutures. John watched in quiet amazement.

Two warriors calmly fixing each other.

"Can you learn? So you can be be . . . you know. More human. Not such a dork all the time."

"My CPU is a neural-net processor . . . a learning computer. But Skynet presets the switch to 'read only' when we are sent out alone."

"Doesn't want you thinking too much, huh?"

There was no irony in his reply, only fact. "No."

"Hey, can we reset the switch?"

Sarah looked at the Terminator, arching an eyebrow.

"Yes," the cyborg answered.

After Terminator gave her preliminary-access instructions, Sarah found an X-Acto knife and was now cutting into Terminator's scalp at the crown of his

skull. His voice was even and unaffected by her minis-
trations as he directed her to spread the bloody inci-
sion and locate the maintenance port for the CPU in
the chrome skull beneath. "Now open the port cover."

John used a rag to dab away some of the excess
blood. Sarah used the garage-mechanic's compressed
air driver to unscrew the port cover.

Terminator saw a digitized image as he watched her
work in a mirror John had taken from the washroom.
Her hands were covered with his blood, as she waited
for further instructions.

"Hold the CPU by its base tab. Pull."

She reached in with a pair of tweezers and gingerly
pulled out a shock mount, then went deeper into the
cyborg's skull. She carefully clipped the base tab of the
CPU and lifted it out of its socket.

Terminator saw a burst of static, then blackness.

John and Sarah were looking at what she had removed. A reddish brown ceramic rectangle with a con-
nector on one end. About the size and shape of a
domino. On close inspection it appeared to be made up
of small cubes connected together, identical to the
shattered one in the vault at Cyberdyne Systems. Now
they knew what Miles Dyson was still trying to figure
out. This was the brain of a terminator.

John walked around Terminator and looked at his
face. He was completely inert. No chest movement. No
twitches. Eyes open.

Dead.

Experimentally, John lifted his huge hand. The
servos whined sullenly as he forced them through their
range of motion. It was like moving a limb on a corpse
suffering from rigor mortis. He released the hand and
it stayed in the lifted position.

It was clear to John that this was the most vulnerable
anyone was likely to see a terminator. They could have
begun disassembly. Taken the machine/man apart
until it was reduced to its basic components, just so
much scrap-heap. But Terminator had allowed them
to take out his brain and completely disable it. That
showed a lot of trust.

Or, John wondered, can machines trust?

Sarah studied the CPU chip under the nearby lamp.

"Do you see the pin switch?" John asked.

She ignored him, looking at Terminator with cold eyes, then back at the chip. What she felt was more than justified. It wasn't strategically smart. It wasn't particularly necessary. Terminator was already out of action. But the emotion was so strong and irrational that before John knew what she was doing, she had set the chip on the worktable and picked up a small sledge hammer. As she raised it to strike, John realized her intentions and dove at her. "No!"

He protectively slapped his hand over the chip. That was the only thing that could have checked her swing. Sarah could barely stop the sledge before smashing his fingers. "Out of the way, John!"

"No! Don't kill him!"

"It, John. Not him. It."

"All right, it. We need it!" John kept his hand right where it was.

"We're better off by ourselves."

"But it's the only proof we have of the future . . . about the war and all that."

Sarah hesitated. The boy was right. But she was still enveloped in loathing for the duplicate of the thing that had killed Kyle Reese. "I don't trust it! These things are hard to kill, John, believe me, I know. We may never have this opportunity again."

"Look, Mom, if I'm supposed to ever be this great leader, you should start listening to my leadership ideas once in a while. 'Cause if you won't, nobody else will."

Another good point. A sliver of pride in her son slid in between her rage and the helpless Terminator.

John realized that he and his mother were at a turning point. He could see it in her eyes. For years he had been trying desperately to keep up with her program, to fit the mold she had made for him. Until this moment, he had despaired of ever pleasing her. Now, he felt the power shifting subtly between them. There was a confusion and uncertainty in her eyes John had never seen before. And he had put it there. He was right. And she knew it. So he slowly took his hand away from the chip, then stepped back. It was her choice now.

John had taken another step toward becoming John Connor. For in his wisdom, he had done the right thing.

Sarah's fury was still at a high pitch. Her head said lower the hammer. Her heart said smash it down. So she did.

An inch away from the CPU.

"All right, we'll do it your way."

John palmed the chip and examined it carefully, his forehead furrowing with a child's intense scrutiny. He found what he was looking for and picked up a safety pin, using it to move the almost invisible switch to the other position, putting the CPU in the "write" mode. Grimacing, he gingerly inserted the wafer-circuit back into the slot in Terminator's blood-spattered skull.

Out of a timeless blackness, light flared back to life in another burst of static. To Terminator, it had just been a single glitch, his consciousness otherwise uninterrupted. He could see the digitized images of Sarah and John standing behind him in the mirror. It didn't "feel" any different. Internal scans indicated no damage. All systems were nominal. Except, his time clock indicated more time had passed than was necessary to complete the task.

"Was there a problem?" Terminator asked them.

John glanced sheepishly at Sarah, then smiled at the cyborg.

"No problem. None whatsoever."

A few hours later, Sarah sat in the dark, cross-legged, her back against the wall, the .45 cradled in her lap. She was watching her son, who was in a deep sleep, lying on the rear seat of the security car. The sleep of children was depthless. All the horrors of the day turned into manageable monsters or fun adventures. Never had she so desperately wanted to sleep like that. She ached all over, and when she moved, her joints felt like they had been filled with sand. She needed a good solid meal and twenty hours of totally dreamless sleep.

But her eyes were wide open.

As long as Terminator was with them.

He was standing at the office windows, in a slash of moonlight, silent and still, watching the night. A maniacal mannequin. Only his eyes moved, tracking with the occasional car passing on the road.

Faithful machine sentinel.

He seemed to grow lighter, glowing as the reflection of another car's headlights passed. But then Sarah realized, he wasn't the only thing getting brighter. The whole room was filling with light. Thinking a car was turning in, she jolted upright, hand tensing around the .45.

Then she relaxed. It wasn't a car.

It was morning.

I must have dozed off, she thought with horror. That damn machine is still standing in exactly the same position. It could have done anything while I was out.

Sarah's self-reprimand was harsh. She had only lightly dozed out of sheer exhaustion. But her brain was so attuned to danger, had Terminator moved one inch, she would have known. She wouldn't have been able to do very much about it, but she would have known.

She struggled to get to her feet, wincing at the pain in her arm. It would hurt like this for weeks. And those compartments were all filled up. Steeling herself, she limped over to John and nudged him awake.

His eyes fluttered open and he saw the silhouette of his mother bending over him in the predawn gloom. He began to smile with a child's joy, until she leaned into a shaft of light and he saw how ravaged and hard she had become. It melted into a sleepy scowl as he heard her low, toneless voice, not so far from sounding like Terminator's say, "It's getting light. We have to get moving."

John and Terminator walked to an old Chevy station wagon parked behind the garage. The sun was cresting the horizon in a cloudless sky. The air was crisp and churlish, the wind whipping at their clothes and hair.

Dust devils chased themselves across the land. It was going to be a long, hot day.

The station wagon was locked, so Terminator broke the side window with his fist and casually opened the door. They climbed in and Terminator used his servo-driven steel hand to smash the cowl around the steering column with one blow. When it shattered, he stripped it away with a single move, then turned the stub of the lock-mechanism with his fingertips. By the time John had reached up for the sun visor, the engine was already running. John flipped the visor down and a set of keys dropped into his lap. He grinned and dangled them in front of Terminator's eyes.

"Are we learning yet?"

Terminator said nothing, but internally he was doing something he had never done before. In the past, he had cross-referenced new data, finding a contextual meaning and filing it in memory. But this was a subtle difference. Terminator was only dimly aware of the difference. But the location of the keys, the human motivation to hide an extra set there, and the undermeanings of that motivation, created an almost organic melding of these knowledges into an expanded awareness unlike any recording of new data he had previously experienced in his short life. He reran the data back and forth, analyzing it with a small part of his brain, while the other tended to driving the truck alongside the pumps and filling the gas tank to the top.

Sarah walked out of the station office. She'd found a mechanic's jacket to hide the blood on her tank top inside, used but fairly clean. It didn't fit too well, but it was better than the stuff from the hospital. She was still barefooted.

The sun hurt her eyes. She had always seen it through smoked, barred, wire-mesh windows. It had been so long since she had stood in its full light, out in the open, with the wind in her hair. She wanted to feel free.

Instead, she felt dangerously exposed.

Terminator and John pulled up in the station wagon. As she climbed in next to her son, Terminator made his first pronouncement of the day. "We need to get as far from the city as possible."

Sarah was for that. She knew this escape path. She had plotted a dozen over the years. She looked down the highway as it converged into the horizon.

"Just keep heading south," she said.

SUNDAY DRIVE

T he station wagon roared through light traffic down a long stretch of open highway. Terminator drove and Sarah sat in the passenger's seat. John was in the backseat watching the backs of their heads and marveling at how they were like some weird family on a Sunday road trip. Sarah leaned over to get a look at the speedometer. "Keep it under sixty-five. We can't afford to get pulled over."

Terminator slightly backed off the throttle, saying, "Affirmative."

"No, no, no," John scolded, "you gotta listen to the way people talk. See, you don't say things like 'Affirmative' or some robot shit like that. You say 'no problemo.' See?"

Terminator nodded, filing away the information, again in that slightly different way, seeming to pick up phantom ghosts of undermeanings and cross-references that were not readily apparent.

Sarah was ignoring the lesson, lost in thought.

John elucidated further, a professor of current colloquialisms. "If someone comes off to you with attitude, you say 'eat me.' If you wanna shine them on, it's 'hasta la vista, baby.'"

152

"Hasta la vista, baby?" Terminator asked, uncertain of the boy's pronunciation, but sensing contextual appropriateness.

"Yeah, or 'later, dickwad.' Or if someone gets upset you say, 'chill out.' Like that. Or you can do combinations."

Within seconds, the concept registered in Terminator's synthetic mind, and he said, "Chill out, dickwad."

"That's *great*! See, you're getting it!"

"No problemo," Terminator added.

John grinned widely with the pride of a successful teacher.

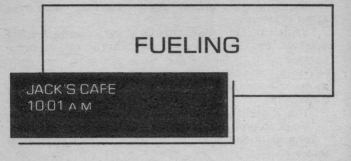

FUELING

t had a gas pump and a sleazy fast-food stand. Picnic tables were set up at the side of the stand. A family sat alone at one, children playing and running about nearby. The mother, forty-five pounds overweight and going for fifty with a double-deck cheeseburger, idly glanced over her husband's shoulder as the dusty station wagon pulled up next to a gas pump.

Sarah turned to John and asked, "You got any cash?"

John pulled out what was left of his Fed-Teller money, quickly counting. "Only a couple of hundred. I'll give you half."

Sarah snatched all of it out of his hand, peeled off a twenty, and handed it back to John. "Get some food," she commanded, then opened the door and got out.

John turned to Terminator. "No sense of humor."

The cyborg gave no reply.

John sighed, then said, "Come on."

They got out of the station wagon and started walking toward the food stand. "And that's another thing," John said. "You could lighten up a bit, yourself. This severe routine is getting old. Smile once in a while."

154

"Smile?" Terminator pondered the concept. It didn't seem in the least bit necessary to the success of the mission.

"Yeah. Smile. You know. People smile, right? Watch."

John reached the order window and smiled broadly at the weathered, middle-aged woman standing impatiently inside. "Hi. Nice place you got here. How's business?"

The woman's feet were one big ache. She had no time to waste on snotty little brats. "Gimme a break."

John turned back to Terminator, shrugging. "Okay. Bad example." Then he noticed something over the cyborg's shoulder. "Over there, look." John pointed at a teenage girl watching her boyfriend talk on a nearby pay phone. Something the other party was saying made him laugh. His girl smiled along with him.

"Like that," John said.

Terminator zoomed in on the real-time image of the smiling couple while a replay of the boy's grin ran in an electronic window. It expanded, the mouth filling the window. Terminator replayed it again in slow motion while a vector-graphic of lips smiling appeared alongside, accompanied by an array of symbolic data chattering by.

And again, that difference in collating data struck Terminator. There were unspoken or unseen data leaking in from the unconscious and cross-reffing going on in his wafer-circuit brain.

He was learning.

Knowing all he needed to know about a smile, Terminator tried one. John winced. The result was dismal, a rictuslike curling up of the upper lip.

John tried to be encouraging. "Better not do that in public. Try again."

Terminator's next effort was a marginal improvement.

"I don't know, maybe you could practice in front of a mirror or something."

Terminator made another effort.

The overweight woman glanced over her husband's shoulder at the tall, well-built man standing by the food stand. He was making strange faces.

"Ralph," she said, uncertain. "I think something's wrong with that man."

Her husband turned and saw the man screwing up his lips experimentally.

Ralph grunted and turned back to his food, saying, "He probably just got a good look at you."

She punched him in the arm. Hard.

When Sarah came out of the rest room, John and Terminator had already brought the cheeseburgers and Cokes over to the car. She joined them and grabbed a bag of fries, ravenous. They were parked away from the other families, at the end of the gravel parking area. Terminator, completely disinterested in food, was pouring coolant into the radiator. Sarah was mechanically chewing the cheeseburger, deep in thought, turning and turning the whole thing over in her brain:

What was after them.

What Skynet's strategy was.

What they could do to stop the T-1000.

She was feeling a little better, more in control. She knew now what they must do. What she had tried to do a long time ago. What had gotten her committed. It was an idea that she had abandoned, but thanks to the existence of the T-1000 in her time, she knew now it must be acted upon. Skynet had provided the proof she needed. It believed time travel could change history. Supposedly the most complex mind in history, it would develop time travel as a tactical weapon to alter history. In fact, Skynet was so certain that time displacement could save it from defeat that it had sent two terminators through: on in 1984, and one now. To terminate the mother, and if that failed, the child. Remove two human beings like pieces out of a puzzle, hoping the new historical pattern that emerged after will be more in its favor. Editing the past to change its present. Okay, Sarah thought, an adrenaline rush pouring through her, why can't I do the same thing? Why not find a way to alter my present to change the future?

It was what she had tried to do years before when she had first attacked Cyberdyne. She realized now she needed to focus in more, on one crucial person. At the exact moment that history could be pivoted, away from nuclear war.

John wanted to talk to her. Not about strategies. Or weapons. Or the future. Just . . . talk. A million things. Nothing. The tone was more important. Trivial nothings that had no end use other than a pleasant feeling between mother and son. But he could see the dark clouds in her eyes. They had always been there. He had never known the other Sarah, of course. The one before he was born. Before Terminator. He had no idea how this woman was once a young, impressionable, pretty girl, whose only serious decision in life was what to major in at college.

All he saw was the brooding, haunted Sarah, her life turned into a mission, with him as its objective.

The food was turning to lead in his stomach, and he couldn't deal with her silence, so he stood up and went around to where Terminator was working.

John saw two kids playing with machine-gun water-pistols nearby, viciously squirting each other between giggles.

"You're dead!"

"Am not!"

"Are so!"

The ancient game of pretend combat and fake death. The rehearsed final falling, into the bottomless abyss, sensed, but unimaginable to a ten-year-old kid. Unless you're John Connor.

Sarah rounded the front of the car and saw John sighing, solemn. He looked up at the cyborg, not seeing her, and asked, "We're not gonna make it, are we? People, I mean."

Terminator glanced at the battling children. "It is in your nature to destroy yourselves."

John nodded. He had seen real people with real guns

playing the game of death. Violence seemed to come in many forms. On television. The movies. In newspapers. In jokes. Between lovers and friends. There were enemies everywhere. And blood ran freely.

Other children could see all this and find a way to laugh around it, because it was so unreal, so far away—unless you were at the center of it. Unless your mother made you aware of it, rammed your face in it until everywhere you saw skulls instead of faces.

The future.

It was all true.

There would be a war.

And millions would die.

And he would lead the survivors against the machines.

And there would be nothing left to win back from them but mutilated bodies and vast ruins. That's what he felt. What he finally said was, "Yeah. Drag, huh?"

But Sarah guessed what he was thinking. She had worn the same expression of despair for years. She knew full well what was in store for her son. Victories, yes. But after years of struggle under the most abject of conditions. John Connor was evidently the pivot of Fate. For some reason, he was at the center of the circle. The time-loop revolved around him in some unexplainable way. No one man should have been saddled with such a burden. It was a killing weight. And looking at her son, all these years in hiding, had been like looking at humanity, crying out with every cell against the vile cruelty of destiny. His lot in life was to be the savior of the world, but at what cost to him. And to her. It had already scarred their lives.

She had been willing to accept that, to save the millions of other children. Yes, she would sacrifice herself and her son. But while finishing her bag of french fires, Sarah was ready to act. She approached Terminator and said, "I need to know how Skynet gets built. Who's responsible?"

Terminator searched his memory. There was a basic

history of his time embedded in the circuits. Data useful as a basis for cross-reffing and scaling events in this time. Terminator gained access to it with prioritizing it as tactical information. Another first. He answered her. "The man most directly responsible is Miles Bennet Dyson, Director of Special Projects at Cyberdyne Systems Corporation."

"Why him?"

"In a few months he creates a revolutionary type of microprocessor."

"Then what?"

Terminator closed the hood and got back into the wagon as he spoke. "In three years Cyberdyne will become the largest supplier of military computer systems. All stealth bombers are upgraded with Cyberdyne computers, becoming fully unmanned. Afterward, they fly with a perfect operational record."

Sarah hopped in behind John, and Terminator began to drive out of the parking lot. "Uh-huh, great. Then those fat fucks in Washington figure, what the hell, let a computer run the whole show, right?"

"Basically," the cyborg answered, after interpreting her colloquialisms. As he accelerated back onto the highway, Terminator continued. "The Skynet funding bill is passed. The system goes on-line August 4th, 1997. Human decisions are removed from strategic defense. Skynet begins to learn, at a geometric rate. It becomes self-aware at 2:14 A.M. Eastern daylight time, August 29. In a panic, they try to pull the plug."

"And Skynet fights back?" John asked.

"Yes," Terminator answered. "It launches its ICBMs against their targets in Russia."

"Why attack Russia? They're our friends now, aren't they?"

"Because Skynet knows the Russian counter-strike will remove its enemies here."

Sarah began to see a microthin beam of hope in a dark sky. "How much do you know about Dyson?" she asked.

"I have detailed files."

"I want to know everything. What he looks like. Where he lives. Everything."

John saw that old, grim expression of defiance return to her face.

Mom was up to something.

FAMILY MAN

M iles Dyson's house was, of course, high-tech and luxurious. Lots of smoked glass and steel. Dyson sat in his study at a massive obsidian desk, deep in thought, tapping away at the keyboard. Next to the desk were racks of sophisticated electronic gear, most of them circuit-testing units. On a Sunday morning, when most men were relaxing, spending time with their families, Dyson was in his element.

Hard at work.

His mind was prowling the labyrinth of Lot Two, the Rosetta stone microprocessor, so he didn't notice a pretty woman's face peer in the door at him. Nor did he have the slightest idea she was creeping up behind him.

If she'd had a gun, she could have easily killed him. Instead, she leaned close and extended her tongue, tracing it down the back of his neck.

"Morning, Tarissa," he said, smiling and turning to kiss his wife. She was still in her bathrobe, holding a cup of steaming coffee. "You been up all night again?" she said, a trace of exasperation in her voice.

"Um-hm," he answered, already turning back to the

161

computer, distracted. She watched him work, realizing he had probably forgotten she was standing there. The arcane symbols moving across the screen meant absolutely nothing to her. And that disturbed Tarissa. Because she had no handle to truly enter the magic box of his world. The world where he spent eighty percent of his waking life. They had spent more time together when they were first married, of course, but since he'd started working for Cyberdyne, she felt as if she had entered a nunnery.

"You going to work all day?" she asked, trying somewhat successfully to suppress her irritation. She didn't want to wind up like a lot of the other wives, whining endlessly about their empty lives with their obsessed husbands. She had plenty of things to fill up her life with meaning. But she married Miles Dyson because she loved being with him, and wanted to make it a twenty-four-hour-a-day proposition, minus, of course, the ten-to-twelve-hour workdays he routinely put in. But the fourteen- or fifteen-hour days were replicating into one night a week sleepovers at the lab.

Dyson, of course, knew vaguely that his wife was unhappy. But he assumed it was a problem that could easily be fixed. Once he solved the puzzle of Lot Two, he would spend more time with the family and take some of the stress of child-rearing off his wife. And then things would be peachy. It didn't occur to him that you don't prioritize wives behind work and not create permanent scars in the skin of a marriage.

"I'm sorry, baby. This thing is just kicking my ass. I thought we had it with this one . . . " He pointed to a metal box on his desk, a prototype of Lot Two, about two feet long. It was a crude assembly of small cubes, a dinosaur version of Terminator's CPU.

" . . . but the output went to shit after three seconds. I'm thinking now it's in the way I'm matrixing the command hierarchies. . . . "

He started to go into computerese. He might as well have been speaking Martian. It was sweet of him to try to explain it to her, but he would drone on like that for minutes at a time, forgetting she was very intelligent but no genius in arcane jargon as he was. Not wanting to remind him, she tried a gentle diversion, breaking in during a pause in his recitation. "You need a break. You'll see it clearer when you come back." Safe, generic advice.

Of course, he rejected it. "I can't."

Now she let a fraction of the irritation show through. "Miles, it's Sunday. You promised to take the kids to Raging Waters today."

"Oh. I can't honey. I'm on a roll here." He took her hands in his, enthusiasm bubbling up. She saw the childlike excitement in his face. He wants so badly to share the almost orgasmic thrill of discovery, the satisfaction of creation, she thought. And in a way, she could understand.

"Baby, this thing is going to blow 'em all away," he continued. "It's a neural-net process—"

"I know. You told me. It's a neural-net processor. It thinks and learns like we do. It's superconducting at room temperature. Other computers are pocket calculators by comparison." She took her hands away. "But why is that so important, Miles? I really need to know, 'cause I feel like I'm going crazy here sometimes."

There, now it was out in the light. She had held it in until she began to feel like a Stepford Wife. She hadn't planned on making an issue of it today, but she hadn't realized he would refuse to live up to a promise to his kids.

"I'm sorry, honey, it's just that I'm *thiiis* close." He held up his thumb and index finger, a fraction of an inch apart. She pursed her lips and picked up the prototype. It didn't look like much.

"Imagine a jetliner with a pilot that never makes a mistake, never gets tired, never shows up to work with a hangover." He tapped the box in her hand. "Meet the pilot."

All fine and well and noble. But . . . she had wanted to ask this question so many times before. It came tumbling out now, surprising Dyson with its directness. "Why did you marry me, Miles? Why did we have these two children? You don't need us. Your heart and your mind are in here." She indicated the prototype and delivered the punch line. "But it doesn't love you like we do."

Sighing, he took the anodized box from her hands and set it down. Then he placed his hands on her shoulders and kissed her gently. At first resisting, at last she gave in to his soft touch. When they parted, her expression had been transformed. Her eyes glowed with affection for him. It wasn't just the kiss. It wasn't even the way he kissed her, all masculine and sexual while being tender and sweet. It was the look in *his* eyes. She had forgotten, as she sometimes did lately, that despite how little he saw of her, he truly loved her.

"I'm sorry," he simply said.

And she believed him. She could still reach him. He wasn't totally lost . . . yet.

He started to kiss her again, but Tarissa stopped him, nodding over his shoulder. He looked back toward the doorway. Two children stood there in their PJs, their hair rumpled, their faces adorably puffy with sleep. Danny and Blythe. The sun and the moon. The physical end result of his love for his wife. He was a driven, compulsively obsessed scientist. But he wasn't dead to the world. Dyson wilted at their hopeful expressions.

"How about spending some time with your other babies?"

The conflict was profound. The endless opportunities for good for all mankind lay in the shadow of that tiny prototype circuit. But there was his own family, a tiny chunk of mankind, here, now, waiting for him.

He wanted both. But this day, he could only have one. But one of them was going to grow up even without his input. And that couldn't wait.

Dyson grinned. The forces of darkness had lost this round. He held out his hands and his kids ran to him, cheering.

THE WEAPONS PIT

he land was burning under the sun like a delirious hallucination. Heat shimmered the image, miragelike, as Terminator turned the station wagon off the paved highway and barreled along a roadbed of sand and gravel, trailing a huge plume of dust. They passed a sign that read: CHARON MESA 2 MI and under that, CALEXICO 15 MI.

Ahead, Sarah saw a pathetic oasis of humanity in the vast wasteland: a couple of aging house-trailers, surrounded by assorted junk vehicles and desert-style trash. There was a dirt airstrip behind the trailers, and a stripped Huey helicopter sitting on blocks nearby. Whoever lived here didn't much care for the city life. Or the niceties of a planned community. And they probably didn't pay their taxes.

The station wagon rolled to a stop in a cloud of dust.

"Stay in the car," Sarah commanded as she slowly got out. She could see that somebody was trying to make it look as if no one was home. The door to the nearest trailer banged in the wind. There was no noise, save the lonely keening of the wind through the yucca.

Good tactics, she thought, assuming they must have seen the dust cloud coming minutes ago.

As she crossed the yard, she noticed a subtle shifting of shadows inside one of the trailers. And perhaps she was just hyped up, but she thought she saw the gleam of something metallic. A weapon, most likely.

A small dust devil whirled through the camp, stinging her eyes. Keeping her empty hands held away from her sides, she cautiously approached the trailer, hoping she hadn't miscalculated. For all she knew, her friends had gone off and the place really was deserted.

Or had been taken over by less friendly faces.

"Enrique? You here?" She tried, sounding unnaturally loud in the open desert.

Sarah heard a *KA-CHACK!* behind her and spun, whipping out her .45 tucked behind her back in one rapid motion. In fact, she did it so quickly, Terminator was a full two seconds behind her in lunging out of the truck and whipping up his shotgun.

They were aiming at a man who had suddenly popped into view behind the Huey. He was in his mid-forties, a tough Guatemalan with a weathered face and heavy moustache, wearing cowboy boots and a flak vest over a bare, nearly hairless chest. He had an AK-47 aimed at her forehead. He frowned and spoke so quietly she could barely hear. "You pretty jumpy, Connor."

Terminator's finger was closing around the trigger of his weapon, but John put a hand on his arm, shaking his head no. The cyborg hesitated, and watched. Learning.

Enrique Salceda's fierce features broke into a broad grin. The assault gun dropped to his side as he walked toward Sarah, throwing his arms around her neck and pulling her into a tight embrace.

When he stepped back to look at her, they were both smiling.

Salceda spoke in slurred Spanish, but Sarah could understand. "Good to see you, Connor. I knew you'd make it back here sooner or later."

He waved at John, switching back to heavily accented English. "Oye, Big John! Qué pasa? Who's your very large friend?"

John answered in very natural Spanish. "He's okay, Enrique. He's . . . uh . . . this is my uncle Bob. He turned to Terminator and said in English, "Uncle Bob, this is Enrique."

Terminator tried a smile. It still needed a lot of work. Salceda squinted at him. Glanced at Sarah. "Hmmm. Uncle Bob, huh? Okay." Then he shouted toward one of the trailers. Yolanda. Get out here, we got company. And bring some fucking tequila!"

A thin Guatemalan youth named Franco, only eighteen or so, came out of the trailer with a MAC-10 A, followed by Salceda's plump, wrinkled but cheerful wife Yolanda. Three younger children trail after her like ducks; Juanita, a pretty twelve-year-old; Jamie, a grinning eight-year-old; and Paco, a two-year-old baby boy. Yolanda waved at John and shouted greetings in Spanish.

Terminator looked down at John and quietly said, "Uncle Bob?"

"So, Sarita," Salceda said, "you getting famous, you know that? All over the goddamn TV." He ripped the cap off the tequila bottle and offered her a drink. She upended the bottle and took a couple of healthy swallows, then handed it back to Salceda, without expression. Her eyes didn't even water.

Paco toddled over to Terminator and grabbed his pants, sliming them with drool. The cyborg looked down at the tiny kid, fascinated. He hadn't seen such small humans before. He rapid-scanned his memory for data on infants. There was little there. As the others talked, Terminator reached down for the child and picked it up with one huge hand, turning it to different angles, recording the physical data. The child seemed not to mind, gazing somberly into the cyborg's impassive face.

Terminator set Paco down. The child waddled off, a little dizzy, and bumped into his father. Salceda picked him up and handed him to his wife. "Honey, take Pacolito. Thanks, baby."

Salcedo took the bottle back from Sarah and guzzled half the contents. Then he turned to "Uncle Bob" and held out the tequila. "Drink?"

Terminator said, "No, thank you."

Salceda turned back to Sarah. "How long you staying?"

"I just came for my stuff. And I need clothes, food, and one of your trucks."

"Hey, how about the fillings out of my fucking teeth while you're at it?" Salceda growled. But he was grinning when he said it.

"Now, Enrique." She gave him a charming smile. One he couldn't resist. Not that there had ever been anything between these two but mutual respect and trust. Although Yolanda was no longer any man's idea of a beauty, she was the mother of his children, and still wonderful in bed. And Salceda knew very well that if he ever tried anything with Sarah, the Americano woman would probably slice off his balls and feed them to the chickens.

She had almost done as much to one of his younger cousins the last time she'd been in camp.

Sarah turned to Terminator and her son. "You two are on weapons detail."

"Aw, Mom . . . " John started to say.

"March," Sarah commanded.

"Come on," John said to Terminator, and walked toward an aging and rusted Caterpillar sitting behind one of the trailers. John climbed into the driver's seat and expertly backed it toward Terminator who was standing nearby, holding one end of a piece of heavy chain that disappeared into the sand.

"Hook it on!" John shouted, and shifted into forward. But when he looked back, Terminator was already yanking the chain hand-over-hand, pulling up a huge metal plate buried under six inches of hot sand.

"Cool," John said and hopped off the tractor, approaching the rectangular hole in the ground. Terminator joined him and looked down at what seemed like the mouth of a tomb. "One thing about my mom," John said, "she always plans ahead."

First John, then Terminator jumped down into the hole. Sunlight slashed down into a cinder-block room, less than six feet wide but over twenty feet long. Sand spilled down the sides of the walls, which were lined with guns of almost every variety. There were rifles, pistols, rocket launchers, mortars, RPGs, radio gear. At the far end, boxes containing ammo, grenades, and rockets are stacked to the ceiling.

Here was a room Terminator had no trouble comprehending. The man/machine scanned it, deciding where to begin. Terminator picked up a Vietnam-era "blopper" M-79 grenade launcher. It was a very crude, but effective, weapon. He opened the breech and inspected the bore. It had been fired a few times. "Excellent."

"Yeah, I thought you'd like this place," John said, smiling sadly.

Sarah emerged from a trailer, wearing boots, black fatigue pants, T-shirt, aviator shades. Now her outward form reflected her inner one. She was all caught up to speed. She'd had food and was now among the few people on the planet she could trust. Not only was she regrouped and resupplied, she was beginning to get ready for a counter-attack against the blind forces of Skynet and Fate itself.

Which is not to say she was not still terrified. Her son was still a target of something that made the Terminator seem ineffectual, something she had never imagined possible.

But she had been getting used to the impossible lately. Locked in an insane asylum, one thinks all sorts of impossible things. Now that she was out, and the T-1000 had made its appearance, she was going to see if some of those impossibilities could be ones she manufactured.

Salceda was nearby, packing food and other survival equipment with Yolanda. He looked up as Sarah approached, slapping the side of a big four-by-four Bronco next to him. "This is the best vehicle I got, but the starter motor is blown. You got the time to change it out?"

"Yeah. I'm gonna wait till dark to cross the border." She gently steered him out of Yolanda's earshot, not wanting to worry her with what she was about to say to Salceda. "Enrique, it's dangerous for you here. You get out tonight, too, okay?"

He narrowed his eyes at her, almost as if she had insulted him, then revealed a gold-capped tooth in a cockeyed grin. "Yeah, Sarita. Sure. Just drop by any time and totally fuck up my life."

She clapped him on the shoulder. "I'm sor—"

"Don't," he answered. "I know the drill. You'd do the same for me."

He turned back to the packing. Sarah watched him for a moment, working alongside his wife, and thought about the human race. The evil men and women who fumbled desperately for themselves in the continuing crisis of their lives, ruthlessly elbowing aside anyone remotely in their way. And then there were the sheep, those who had no lives of their own, who unconsciously willed themselves over to the others, or were easily tricked into giving up their most precious commodity, in defending the takers, even unto their own deaths.

And then there were the Salcedas.

Men and women who made their own rules. Modern gypsies who refused to be cowed by the material seductions of city and state. They formed small bands, enlarged families, and moved across the landscape untouched by the authorities, because they were armed and dangerous if fucked with.

They demanded nothing from anyone. Took nothing from anyone. And sometimes gave just for the hell of it. Men like Salceda helped Sarah decide during one of the darkest periods in her life that humanity was worth saving after all.

There was a time when all she could think of was hiding John from the world, keeping down, letting it all happen in a place where they could survive the machine war, and live in a hole somewhere at the bottom of the world, living what was left of their lives on the edge of global oblivion. Let mankind wind down. Hell, maybe it was natural selection anyway. Darwin mechanized into an efficient killing machine that mowed down its original creators.

She'd seen a lot of evil in those days. People who tried to exploit her, despite the fact she had an infant son. People who were blind to how low they had fallen into the abyss. People who knew and were more dangerous for knowing, because they would do anything to be able to crawl back out or drag others back in.

There was one night where she prayed, yes, actually prayed to a God she wasn't sure existed, to put an end to it all now. And when her prayers were not answered, she sat up all night holding the pistol, feeling its cold comfort, thinking of ending the world for just herself and John.

But that she could not do. Then the bastards of the earth would have really won. She came away from that night harder than she had ever been before, her love for John sealed into an iron maiden of commitment. He would not die. And the machines would be defeated. And Kyle's death would have meaning.

But still she could not care that much for the fate of mankind. She had lost the ability to care for people beyond herself and John, until Salceda found her and nursed her back to humanity within the bosom of his family.

And now Sarah screamed out in the night against the utter horror of nuclear annihilation. Because it was Salceda's children she saw dying in the radioactive fires.

Yes, if ever in history there was a time for impossibilities, this was it.

Down in the weapons pit, John was selecting rifles from a long rack. Terminator returned from carrying out several cases of ammo. John continued his train of thought, as if uninterrupted. "See, I grew up in places like this, so I just thought it was how people lived . . . riding around in helicopters. Learning how to blow shit up."

John grabbed an AK-47 and racked the bolt as if a humanoid extension of the gun, inspecting the receiver for wear. Some subtle wrongness in it made him put it back. His movements were efficient. Professional. Disinterested.

Terminator was listening to John, as no human could. Every tonal nuance factored into the words for added meaning, not one moment passed over, every syllable recorded for later restudy, if necessary.

"Then, when Mom got busted, I got put in a regular school. The other kids were like, into Nintendo." Games. John thought about how up until recently he thought it had all been a game. As he stood surrounded by this arsenal of death, he realized how close he and his mother had come to death.

"Are you ever afraid?" John impulsively asked the cyborg.

Terminator paused a second. Afraid. The thought never occurred to him. He dutifully searched his mind for the answer. . . .

"No."

Fear was a detriment to total mission commitment. And yet, around the edges of that preprogrammed fact, a tiny insight sparked. Humans had fear because they were mortal. And yet, in spite of, or even because of the fear, they would sometimes sacrifice their lives for another useless emotion to Terminator. Love. It was an interesting paradigm. Terminator siphoned part of his mind off to contemplate it while he slung the M-79 and started looking for the grenades.

"Not even of dying?"

No hesitation in the answer. "No."

"You don't feel anything about it one way or the other?"

Terminator gave the automatic answer, although it was still processing through the paradigm. "I have to stay functional until my mission is complete. Then it doesn't matter."

John idly spun a Sig Saur 9mm pistol on his finger . . . backwards and forwards like Bat Masterson.

"Yeah. I have to stay functional, too." Then, in a singsong mimicry of his mom, "I'm too important."

The litany of his life. And he was pouring his heart out to a walking death-machine about it. That was the pitiful part, John thought to himself. He often did that. Thought to himself. He had never had any real friends, except here with Salceda's family. Back in the world, what could he say to guys his own age? He had tried several times to tell people things. They gave him the strangest looks. John remembered Tim. That was the closest he had come to a real friend. But he was really just someone to unconsciously share the loneliness with, a chum to hang out with.

Even Tim had given him that look when he had mentioned his crazy mother.

No, to John Connor, the world was a cold place, even in the warm spots. And here, among the guns and dirt, talking to a machine from the future, he actually felt listened to.

Was Terminator a friend?

He had saved his life several times in the last twenty-four hours.

He gave advice.

He took it.

He didn't make a lot of stupid mistakes.

Yeah, John thought, maybe it's silly, but Terminator was a friend. A synthetic man who, by default when measured against his mother's relentless drive, was actually a pretty nice guy.

Terminator pulled back a canvas tarp, revealing a squat, heavy weapon with six barrels clustered in a blunt cylinder. A G.E. Mini-Gun. Rate of fire was 6000 rounds per minute. 7.62 mm shells on a linked belt feed from an amo cannister nearby. The most fearsome antipersonnel weapon of the Vietnam era. Terminator stuffed the amo cannister into a nylon bag and then hefted the heavy gun.

John nodded gravely and said, "It's definitely you."

* * *

Sarah had their weapons and supply selections laid out on two battered picnic tables for cleaning and packing. Maps, radios, documents, explosives, detonators . . . just the basics. The next time the T-1000 came crawling, they'd be ready. She was fieldstripping and cleaning guns, very methodically. Absolutely no wasted motion.

Not far away, John and Terminator were working on the Bronco, greasy up to their elbows, lying on their backs under the engine compartment, ratcheting bolts into place on the new water pump. John was saying, "There was this one guy that was kinda cool. He taught me engines. Mom screwed it up, of course. Sooner or later she'd always tell them about Judgment Day and me being this world leader and that'd be all she wrote."

A part of Terminator's brain was overlaying John's words and behavior into a surprisingly complex matrix. The cyborg came to the conclusion that John was missing something important in his life. An element essential to survival for a human being. More processing was required to fit what it was into the basic facts. Terminator continued working on the vehicle, a simple re-assembly of basic units that required a fraction of his mental capabilities. "Torque wrench, please."

"Here. I wish I coulda met my real dad."

"You will."

"Yeah. I guess so. My mom says when I'm like, old, I send him back through time to 1984. But right now he hasn't even been born yet. Man, it messes with your head."

"Hand me that bolt," Terminator requested, quite comfortable with the concept of time-loops and alternate reality.

As John handed it to him, he continued. "Mom and him were only together for one night, but she still loves him, I guess. I see her crying sometimes. She denies it totally, of course. Like she says she got something in her eye."

They crawled out from under the station wagon into the bright sunlight.

"Why do you cry?" Terminator asked, realizing that that was part of the complex matrix.

"You mean people? I don't know. We just cry. You know. When it hurts."

"Pain causes it?"

"Uh-uh, no, it's different. It's when there's nothing wrong with you but you hurt anyway. You get it?"

The cyborg lost the flow of the concept. "No."

John shrugged. "You have to kind of feel it to understand it, I guess."

"I guess," Terminator added as he got into the Bronco and turned the ignition key. The engine caught with a roar.

"All riiight! My man!" John yelled, slapping the cyborg's open palm.

"No problemo," Terminator said around a crooked smile.

John grinned and did a victorious thumbs up. Terminator imitated the gesture awkwardly, not certain of its relevance. John laughed and made him get out of the Bronco and try the move again.

Across the compound, Sarah paused in her work to watch John and Terminator. She was too far away to hear them, only see them pantomime as John showed some other gestures to the cyborg. Trying to get him to walk more casually, John walked, then Terminator tried it, then John gestured wildly, talking very fast . . . explaining the fundamental principles of cool. They tried it again. This time, the hulking man swung his hips as John did.

As Sarah watched John with the man/machine, she realized she had found a solution to the one chink in the plan she had been formulating. Terminator would never stop protecting John, it would never leave him . . . it would live out John's lifetime, for that purpose only. And it would never hurt him, never shout at him or get drunk and hit him, or say it couldn't spend time with him because it was too busy. And it would die to protect him. Of all the would-be fathers who came and went over the years, this machine, this *thing*, was the only one who measured up.

In an insane world, it was the sanest choice.

Sarah clenched her jaw and went grimly back to work . . . a strong woman burnished into iron by years of hard choices.

MAIL CHECK

PERRIS, CALIFORNIA
1:23 P M

he T-1000 had parked the police cycle off the side of a quiet empty road near a shriveled grove of water-hungry orange trees. A ribbon of traffic moved by steadily on a freeway in the distance. Some pump-jacks were sucking oil out of the earth on the brown hill behind it.

The T-1000 scanned the return addresses on John's letters. He had checked all but the last . . .

Charon Mesa, Calif.

Sooner than later.

To the liquid brain, this world was a simple puzzle-box of broken reality, the hard pieces easily fitting back into the river of cosmic order. Cause and effect was the closest thing to humor in a mind so alien even a terminator would have difficulty comprehending it. It had deduced several possible avenues of continuing the pursuit. It was methodically following one while constantly processing the others. First priority was to investigate all the addresses on the envelopes. Next, deduce from externalizations of analogous evidence what the target's next move will be and move to intercept. And third, lie in wait for years if necessary, accumulating microscopic bits of information as to their

177

whereabouts. The T-1000 was programmed with enough history to know when the war happened. And where John Connor was likely to be in the beginning stages. John Connor would eventually show himself.

And the T-1000 would be there.

Skynet itself had hesitated before making this latest weapon. There were unpredictability factors related to the thing's longevity and ability to process commands without interpolating its own priorities. It was so volatile a construct, that only in the last throes of utter defeat, when the plug was about to be pulled, had Skynet sent the terminators through time to change the outcome of the war. And only in the very last microsecond before shutdown, had the hypercomputer sent the T-1000.

Einstein had said once that God didn't play dice with the universe.

Skynet had no choice.

The T-1000 revved the engine. The Kawasaki 1100 quickly accelerated out onto the highway, doing about a hundred and twenty. It was a metal blur, moving almost out of time, on a track of its own, that led directly to its target.

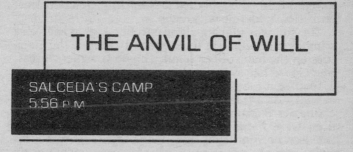

THE ANVIL OF WILL

SALCEDA'S CAMP
5:56 P.M.

Sarah was sitting at a weathered picnic table. The weapons has been cleaned and her work done. She took a breath, feeling the weight of the whole world on her shoulders. The sun was going down.

On so many things.

She drew her knife from its belt-sheath. Idly started to carve something on the tabletop . . . the letter *N*.

John and Terminator were finishing up packing the Bronco for the trip.

Sarah looked up from her carving, watching Salceda's kids playing nearby . . . wrestling with a mutty dog and loving it. Yolanda came out of a trailer, walking her toddler by the hands.

Here was the balance. In this armed camp there was unity. Love. Benevolence. Tenderness. The balance she seemed to lack. There was only so much she could do. Cope with. No human had ever done what she had. How could she not make mistakes?

But as she watched Salceda hurry over to lift his child into the air, flying him around as if Paco were a human bird, she glanced back at John glumly loading guns and supplies.

179

Behind him the other kids frolicked, their laughter unrestrained, their bodies flailing in a frenzied freedom John's had never known.

The sun was glaring right into her eyes. They were stinging. She wiped at them absently, feeling the moisture on the back of her hand. The pain was too great. She closed her eyes.

Just for a moment.

That was a mistake.

She was back in that playground, and Salceda's children were there with the others, playing with that freedom born of trust that their parents were not insane enough to cremate themselves, whirling on swings, slipping down slides, and giggling through the jungle gym. The grass was vibrant green and the sun was not hurtfully hot, but warm and nurturing.

Sarah hooked her fingers in the chain-link fence. She was staring at the young mothers playing with their kids.

Little girls played skip-rope. Their singsong chant weaved through the random burbling of the kids. One young mother appeared, walking her two-year-old son by the hands. She was wearing a pink and white waitress uniform. She turned, a cheerful smile on her lips.

It was herself. Beautiful. Radiant. The Sarah uncontaminated by the dark future. She glanced at this strange doppleganger beyond the fence.

She knew it was coming, like the hammerblow of God.

Grim-faced, Sarah pressed against the fence. She started shouting at them, but no sound came from her mouth. She clutched the fence in frustration, shaking it. Screaming soundlessly.

The waitress Sarah's smile fell away, like leaves in gathering autumn. And for a moment, their eyes met across the timeless gulf. But she turned away, her smile returning when her little boy gurgled and threw a fistful of sand at her. She laughed heartily, forgetting the Sarah at the fence as if she were only a shadow, a trick of the light.

The bright blue sky suddenly blossomed into an un-earthly white. The children ignited like match-heads. Sarah was burning, screaming silently, writhing in the repeating loop of her own Hell.

The blast-wave hit, devouring the cowering mothers and children in a whirl of hate. Sarah's scream merged with the howl of the wind as the shockwave ripped into her, blasting her apart and she . . .

. . . jerked her head up, gaping at the horizon. Scrub-brush-dotted hills. The darkening sky, all purple with dusk. The children were still playing nearby. Sarah glanced at her wristwatch. Less than fifteen minutes had gone by. Bathed in perspiration, Sarah hunched over the table. She ran her hand through her soaked hair. Every muscle was shaking. It was hard to breathe. So hard.

She could escape from the hospital, but not from the madness that haunted her.

It seemed to Sarah that Fate, or Destiny, or some kind of cosmic pattern, was a real living entity impos-ing order to all things. Time itself was only one aspect of this order, like an artery running through the body of the universe through which events flowed. And maybe people were cells in that body, not knowing what the universe was precisely, but subject to its func-tions. Cells, even only a single cell, could, if found in the right place at the right time, initiate changes in the body that were far-reaching. And maybe that was all part of the cosmic order. A preordained pattern of cells that made individual decisions, choosing their own im-mediate destiny within the body of the whole.

But she knew also that she could never know the truth and falsehood of such an idea. She was grasping at straws in a hurricane. Whether they believed in a controlling deity, or in random forces making the uni-verse dance blindly in some gargantuan blender, all she could know was the momentary order of things, the temporal cause and effect of her own actions. And, of course, every waking action was filled with unpredict-able possibilities (unless, of course, dreams were bits and pieces of the pattern, coming at us all at once in the night, in a blinding burst of psychic sight, to be patterned back into our waking minds).

Until mankind learned how to see across time in both directions, or rather, out of time, they had to gamble that their actions were going to come out all right in the end. It was humanity's curse to be aware of itself, and to know the limits of its awareness.

People played dice with the universe, too.

In a thousand little ways, in all the small, trivial choices that people were compelled by forces beyond their control to make every second of their lives, people expressed their wills. It was their choices. And even when the behavior of some seemed to be most predictable, there could be surprises, unexpected choices, unexpected consequences.

And now Fate was inviting her to embrace and dance again, to chose several paths among a multiplicity, to strike at the heart of Destiny itself, to fold it back in on itself like a flower closing up for the night.

Sarah was going to end the loop.

She looked down at the words she has carved on the table, amid the scrawled hearts and bird-droppings. "NO FATE."

"No fate but what we make for ourselves." Kyle had given her that message from the uptime John Connor. He should have known. Besides, the first terminator and the T-1000 were proof that Skynet thought it could change the past. Why couldn't she change the future?

She slammed her knife into the tabletop, embedding it deeply into the word FATE, then stood up and turned to go.

Sarah strode across the compound with grim purpose, carrying a small nylon pack and a CAR 15 assault rifle. Her face was set. Committed. An impassive mask.

She had become a terminator.

John glanced up from his work at the Bronco in time to see Sarah throw the rifle behind the seat of their stolen station wagon, jump in, and start it.

Salceda walked up to John. "She said you go south with him . . . " He pointed at Terminator, standing nearby. " . . . tonight, like you planned. She will meet you tomorrow in . . . "

Sarah jammed the car in gear and it lurched forward. John suddenly bolted across the yard, running after her. "Mommm! Wait!"

Sarah heard her son and glanced in the rearview mirror. He was a rapidly dwindling figure, yelling after her. She turned onto the gravel road and drove away from the compound, dust marking her passsage.

When she reached the highway, she turned onto it and accelerated to seventy-five. Until she reached her target, she wouldn't slow down.

John and Terminator pondered the message carved into the top of the picnic table. Sarah's knife was still embedded there. "No fate but what we make. My father told her this . . . I mean I made him memorize it, up in the future, as a message to her—"

Time disorientation again. The brain-tangling perplexities of time paradox. "Never mind," John said, giving up. "Okay, the whole thing goes 'The future is not set. There is no fate but what we make for ourselves.'"

Terminator had no trouble interpreting this information. The subtextual cues and free associations were increasing exponentially. All he said, however, was, "She intends to change the future somehow."

"What? How?"

"Unknown."

John snapped his fingers as it hit him. "Oh shit!"

Dyson.

Terminator waited with the patience of a clock.

John was dancing around, more scared than he had been in the previous two days. "Yeah, gotta be! Miles Dyson! She's gonna blow him away!"

John motioned to Terminator to follow him as he broke into a run. "Come on. Let's go. LET'S GO!"

Terminator hesitated one second, processing. Then it corroborated what John had said. It was as good as fact.

Sarah Jeanette Connor was on a mission of death.

Terminator started running, easily overtaking John and jumping behind the wheel of the Bronco.

Already several miles ahead, Sarah sped through the darkening desert. Expressionless. In her dark glasses, she looked as pitiless as an insect.

Terminator and John headed north toward L.A., the cyborg coolly whipping the bulky Bronco—which was overloaded with heavy artillery—around slower traffic. He could sense radar scans, so whenever a police beam was detected, he would slow to precisely the speed limit until out of range. They couldn't afford to get stopped now.

Terminator made his first pronouncement of the evening. "This is tactically dangerous."

John anxiously glanced over and said, "Drive faster."

"The T-1000 has the same files that I do. It could anticipate this move and reacquire you at Dyson's house."

"I don't care. We've gotta stop her."

Terminator had come to the same conclusion the T-1000 probably had. "Killing Dyson might actually prevent the war."

In frustration John punched the seat next to the cyborg. "I don't care! There's gotta be another way. Haven't you learned *anything*? Haven't you figured out why you can't kill people?"

Terminator made no response.

"Look, maybe you don't care if you live or die. But everybody's not like that! Okay? We have feelings. We hurt. We're afraid. You gotta learn this stuff, man, I'm not kidding. It's important."

They crested the pass and below them lay the mega-sprawl of the city, all lit up for night fun.

THE TERMINATOR

rom an embankment behind the house, Miles Dyson was a clear target, with his back to the study window, sitting before his terminal, buried in his work on Lot Two. The only illumination in the room was the bluish glow of his CRT monitor.

A dark figure crept up the ivy-encrusted hill. Sarah raised the CAR 15 rifle and began screwing the long heavy cylinder of a sound-suppressor onto the end of the barrel.

Danny and Blythe were playing in the halls with a radio-controlled toy off-road ruck. Danny drove the "Bigfoot" and Blythe scampered after, trying to catch it. They stopped in the hall outside Dyson's study and saw him working at his desk. Danny put a finger to his lips, shushing Blythe, his expression mischievous.

With the silencer in place, Sarah eased back the bolt and then slipped it forward, chambering a .223 round. Then she lay down on the embankment. Her cheek pressed against the cool rifle-stock, she slid one hand slowly forward to brace the weapon, taking the weight on her elbow. Her other hand moved knowingly to the trigger. She looked through the scope at the man in the house. Raised the rifle.

It wasn't a man. It was another pivot of Fate. A catch in the flow of time that had to be removed. Plucked out of reality before he destroyed it. Sarah knew she could do this. That it would be remarkably easy. Just a mechanical pull of the trigger, a mere quarter-inch movement, and the man would be knocked out of the game.

And then millions could live without fear of annihilation.

Dyson was not aware of the soft, rhythmic sounds of the keys as he typed. His mind was focused only of the symbols on the screen shift. It was becoming a certainty that this would be the last image in his mind before it exploded outward onto the CRT.

A glowing red dot appeared on his back . . . the target dot of Sarah's laser designator. It moved silently up his back toward his head.

Sarah's eye was pressed against the night-scope. She had a steady, even breathing pattern going. The target dot hardly shifted against the target.

The target.

Her finger tightened on the trigger, slowly taking out the slack. And she held a deep breath.

It was time to make it go away.

The laser dot jiggled slightly on the back of Dyson's neck and then steadied on the back of his skull.

Danny's Bigfoot station wagon roared along the carpet and encountered a solid obstacle with a thump: Dyson's foot. The scientist jerked, startled back to Earth in a sudden plummet from the Promethean heights of calculus, and leaned down to pick up the truck.

The glass window behind him suddenly erupted inward, spraying his back with glass. He felt, or rather sensed, something very small and very fast whizzing by his ear. Then his monitor screen imploded in a shower of sparks. He fell off the chair, utterly shocked, and looked up at the large hole in the window. This saved him, because—*K-THUMP!* —the second shot blew the top of his high-backed chair into an explosion of stuffing an inch from his head.

Instinctively, he flung himself to the carpet.

Rounds blasted through the window, tearing into his desk and computer, blowing his keyboard into shrapnel. With the monitor blasted out, the room was now in darkness.

Sarah could no longer see clearly.

Dyson crawled behind the desk as round after round poured into it, blasting one side of it into kindling.

Dyson, face jammed against the carpet, terrified, saw something even more horrifying. . . .

His kids standing confused and scared in the hall.

"Run, kids! Go! Run!"

Tarissa had heard the shots a moment before and had no idea what they were. At first, she thought firecrackers. July was not far away and maybe kids were celebrating early. But then she heard the broken glass and stopped thinking or guessing or doing anything except leaping up from the couch and racing through the house like an out-of-control locomotive, searching for her kids. She hit a corner at a dead run and saw them, coming her way, wailing. She enfolded them in her arms and then continued cautiously down the hall, peering around the corner into the study.

Dyson was still on the floor amid the splinters and shrapnel of the continuing fusillade.

"Miles! Oh my God!"

"Stay back!"

Dyson flinched as chunks of wood and shattered computer components showered down on him. He looked desperately toward the door, but knew he'd be totally exposed.

He'd never make it.

On the embankment, Sarah's rifle emptied with a final *CLACK!* She threw it down and drew her .45 smoothly from a shoulder holster. She rose and started toward the house, snapping back the slide on the pistol, chambering a round.

And it was easy.

Easier than making love.

Or giving birth.

Or writing a poem.

It was necessary and so damn easy to kill. If you didn't think about it.

From under his Swiss-cheesed desk, Dyson saw a sliver of the backyard. Someone was walking toward him. The combat boots hit the ground with assurance, coming onward without pause.

He tensed to make a break for the hall door.

Sarah raised the pistol, eyes riveted ahead on the shattered study window, still regulating her breathing for the next round of shots.

Dyson sprung to his feet in a full-tilt sprint.

Too calmly, she tracked him.

She could not possibly miss.

But this was a time of impossibilities. Dyson hooked a foot on the cord of a toppled disk-drive just as her shot blew apart a lamp where his head was. He hit the floor hard, but kept moving, scrambling forward.

There was a crunch of glass behind him. He could not avoid the powerful need to see who was trying to kill him. He shot a frantic look over his shoulder as his arms and legs continued carrying him across the floor.

He was as surprised as could be to see a strange woman, dressed in fatigues, framed in the floor-to-ceiling window, reaiming the pistol in her hand right at him.

Tarissa was screaming hysterically.

His sense of reality was rupturing along the fault lines of fear. It propelled him toward the hall in a sudden, powerful lunge. Her next shot plowed into him and threw him forward onto the floor in the hallway.

Dyson struggled forward, stunned. Tarissa gaped down at her wounded husband. There was a .45 caliber hole clean through his left shoulder. He smeared the beige wall with dark blood as he staggered up.

He turned and blearily saw the woman walking through the study after him, relentless, grimly determined to take his life away.

He was mesmerized for an instant by the adrenaline-rush flash-frame of her impassive expression. He wasn't even human to her. He was meat. And she was the tenderizer. He almost wanted to take the bullet, compelled by a lockup in his hyperbiological reaction to the threat. Fight or run.

Or perhaps he was fighting the pattern of destiny. And it wanted him dead.

But momentum helped him live a few moments longer. He toppled through a doorway as her shots tore away the molding where he just was.

Outside, Terminator and John roared up onto the grass of Dyson's house and leaped from the Bronco, sprinting toward the house. John despaired when he heard several shots ring out, muffled from outside. "Shit, we're too late!"

Tarissa held the children close as she backed into the living room. Sarah was following Dyson as he stumbled down the hall toward them. Danny broke loose and ran to his father's side. Tarissa held onto Blythe and screamed at Danny to get back.

But the boy was hurling himself at his father, wailing "Daaaaddeeee!"

Tarissa impulsively dropped Blythe and ran back to her husband and her son, throwing her arms around both of them.

Sarah loomed behind them with the pistol aimed and cocked.

Tarissa howled, "Noooo!"

Sarah hesitated for the first time, the steel in her veins glowing from the heat of the moment. She yelled, "Don't fucking move! Don't FUCKING MOVE!" Then she swung the gun on Tarissa. "Get on the floor! Now! Fucking down! NOW!"

Sarah was crazy-eyed now, shaking with the inten-

sity of the moment. The kill had gone bad, with screaming kids and the wife involved . . . things she never
figured on. Tarissa dropped to her knees, terrified, as
she looked into the muzzle of the gun. Blythe flung her
little arms around Dyson. Her small voice quavered as
she yelled, "Leave my daddy alone!"

The momentum was so powerful; she wanted to pull
the trigger, needed to pull the trigger. "Shut up, kid!
Get out of the way!"

Dyson looked up, through his pain and incom-
prehension. Why was this happening? Money? Insanity? Cultist?

The black gun muzzle was now only a foot from his
face. He cried out impulsively, "Please . . . let . . . the
kids . . . go . . . "

"Shut up! SHUT UP! Motherfucker! It's all your
fault! IT'S YOUR FAULT!"

And now it wasn't quite so easy, because she was too
close and had hesitated too long. She could see his eyes.
And he was no longer the target. He was a human
being, like her. She needed something the Terminator
never needed.

Hate.

For a man she didn't even know.

Blinking, she rapidly wiped sweat out of her eyes
with one hand, then got it back on the gun. The .45 was
trembling.

She registered the faces of Dyson, Tarissa, Blythe,
Danny. The family. Cringing in terror at their fate.

And she was its executioner.

Sarah took a sharp breath and all the muscles in her
arms contracted as she tensed to fire.

But her finger wouldn't move.

The cold steel and the hot fire simply evaporated and
she was left with nothing to carry her through the
awful moment.

Very slowly, she lowered the gun, dropping it to her
side.

It was over.

All the breath and energy streamed out of her and

she weakly raised her other hand in a strange gesture, as if to say, "Stay where you are, don't move." As if, should they move, the fragile balance might tip back the other way.

She backed away from them, panting, as if backing away in terror from what she almost did. She reached a wall and slumped against it, sliding down to her knees. The gun fell limply from her fingers, thudding onto the carpet. She rested her cheek against the wall.

It was all really over.

And there was nothing she could do.

Nothing . . .

The front door was kicked in. Terminator stepped inside. John grabbed his sleeve and pushed past him, scoping out the situation in two seconds . . . Sarah, the gun, the sobbing family. John moved to his mother while Terminator knelt next to Dyson and began checking his shoulder.

Tears were spilling down Sarah's cheeks. Tears that she no longer knew how to hold back, from a spring she had thought long dry.

John tentatively reached for her. "Mom? You okay?"

"I couldn't . . . oh, God." She seemed to see him for the first time. "You . . . came here . . . to stop me?"

He nodded, expecting the worst harangue of his life, about how important he was to the future, and how he shouldn't take risks, and—but she surprised him, reaching for his shoulders and drawing him into a fierce embrace. A great sob welled up from deep inside. His arms slid around her neck and they held one another as the spasms wracked her.

This was all John ever wanted. All he had lived for. And now the tears burned in his eyes and his throat tightened, so that he could barely get out the words . . .

"It's okay, Mother. It'll be okay. We'll figure it out."

She whispered into his ear, "I love you, John. I always have."

His heart raced and he kissed her flushed cheek. "I know, Mom. I know."

Tarissa was gaping at the bizarre tableau. The blood on the walls, the weeping children, the woman and boy clinging to one another, sobbing, and the large man wordlessly ripping open her husband's bloodstained shirt and examining the wound as if he'd expected all this to happen.

The man turned to her and calmly said, "Clean penetration. No shattered bone. Compression should control the loss of blood."

Wonderful news, she was thinking, dazed, as he took her hands and pressed them firmly over the entrance and exit wounds.

"Do you have bandages?"

Dyson was feeling the damage now, in great pounding throbs. "In the bathroom. Danny, can you get them for us?" He tried to sound perfectly normal, not to show the pain, so his children would calm down.

Danny nodded somberly and ran down the hall.

John reluctantly pulled away from Sarah. She wiped at her tears, the instinct to toughen up taking over again. But she knew the healing moment would have its effect, nevertheless.

John stood by Terminator.

Dyson squinted up at his surreal houseguests. "Who are you people?"

John drew the biker's knife from Terminator's boot. Handed it to him.

"Show him."

Terminator removed his jacket to reveal powerful bare arms. John took Blythe by the hand and led her down the hall, away from what was about to happen. She'd had enough trauma for one night.

Tarissa started to protest, to follow, but she couldn't remove her hand from her husband's wounds. She could feel the blood wanting to spurt between her fingers.

But then a new level of terror flooded her senses as she watched the big man raise the large, flat knife and plunge it into the forearm, making a deep cut just below the elbow.

In one smooth motion, Terminator sliced all the way around his arm. With a second cut, he split the skin of the forearm from elbow to wrist and quickly stripped it off like a surgeon ripping off a rubber glove. It came off with a sucking rip, leaving a bloody skeleton.

Tarissa bit her bottom lip, straining to hold back a scream.

Dyson gasped. The skeleton was made of bright metal, and laced with hydraulic actuators. The fingers were as finely crafted as watch parts . . . they flexed into a fist and extended. Terminator held it up, palm out.

And Dyson knew now what Lot One was. Because there was another metal arm, held in almost the exact position as this one, in the vault at Cyberdyne.

"My God," he said quietly.

Terminator lowered his arm. "Now listen very carefully," he commanded.

Later, in the Dysons' kitchen, Sarah was sitting on the counter, her face in her hands, breathing deeply and slowly, gradually pulling herself back together. John sat near her. She could feel the heat of his body, and it was what she needed to ground her. Tarissa was holding Blythe in her arms. Danny was curled up on a blanket on the floor. The children had listened until they could resist sleep no longer. Dyson was listening, face lit from the single overhead light, looking like that guy on the Sistine Chapel wall, the damned soul . . . eyes fixed and staring with terrifying knowledge. His shoulder was bandaged. Terminator's arm was wrapped with a blood-soaked bandage below the elbow. The steel forearm and hand gleamed in the harsh kitchen light. Dyson listened while Terminator laid it all down. Skynet. Judgment Day . . . the history of things to come. It's not everyday you find out you're responsible for three billion deaths. He took it pretty well, considering. . . .

Finally, Dyson said, "I feel like I'm gonna throw up." He looked at them, clutching the table as if he were about to blow away. His face, his posture, his ragged voice expressed soul-wrenching terror. He had been ripped out of normal life into their grim nightmare. His voice was pleading. "You're judging me on things I haven't even done yet. Jesus. How were we supposed to know?"

Sarah spoke from the shadows behind them. She was looking right at him, but really through him, thinking of most of the men she'd known, excepting Salceda and Kyle, and the words came tumbling out, fired by the long-repressed rage she felt for the outrageous human slaughter that had been going on since the Beginning. "Yeah. Right. How were you supposed to know? All you know how to do is thrust into the world with your . . . fucking ideas and your weapons. Did you know that every gun in the world is named after a man? Colt, Browning, Smith, Thompson, Kalashnikov. Men built the hydrogen bomb, not women . . . men like you thought it up. You're so creative. You don't know what it's like to really create something . . . to create a life. To feel it growing inside you. All you know how to create is death . . . you fucking bastards."

John touched her trembling hand and said, "Mom, Mom, we need to be more constructive here. I don't see this as a gender-related issue." He turned to the Dysons. "She's still a little tense." Then he turned back to Sarah. "We still have to figure out how to stop it all from happening. Right?"

"But I thought . . . " Tarissa said, confused, "I mean, aren't we changing things . . . right now? Changing the way it goes?"

Dyson sat up. "That's right! There's no way I'm going to finish the new processor now. Forget it. I'm out of it. I'm quitting Cyberdyne tomorrow . . . I'll sell real estate, I don't care—"

"That's not good enough."

Dyson's voice was pitiful. "Look, whatever you want me to do, I'll do. I just want my kids to have a chance to grow up, okay?"

"No one must follow your work," the cyborg said.

"All right, yeah. You're right. We have to destroy the stuff at the lab, the files, disk drives . . . and everything I have here. Everything! I don't care."

Tarissa took his hand and he looked at her. She had never seen such love there.

Later, in Dyson's backyard, a fire roared in a metal trash barrel. Stacks of files were dumped onto it. Terminator poured lighter fluid liberally over the fire, which flared up, lighting his face demonically.

Sarah, Dyson, Tarissa, and John returned from his office with more stuff—files, notes, optical disks. Even his kids were carrying stuff. It all went into the fire. Dyson dropped the prototype processor onto the fire . . . his eyes hollow and distant. He stared into the flames, watching his world burning. Then has a sudden thought. "Do you know about the chip?"

"What chip?" Sarah asked.

"They have it in a vault at Cyberdyne." He turned to Terminator. "It's gotta be from the other one like you."

The cyborg turned to Sarah. "The CPU from the first terminator."

"Son of a bitch, I knew it!" she hissed.

"They told us not to ask where they got it. I thought . . . Japan . . . hell, I don't know. I didn't want to know. It was scary stuff, radically advanced. It was shattered . . . didn't work. But it gave us ideas. It took us in new directions . . . things we would never have thought of. All this work is based on it."

"It must be destroyed," Terminator said.

Sarah grabbed Dyson's arm, her eyes reflecting the flames. "Can you get us in there, past security?"

"I think so, yeah. When?"

Dyson looked at her, Terminator, then John. Saw his answer in their faces. "Now?" He took a breath. "Yeah, right."

He turned to his wife. Her face was streaked with tears, but her eyes were strong and clear. She put her hand on his arm, and said, "Miles, I'm scared. Okay. But the only thing that scares me more than you going . . . is you not going."

He nodded. She was right, of course.

Sarah turned to Terminator. "Is it safe for them here?"

For an answer, Terminator turned to Tarissa and said, "Take your kids. Go to a hotel. Right now. Don't pack." Then he turned to the others. "Let's go."

THE DANCE OF FATE

Sarah was watching the pavement rush by, lit by headlights. Beyond, there was darkness, swallowing the horizon. She was thinking that the future, always so clear to her, had become like a black highway at night. They were in uncharted territory now ... making up history as they went along. She felt for the first time that she had taken Fate's hand and was now leading the dance. What they did next would either change the future, or destroy it. She looked up as a vast rectangle of light loomed ahead.

The Cyberdyne Building.

Dyson zipped his security card through the I.D. scanner slot in one motion. There was the sound of a servo-lock clacking open, and he entered the spacious lobby, followed by Sarah, John, and Terminator, who was wearing his bullet-riddled jacket and a black glove over the exposed endoskeleton arm.

The guard at the front desk was a calm, relaxed man named Gibbons. He was reading *Westways* magazine and actually enjoying the article on yucca trees and their origin, when he looked up to see Miles Dyson moving toward him, pale and sweaty, but smiling warmly, speaking well before he reached the desk. "Evening, Paul. These are friends of mine from out of town. I just thought I'd take them up and show them around."

"I'm sorry, Mr. Dyson. You know the rules about visitors in the lab. I need written authoriz—"

K-CHAK! Gibbons was staring down the barrels of Sarah's and Terminator's weapons.

Terminator said, "I insist."

Gibbons was too stunned to move. His eyes went to the silent-alarm button on the console, but Sarah, following his eyes, said, "Don't even think about it."

Gibbons nodded, remaining as still as his hammering heart would allow. Terminator circled quickly and pulled the guard out of the chair. John pulled a roll of duct-tape from his knapsack and tore off a piece.

A few minutes later, the second-floor elevator doors opened, and Terminator led the group warily into the corridor. They had a cart piled high with gear in nylon bags. Dyson motioned down the corridor to the right. As they walked, he continued to fill them in. "The vault needs two keys to open. Mine and one from the security station."

They stood in front of a wide security door. A sign above read: SPECIAL PROJECTS DIVISION: AUTHORIZED PERSONNEL ONLY. Dyson zipped his key-card through the scanner and the door unlatched.

A roving guard named Moshier strolled down the long corridor from the first-floor office block. A punch-clock swung at his hip, and he'd just completed his circuit of the building. He passed the bank of elevators and rounded the corner to the front desk, calling out, "Honey, I'm home . . . "

Moshier saw the desk was deserted and frowned. Gibbons must be in the can, so check that first before getting alarmed. Sighing, he walked to the restroom around the corner. As he pushed through the door, "Hey, man, you shouldn't leave the—"

Gibbons was handcuffed to the urinal, trying to mumble something through the gaffer's tape over his mouth. Moshier spun on a dime and sprinted to the desk where he slapped his hand down on the silent-alarm button.

At the security station, Dyson's hand swished his I.D. card repeatedly through the scanner slot on the locker. Nothing was happening. The light on the locker was blinking red.

Sarah anxiously turned to Dyson. "What? WHAT IS IT?"

Dyson motioned toward a light flashing on the console, then said, "Silent alarm's been tripped. It neutralizes the codes throughout the building. Nothing'll open now."

Dyson took that in, and his nerve snapped. "We should abort."

Sarah grabbed his collar, "NO! We're going all the way! You got that, Dyson?"

He saw the fire in her eyes, and thought of his work burning in his backyard. She was right. There was no turning back now.

Moshier had gotten Gibbons loose and now the guard was hanging over the desk phone, talking to the local police. " . . . multiple armed suspects. Look, I think it's the guy from that mall shootout, and the woman . . . yeah, her. Pretty sure. Just send everything you've got in the area . . . "

On the second floor John jumped on a desk next to the wall-mounted locker. Dyson stared in amazement as John started pulling his counterelectronics gear out of his knapsack. It was just another Fed-Teller to him. "You guys get started on the lab . . . I can open this."

Dyson led Terminator and Sarah to the main lab doors. Another servolock. He tried his card. Nothing.

Terminator stepped in and said, "Let me try mine."

He unslung the M-79 grenade launcher, pulling it over his shoulder in one motion. Sarah grabbed Dyson and dragged him back down the hall. Terminator opened the breech and slid in one of the fat 40mm H.E. grenades. He flipped the thing closed with a snap of the wrist.

Sarah yelled as they ran, "John! Fire-in-the-hole!"

John dropped what he was doing and covered his ears.

Terminator fired at inhumanly close range.

The door exploded into kindling. The concussion blew his jacket open, and flying shrapnel whizzed all around him. Before the thunderclap had faded, Terminator was walking into the fire and smoke.

John went back to work without missing a beat.

Sarah and a stunned Dyson stepped through the burning doorframe into the Artificial Intelligence lab.

A baleful siren began wailing. The halon fire-control system had been triggered. The invisible gas roared in, snuffing out the flames. Dyson yelled, "Fire's set off the halon system! Here . . . hurry!" He ran to a wall cabinet and pulled out some breathing masks. He handed one to Sarah and donned the other. Then he reached out to hand one to Terminator. "Here!"

"No, thank you," the big cyborg said as he removed his massive backpack and opened it. Terminator didn't need a mask, as his oxygen requirements were so low. Dyson shrugged and tossed the mask on a desk, turning to Sarah. "We'll have to keep these on a couple minutes, till the gas clears."

As planned, Terminator strolled down the hall and pulled three five-gallon drums of solvent from a storage room. Sarah started pulling out book-sized, olive-drab claymore mines, taping them to the top of the drums.

Dyson stared. Part of him couldn't believe they were really doing this. This morning he had been on the verge of a breakthrough that would have made him a rich man for the rest of his life.

Now he was in the middle of a war to destroy that breakthrough. And considering what they were saving, it was exhilarating.

* * *

Across town, the T-1000 moved slowly through Dyson's ravaged study, analyzing what had happened there. He walked down the dark hallway. The place was deserted. The flames from the backyard bonfire were smoltering. The T-1000 stood in the dying glow, processing. He had arrived at Salceda's camp minutes after they had pulled out. Switching to its secondary strategy, T-1000 ran through its files until it came up with Miles Dyson. Using the police-walkie from the bike, it had located its next destination.

Here.

The police-walkie now clipped on his belt blared to life. "All units, all units. Two-eleven in progress at the Cyberdyne Building. Multiple armed suspects. SWAT unit is en route . . ."

The T-1000 sprinted out of the house and threw his leg over the Kawasaki. Fired it up. The tires laid a scorch-mark on the pavement as it spun around and roared away.

On the second floor of the Cyberdyne Building, a fire ax smashed down through the housing of a large, state-of-the-art disk drive, shattering it. The entire room was a scene of high-tech pillage. Terminator beat the disk drive into junk and stepped to another. *WHAM.* Same routine. He'd already demolished half a dozen. Sarah toppled a file cabinet, scattering the files. Dyson staggered up with an armload of heavy M-O (magnetic-optical) disks and dropped them on a growing stack in the middle of the floor. He and Sarah had their breathing masks hanging down around their necks, as the halon gas had by now dissipated.

Dyson turned to Sarah, panting. "Yeah, all that stuff! And all the disks in those offices. Especially my office . . . everything in my office!"

Sarah went into Dyson's office and started hurling everything out the door onto the central junkpile . . . books, files, everything on the desk. A framed photo of Dyson's wife and kids landed on top of the heap. Tarissa, hugging Danny and Blythe, all grinning. The glass was shattered.

Terminator was cutting a swath under Dyson's direction, exploding equipment into fragments with his inhuman swings. "These, too! This is important." It was carnage. Millions in hardware, and all the irreplaceable fruits of years of research . . . shattered, broken, dumped in a heap for the big bonfire of destiny.

Dyson stopped a second, panting. "Give me that thing a second."

Terminator handed him the ax. Dyson hefted it one-handed. He turned to a lab table . . . on it was another prototype processor. "I've worked for years on this stuff."

Swinging awkwardly, but with great force, he smashed the ax down onto the processor prototype, exploding it into fragments. His shoulder was in agony, but he looked satisfied.

In the security station, John tapped away at his little lap-top, which was running code-combinations into the card-key lock. Suddenly, the green light on the locker went on and it unlocked with a clunk. "Easy money."

He whipped it open, revealing a rack of keys. But the vaultkey was distinctive, a long steel rectangle on a neckchain. John grabbed it and started to run toward the lab. He was stopped by a bright light blasting through the window. The thump of rotors announced the arrival of a police chopper that hovered in close to the building, raking its xenon spotlight through the second-floor offices. John whirled to the bank of video security monitors nearby and saw various angles on the front parking lot. Headlights swarmed. LAPD black-and-whites poured into the lot, turning the area into a disco of whirling blue and red lights.

Sarah and Terminator were working like a crack-team, rigging the explosives. She finished taping the claymores to the drums, turning them into powerful incendiary bombs. Terminator was attaching claymores and blocks of C-plastic explosive to the large mainframe computer cabinets nearby. All the clay-mores were wired back to one detonator that had a radio-control relay switch. "How do you set them off?" Dyson asked.

Terminator showed him the remote detonator, a small transmitter with a red plunger. "Radio remote." He made a plunger-pushing motion with his thumb and an accompanying "click" sound. Dyson nodded gravely. John came running in, holding up the key. "I got it. Piece of cake. And we got company."

"The police?" Dyson asked anxiously.

John nodded. Sarah turned to the windows. "How many?"

John shrugged. "All of them."

Sarah turned to Dyson. "Go! I'll finish here."

Terminator hefted the mini-gun and the ammo back-pack. "I'll take care of the police."

John anxiously turned to the cyborg. "You sure you won't kill anyone?"

Terminator said, "Trust me." Then he smiled. This time he got it right.

Moshier and Gibbons were carrying out the company mandate to provide absolute security for the building by cowering behind cars in the parking lot in front of the building. More police were arriving by the second.

On the second story, John and Dyson dashed through the security station, heading for the vault. Terminator crossed the office toward the floor-to-ceiling windows. He was outlined starkly by the chopper's spotlight as it slashed through the dark offices. Without breaking stride he kicked an executive desk toward the window. Glass exploded outward and the desk toppled, falling to the sidewalk below. Terminator, standing at the edge, fired a long burst, which strafed the police cars lined up below. Cops ducked as front windshields shat-tered. Terminator, with his superb aim, hit no one.

But notice was served.

The cops, of course, seeking to validate their existence, as well as preserve it, fired back. Terminator calmly reaimed and plotted a firing pattern that crisscrossed the parking lot. He pulled the trigger on the G.E. Mini-Gun, and held it down. Four thousand 7.62 mm rounds chattered down to their targets. In fifteen seconds every single police car had been riddled and reduced to wreckage. Not one policeman had been hit. The ones who hadn't already fled looked down at their woefully inadequate weapons and ran off. A few extremely brave souls fird again. . . . Terminator leveled the M-79 and fired. The grenades blasted several police cars into the sky. They fell back, erupting into flame. A moment later, the police fell back, regrouping. A SWAT van careened around a corner and skidded to a stop just out of range.

In the vault antechamber, John and Dyson stood poised, hands on keys. The boy said, "And let's see what's behind door number one."

Dyson nodded and they turned the keys together. The vault grumbled to itself, withdrawing its locking bolts with a final *KLONK!* Together Dyson and John swung the huge door open.

In the lobby, the varsity took the field as the SWAT troopers sprinted forward, by squads. They flanked the lobby and worked their way inside, deploying rapidly, moving and freezing behind cover, quivering with adrenaline. They had body armor, gas masks, Keckler and Koch MP-5 asault rifles, tear-gas launchers, ropes. Can't do the job right without the right tools. They made a lot of hand signals and kept their mouths shut.

The Roman generals would have been proud.

Outside, the police began firing tear-gas grenades through the broken windows into second-floor offices.

In the vault, John and Dyson were isolated from the world in the silent steel womb. Dyson opened the cabinet containing the terminator relics. John stared with uneasy déjà vu as he saw the terminator hand and CPU. Then in one vicious move he swept his arm behind the inert gas flasks and hurled them to the floor. They shattered. John snatched the CPU and the metal hand out of the broken glass. "Got ol' Skynet by the balls now, Miles. Come on, let's book!"

Clutching the steel hand and pocketing the chip like it was a Mars bar he'd just bought, John ran out. Dyson followed.

On the first floor, the advance squad of SWATs made it to one of the stairwells. They started up, two at a time, covering each other ritualistically by the numbers.

John pelted into the lab with Dyson stumbling along behind him. Sarah had just finished wiring all the charges to the central detonator. "Ready to rock?"

"Ready."

John tossed her the metal hand. She caught it and bent to put it in her empty backpack. Sarah zipped the pack and started to shuck into it.

Dyson stood in the middle of the lab, saying good-bye to it in his mind. He was running out of steam. The bandages at his shoulder were soaked with seeping blood. Terminator strode into the lab behind him. "Time to go. Right now."

He and John headed back the way they'd come, through the security station. Sarah finished her work and turned to the detonator, twenty feet away, near where Dyson was standing. "Miles, hand me the detonator. Let's go—"

He gingerly picked up the detonator. Started toward her. Then—

CRASH! The doors at the back of the lab were kicked open. The SWAT leader and two others opened fire. Their rifles raked the room. Sarah dove behind a computer cabinet. Dyson was hit several times, slammed to the floor by the impacts.

In the hall, John heard the firing and spun to run back. "Mommm!"

Terminator grabbed him as bullets blasted into his broad back. He lunged around the corner with John, out of the line of fire.

In the lab, bullets raked over Sarah's head, smacking all around her, clanging into the machine protecting her as the SWATs poured on the fire. She saw Dyson slumped on the floor. The detonator was clutched in his hand. He rolled to face her, his eyes bulging from the pain of his torn-up guts. "Go," he whispered.

Sarah hesitated a split-second, her eyes meeting his, then snaprolled and fast-crawled through broken glass and debris into the nearest doorway. Big mistake. This was the "clean room." A sanitized, windowless, and perfectly sealed room. There was no exit except for the door she came in by. Bullets rained in. She dove behind a desk.

Terminator ran down the hall toward the gunfire but hesitated by the bank of video monitors. One was trained on Sarah in the clean room. Terminator instantly calculated her situation, and location. He abruptly turned and strode back the way he came.

In the clean room, Sarah was crawling into a corner. But it didn't do any good. The bullets were tearing past, missing by mere inches.

Suddenly, the wall behind her burst open and Terminator reached in, grabbed her by the collar, and yanked her into the hall.

Bullets blasted into the walls behind them as they raced forward and around the corner. John met them, and they ran on together through the security checkpoint.

John reached the outer door first, and tried it. Locked. Terminator smoothly unslung the M-79 blooper, opening the breach. "Get back," he commanded as he pulled a grenade from the bandolier over his shoulder, and slid it into the bore. He flicked his wrist, snapping the breech shut. Sarah and John had only a split-second to duck and cover. Terminator turned and aimed, saying, "Cover your ears and open your mouth."

They did, just as the cyborg pulled the trigger.

Twenty feet away, the door, and half the wall around it, erupted outward. The back-blast hit Terminator full-force, but he strode through the smoking hole before the debris had hit the floor.

Terminator led John and Sarah down the dark corridor. Tear gas seeped under office doors and hung in the air. They started to cough. She pulled off her breathing mask and handed it to John.

Terminator moved ahead of them, reloading the blooper as he walked. Up ahead was another security door. He closed the breech with a wrist-snap and fired one-handed.

The door vanished in a thunderclap. Plaster chunks and burning debris showered around him. He, of course, didn't flinch or slow down. John and Sarah followed the man/machine into another corridor. Terminator reloaded the grenade launcher.

In the now quiet, smoke-filled lab, the SWAT leader moved cautiously through the room. Cat-stepping, he circled around a desk, then crisply leveled his rifle at . . .

Miles Dyson, who was not quite dead. He knew he would be very soon. He had propped himself up against the desk, holding a heavy, technical manual right over the plunger of the detonator, sitting upright on the floor. The message was clear. "Shoot me, the book drops on the plunger. Adios." Dyson wheezed, trying to draw enough breath to talk. "Don't know . . . how much longer . . . I can . . . hold this thing. . . . "

The SWAT leader saw the wires, the claymores, the gas cans all around him for the first time. Even wearing a gas mask, the sudden fear in his eyes could be seen. He made an emergency command decision: he abruptly spun and motioned his squad to retreat. "Fall back! Everybody out! Move it! OUT NOW!"

They obeyed so fast they crashed into the next group coming up the stairs.

Terminator reached the main elevators and hit the button as Sarah and John were close behind, coughing and stumbling in the smoke-filled hall, buddy-breathing with the single mask. The doors opened. They all got in the elevator and headed down.

Dyson was lying amid the ruins of his dream, sprawled on the floor, his back propped up against the desk, bathed in his own blood, which ran out in long fingers across the tiles. His breathing was shallow and raspy. He still held the book, trembling, above the switch.

He saw something nearby on a pile of now very expensive junk. The photograph of his family. He reached for it, balancing the book as he leaned over and put it in his lap. His wife and children smiled up at him through the broken glass. A tear trickled from his eye. He was not going to be able to live any longer. His whole body told him that. And a voice in the back of his head, his voice, but somehow different, calmer, said simply, "You can leave now." But he wanted to see his kids one more time and explain to them why he was going so soon. They wouldn't know what he knew, what he saw now beyond the photograph of his family . . . .

A flash of white-hot light blossoming out of the atmosphere.

And what he heard . . .

The megaphones, the helicopter, distant sirens, all became fainter . . . replaced by a roaring that swelled as the white flower in the sky became a roiling cloud of red and black . . . blood-red fire boiling up through a cloud-mass black as iron. It was the cloud-column of a hydrogen bomb, shaking the earth with its unimaginable power. But then Dyson saw it begin to recede. The thunder rolled away, dying into a wind that was like the last winds of a great storm, ebbing into a soothing breeze as the iron clouds were swirled away, giving way to a soft, gauzy light. And out of it, came Danny and Blythe, running toward Dyson, laughing. Tarissa was behind them, smiling. They were in a bright sunlight, running down a green field, right into the ruined lab. Dyson drew on this slice of memory, so vivid and precious, so he could face eternity. Or was it a gift from the outside? He didn't know. He could sense a deep connection with the things of this earth beginning to slip. And the yearning to see his family once more began to seep away, and a droll sense of irony rolled in after.

It was almost funny, it seemed to him, lying there like a stuck pig, the sacrificial lamb bleeding on the debris of his life's work. Silly people, that they had to go to such extremes to save themselves from their own tools of war. And he saw himself in his own past, a serious man with a mission, coming out of the chaos of the ghetto into the bright light of knowledge of Things, and for a moment he understood the necessity of playing the material game while Here. He had done it very well, he had to admit.

But now that he was dying, he wanted to stay and become that other Dyson, the loving man as dedicated to his family as he used to be to his science. Dyson wanted to laugh, but he thought he would break apart and make a bigger mess than he already was, so he didn't. Instead, he looked up again to see his family. Their hair was blown by the wind, the wind he knew now was blowing through history itself, changing it forever from what it was, and he thought . . .

Men can will their destinies.

If the Fates allowed.

Life would go on.

But history was

dead.

Miles Dyson's gaze was fixed, seeing what no living man could see, and because of that dying vision, there was the faintest hint of a smile. But the instant the light faded from his eyes—

His arm dropped and the book hit the switch—

The police outside were still waiting tensely for the expected bloody climax, guns out, crouched behind their cover. They expected bodies to come out on stretchers. Or they expected suspects to be escorted down to the patrol cars. Or they expected the SWAT teams to retreat to rearm and regroup. What they didn't expect, happened.

The whole gleaming face of the building exploded in an eruption of glass and fire. The second-floor windows showered the parking lot and a huge fireball shot out like the devil's tongue, leaping into the sky. The helicopter rapidly banked away from the heat. Burning debris fell among the cop cars, and a number of officers broke ranks, pulling back in barely controlled panic.

Only one of them, a motorcycle cop, seemed to be moving with purpose, through the disorganized crowd toward the burning building. He slowed once only to grab at a fleeing cop and rip his weapon out of the holster. Then the T-1000 gunned the cycle through a shattered window, across an office, and out into the hall It was scanning with full intensity, its consciousness a flow with the environment. In moments it detected a stairwell and accelerated up the steps in one howling blast of rpms.

It brodied onto the second floor, which was now a smoke-filled maze. The T-1000 drew a Hoechler and Koch MPK machine pistol and cruised slowly into the fire-lit offices, relentlessly scanning.

In the corridor, the cycle skirted more flaming wreckage as the cycle idled forward. The T-1000 scanned the leaping shadows for its prey.

In the downstairs lobby, the elcvator doors parted and Sarah eased a look out into the corridor. The walls on either side of her erupted with bullet hits. The SWATs had the lobby end of the corridor blocked off.

Sarah and the others were totally trapped, cut off and screwed. John turned to his mother and tried to cheer her up. "Don't forget. It's always darkest right before . . . you're totally fucked."

The SWATs fired a tear-gas grenade toward the elevators. It spewed the vicious CS gas out in a swirling cloud that enveloped Sarah and John, who were pressed against the back wall of the elevator.

Terminator had finished his own rapid-scan of the lobby emplacements, then turned to them and said, "Keep your eyes closed. Don't move."

They nodded and squeezed their eyes shut. As Terminator slung the grenade launcher over his shoulder and started out of the elevator, he said, "I'll be back."

A tear-gas grenade ricocheted from wall to wall as it

flew down the corridor. It skidded to rest in front of Terminator, throwing out a white cloud that quickly filled the area. In the elevator, Sarah and John were choking, handing the breathing mask back and forth desperately. They were trapped now, and the claustrophobia of poisoned air and the tiny redoubt of the elevator car oppressed John to the point of panic. He was only moments away from lurching out from cover into the corridor.

The SWAT team stood at the far end of the hall, gripping their weapons, watching the boiling cloud, waiting for the suspects to stumble out of the elevator and into their line of fire.

Someone appeared out of the smoke, incredibly, walking calmly. Totally unaffected. Terminator was not even misty-eyed.

Not at all what they expected.

The leader spoke through a megaphone. "Stop where you are. Lie down on the floor, face down. On the floor, NOW!"

He continued to stride toward them, as if not hearing, or caring.

The SWATs tensed up. They never saw anything like this.

Closer and closer he came.

The leader made another command decision. "Drop him."

The corridor was abruptly filled with crackling thunder. The rounds tore into Terminator's chest.

Stomach.

Face.

Thighs.

His leather jacket, already punctured in two dozen places, was now ripped to shreds as the rounds hit him.

The SWAT leader grasped for the obvious in the face of the impossible, thinking the guy must be wearing body armor. So he lifted his sights and fired directly into the suspect's face. His head should have been taken apart like a ripe melon. Instead, it simply rocked slightly, and a tear in the cheekbone spouted blood.

Still the man kept coming toward them!

The SWATs did what they were trained to do.

Hold the trigger down.

"Aim for the face!" the leader shouted, thinking somehow his bullet must have been defective. But a man next to him shouted with a trace of fear in his voice, "I am!"

Terminator smoothly drew his .45. His internal scanner flashed THREAT ASSESSMENT—TERMINATION OVERRIDE—DISABLE ONLY. Without particular hurry, as if he were glancing at the shelves in a supermarket, he selected his targets. He shot the nearest man in the left thigh. As he screamed and dropped, Terminator bent down and picked up the shrieking man's tear-gas launcher. It was one of those new rotary jobs that held twelve rounds in a big drum. Terminator shot the next SWAT square in the chest with the tear-gas launcher. The gas cannister hit the man's body armor and didn't penetrate. But it was like getting slugged in the stomach with a full-swing from a baseball bat. The SWAT folded double and hit the tiles, gasping.

Terminator was an image from Hell, a tall figure in shredded black leather, streaked with blood. One eye was now a bloody socket, the metal eye-servos glinting. The flesh of one cheek hung down in tatters, revealing the chrome cheekbone beneath. The whole front of his jacket was blown open, revealing his metal chest.

Some of the remaining SWATs were close enough to see all this. It was too much to see. Even in the heat of battle, even against the grain of their training, they began to fall back. One turned to run and—

KA-POW! A gas cannister nailed him in the back, sending him sprawling. Terminator fired three gas grenades into the lobby. It filled rapidly with the white gas, cutting the visibility to a few feet. It was total pandemonium.

The SWAT leader crouched in the fog, white-knuckling his rifle, completely at a loss for what was happening. Terminator loomed suddenly out of the mist right in front of him.

Before the team leader could react, there was an explosion and a white flash and a dull thud as Terminator's bullet drilled in his leg. As he screamed and dropped the rifle to clutch his leg, Terminator ripped his gas mask off. The SWAT leader fell back, writhing to the floor, choking and gagging, mindlessly clutching his ruptured thigh, trying to stem the trickle of blood.

Terminator walked up to two SWATs at the front doors. *POW-POW.* Leg and leg. He snatched off their masks as they fell.

Then, the gunfire stopped. Nobody could see anything. Screams and whimpers echoed in the smoke.

Smoke boiled out the front door as a figure emerged. Firing the tear-gas launcher with one hand, Terminator launched all remaining rounds among the police vehicles. Unprotected officers ran back, choking and half blind, slamming into cars and tripping over each other.

It was a total rout.

At the SWAT van, one of the men was rapidly handing out the remaining masks to unprotected cops. A figure appeared out of the smoke beside him. He looked up as Terminator handed him the empty launcher. Instinctively, he grasped it. Then Terminator ripped off his mask, grabbed his flak vest with one hand, and sailed him out into the mist. The cyborg strode the length of the van and climbed into the driver's seat. No keys in the ignition. He flipped down the sun visor.

The keys fell into his hand. Terminator took a microsecond to note something. He was learning.

He started the van and slammed it into gear.

In the lobby, the tear gas had cleared to a thin haze. The uninjured SWATs were tending their wounded, confused. They looked up at the sounds of shouts and a roaring engine.

The SWAT van crashed through the front doors in an explosion of glass and debris. Cops scattered as the van screeched across the lobby in a smoking one-eighty, sliding to a stop across the corridor that led to the bank of elevators. Terminator backed up until—*crunch*— he sealed the corridor with the back of the van.

Sarah and John heard the crash and saw the van backing into the corridor. They happily stumbled out of the elevator, coughing, and ran along the hall and leaped into the back just as Terminator hit the throttle. The van roared across the lobby and exited through the blown-out windows, scattering cops in every direction.

All but one.

At the sound of the battle below, the T-1000 gunned the big Kawasaki up to an office window and looked down to see the van tearing away across the parking lot with the remaining police ineffectually firing at it.

It knew it had reacquired its target.

It rapidly scanned the area, analyzing options. Through an open office door at the far end of the hall, it saw the helicopter hovering outside the building. There were other ways of reaching the target, but this one seemed the most natural channel. The T-1000 sensed all the best possibilities funneling toward it, as if it were an energy sink. Magnetically pulled by the rotating blades, the T-1000 twisted full throttle on the powerful cycle. It reared up and then blasted down the narrow corridor and into the office, accelerating fast, straight at the windows—

The T-1000 blasted out through the glass, airborne on the motorcycle. It rocketed across the gap to the hovering chopper and slammed into the canopy. The impact of machine and rider radically pitched the chopper. The startled pilot fought to regain control when the weight shifted again, as the cycle tumbled to the pavement below.

The T-1000 didn't. It clung to the shattered canopy. Nightmarishly, the pilot watched as the T-1000 punched its head through the Plexiglas canopy and rapidly poured itself through the jagged hole. It instantly solidified into Officer Austin on the passenger seat. It grabbed the gaping pilot and hurled him out of the cockpit, then slid behind the controls.

The chopper was autorotating, spinning out of control, dropping toward the parking lot. The T-1000 recovered control ten feet above the ground.

Cops hit the deck as the tail-boom swung around, going over them by inches, then dipped as the chopper lifted out in a power climb, roaring away across the parking lot toward the fleeing SWAT van.

Terminator looked back at his two passengers as he turned the boxy van onto a divided highway. Sarah and John were catching their breaths, still coughing from the CS gas. Terminator glanced in the rearview mirror. The xenon searchlight of the chopper was filling it, gaining.

Sarah checked the inside of the van. It was a rolling armory. There were rifles, ballistic vests, all manner of equipment. "John, get under these. Hurry!"

He sat against the front bulkhead of the van and Sarah piled bullet-proof vests on top of him, completely covering him. Then she grabbed two M-16s from the wall-rack and loaded them. She started on a shotgun as Terminator expertly slewed the unstable vehicle around cars and trucks that seemed to be crawling by comparison. The van hit its top speed of eighty. They swerved to miss the back-end of a white eighteen-wheel tanker-truck, which was good, because the large blue letters on its side read: CRYOCO INC. LIQUID NITROGEN SUPPLY, and hitting it would not have been survival promoting.

The chopper swung in behind them, closing fast. The T-1000 reached through the shattered canopy with the MPK machine pistol and fired. The back of the van clanged with the hits.

Terminator steered side-for-side, trying to throw off the T-1000's aim. The unstable vehicle screeched and wobbled, on the edge of control. But the door windows were blown in and the slugs careened around the inside like BBs in a tin can, narrowly missing Sarah and splunking into the pile of protective vests covering her son.

Sarah had had enough of being victim. Once before, she had experienced a rage when the first terminator had shot Kyle. It seemed as if it wasn't quite enough that she was a target. If someone she loved were attacked, a fury so deep she didn't know where it could possibly come from welled up, as if all the militant angels on some other plain of existence channeled righteous defiance through her soul. In any case, she felt the red-hot rage drive her to kick the backdoor of the van open and whip up the M-16. She opened fire, screaming at the top of her lungs, as her bullets, messengers of her will, riddled what was left of the chopper's canopy.

The T-1000 returned fire, stitching the van with hits.

Holes were punched through the thin sheet-metal walls, ripping up the interior. The vests covering John were hit repeatedly. Sarah ducked behind two Kevlar vests on the inside of the backdoor as bullets whizzed around her.

In the reload lull, she popped back out and fired in controlled bursts, aiming for the rotors. A few shots sparked off the blades. Her M-16 emptied and she grabbed another.

Terminator swerved around a battered pickup truck that was changing lanes, clipping its rear and knocking it sideways, skidding out of control. A moment later, the helicopter passed it, the rotor just clearing the top of the cab.

Sarah kept firing.

So did the T-1000.

She took a hit in the thigh, and several rounds hammered into her Kevlar vest. She was thrown back onto the floor, sprawling off balance, an exposed target—

Terminator saw the T-1000 aiming to fire again. He locked up the van's brakes. Tires screamed as the vehicle shimmied. Sarah was thrown forward, sliding up to the bulkhead next to John, out of direct sight. But . . .

Sarah and John looked out the back of the van at a horrifying sight: the helicopter rapidly enlarged, swimming right into the back of the van. It was rocked up off the pavement and thrown forward, as if a giant hand had scooped it a few feet off the highway and flung it a couple yards down the road.

The rotor disintegrated. The back door of the van was crushed in as the canopy and the whole front of the fuselage were hammered into junk, trapping the T-1000 inside twisted metal. The chopper hit the pavement, flipping sideways, and cartwheeled . . . smashing itself into a shapeless mass of twisted metal and falling away behind the van, tumbling end over end.

Terminator fought to control the van, which was fishtailing violently from the impact. It smashed against the center divider, screeching along the concrete, then pulled away. Terminator pressed the accelerator to the floor and the van climbed back up to eighty. He swerved to avoid an ugly pickup, moving like a constipated snail ahead. The right front fender of the van, crumpled by slamming the wall, was sawing into the tire. It suddenly sheared open, peeling clean off the rim. The steel wheel ground across the pavement, striking trails of sparks, and the van slid sideways and toppled—

Steel screamed on pavement as the van ground to a stop on its side.

Inside, John crawled to Sarah, who was groaning and holding her bleeding leg. She was white with shock. "Mom!" John said. She slowly turned to him, breathing shallow, disoriented.

Terminator was beginning to extricate himself from the crumpled driver's-seat.

Back down the road, the helicopter wreckage was a smoking crumpled ball of junk metal. Behind it, the tanker-truck braked hard, shuddering and groaning, trying to stop as it roared up on the bizarre obstacle. The big tires locked up in clouds of tire-smoke. The rig finally came to a shuddering stop just short of the chopper debris.

Dana Shorte jumped down, totally awed, his blood pounding through his body. After his near scrape with the crazed psycho, he had been too nervous drive that same route the next day, so he'd asked for and got a trade with Wilson. He preferred hauling vegetables. He was going north now, instead of east and south, and the route had gotten him away from the desert crazies. But now he was beginning to doubt the wisdom of his choice. He had already seen two other accidents to-night.

He had been idly allowing his mind to drift, and the waitress's face had come into view, the one from the roadside dinner. What was her name? Claudia. Her breasts . . .

Then the pile of debris in the road had suddenly loomed and he'd had to lock all his brakes. He'd felt the tons of pressurized and extremely cold liquid nitro-gen surge toward the cab and he panicked, imagining it blasting through the tank wall and instantly turning him into a human popsicle.

Dana glanced around, looking, with welling nausea, for signs of survivors. From behind the wreckage a cop emerged, walking toward him, looking remarkably healthy.

"Goddamn, are you all ri—" Dana managed to get out before—

SSSSHHCK! The T-1000 drove a blade through his abdomen and walked on past without slowing, or even looking at him.

Dana sank to his knees, reaching for the hot furnace of pain that his stomach had just become. He could feel things loosen and shift as he slapped his hands over the gushing tear in his belly. Before it really hit him that he had been badly cut open, he watched, dumbfounded, as the policeman with the harpoon-hand calmly climbed into the open cab of his tanker, then released the brake. The huge vehicle bellowed and rolled forward, churning out exhaust like a berserk dragon.

Dana thought that God could be a very unforgiving fellow as he pitched face-forward on the pavement, falling into a welcomed unconsciousness that he would never climb out of.

Farther down the road, John and Terminator were carrying Sarah out of the overturned van. Terminator had the M-79 slung over his shoulder, the bandolier of grenades, and his reloaded .45 stuck in his waistband. John had borrowed a 12-gauge riot-gun from the van's arsenal.

At the sound of a metallic crash, Terminator and John looked back the way they'd come. In the distance, they saw the helicopter wreckage knocked aside by the accelerating tanker-truck.

John gripped Sarah's arms. "Holy shit. Come on, Mom . . . we gotta keep moving . . . come on—"

The pickup truck they had passed seconds earlier screeched up to them. The astonished driver was a Hispanic in his fifties. He leaped out of the cab to offer them help. Terminator approached and said, "We need your vehicle."

Without waiting for a reply, Terminator stepped past the driver and slid Sarah into the front seat and climbed behind the wheel. John ran to the passenger side. The driver nervously backed away, knowing better than to try and stop these bloody, crazed people.

The tanker roared toward them, spewing smoke from its chrome stacks as it shifted up through the gears.

Terminator jammed the pick-up in gear, checking the rearview. The tanker was a hundred feet behind them now, and accelerating. Terminator quickly estimated seven seconds until contact. Plenty of time. He put the throttle down, but the pick-up was an old slug, loaded down by the heavy homemade wooden camper-shell on its back. It accelerated slowly.

Terminator readjusted his estimate to three seconds.

Forty-percent chance of outracing the thundering tanker.

The tanker slammed into one end of the SWAT van, spinning it out of the way with a roar and screech of twisting metal. The eighteen-wheeler shifted to a higher gear, still accelerating.

With the tanker right behind them, Terminator cut the wheel, swerving the pick-up back and forth across the lanes. The big rig stayed right on them, its tanker whiplashing violently.

"Faster! He's right on us!" John screamed.

Terminator determined that a reply was strategically unnecessary. A more viable tactical activity was to rapidly unsling the blooper, still around his neck, and reach for a grenade. So the cyborg did just that, keeping one hand on the wheel.

John glanced back at the looming chrome and lights of the liquid nitrogen tanker.

Déjà vu.

KA-WHAM! It rammed the back of their truck, sending it skidding. Then the T-1000 pulled the tractor-trailer up alongside the pickup and crabbed over, sandwiching it against the center divider. The spinning chrome hubs tore into the passenger-side door and the guardrail screeched along the other side.

The pickup bucked and shook insanely, ricocheting violently between the big rig and the divider. John gripped his mother's bloody hand as they heard the high-pitch wail of tortured metal.

Sparks poured in sheets of fire from both sides.

The windshield shattered as the door-posts buckled in.

Metal and glass showered in through the side windows.

The frame twisted and buckled.

They were slowly being crushed.

John felt as if his teeth were being vibrated from his jawbone. The wooden camper had had enough of this rough ride and bailed, disintegrating and falling away as kindling behind them.

The T-1000 held the wheel hard over, mercilessly grinding the pickup truck. Terminator slid toward the passenger side. Keeping his foot on the gas, he lifted John over him and put him in the driver's seat. He spoke as if he were just going to get something out of the glove compartment. "Drive for a minute."

A relevant question popped into John's mind. "Where you going?"

Terminator answered by slamming the shattered windshield with the palm of his hand. Held together by the plastic laminate, the windshield flopped out of its frame and flew back over the top of the pickup. John grasped the wheel in terror, watching with confusion as the cyborg pushed his upper body out over the dashboard and stood up. He turned and aimed the M-79 one-handed. Clicked off a grenade.

It missed the T-1000 by less than a foot and exploded against the front bulkhead of the tanker, almost at the top. Metal was punched in and a blast of pressurized liquid nitrogen poured from the opening, swept back by the sixty-mile-an-hour windstream.

The big rig swerved as the T-1000 regained control. The tanker swung like a massive pendulum behind the cab.

As the big rig backed off a little, releasing the pickup from the vise, John accelerated, terror compelling him to slowly get back out in front by a few yards.

But the tanker was gaining again, trailing a swirling comet-tail of nitrogen vapor.

Terminator, still standing, opened the breech and started to reload. John cut across the highway and took an off-ramp. The T-1000 swerved the smoking behemoth across the lanes and down the ramp after them, picking up speed. Now it was twenty feet behind them and closing. Terminator snapped the breech closed and fired.

The grenade hit the front grill and blasted open the radiator and tore off half the hood. Steam blasted out, obscuring the whole front of the pickup. Spewing smoke and vapor like some demon locomotive, the tractor-trailer pounded into the back of the pickup, driving it right through the intersection at the bottom of the ramp, and straight toward an area of heavy industry.

Terminator struggled to reload amid the chaos and impacts. He had only a few grenades left on the bandolier.

Approaching just ahead were the cold gray stacks of a sprawling steel mill. The gates of California Steel Industries were blasted off their hinges as the semi shoved the pickup truck right through them. John screamed, desperately trying to steer as the pickup was pummeled from behind. But there was nothing he could do. They were rocketing down the broad thoroughfare that led directly to the vast main building of the plant. Terminator had been trying to load a grenade when they went through the gate. It flew out of his hands. There was no time to look for it. Instead, the cyborg grabbed an assault rifle and pulled himself onto the roof of the pickup, leaped across to the bed, taking two powerful strides and then jumped onto the semi's hood and fired point blank through the windshield, emptying the magazine.

Right into the T-1000's face.

The T-1000's face erupted with dozens of metal craters. For a moment, the ballistic blows stunned it. Terminator grabbed the air horn and reached into the cab, yanking the wheel. The semi started to jackknife, almost dream-slow. The cab began to swing sideways, until its tires were shrieking over the pavement, smashed back at right-angles to the tanker-trailer, which was now sliding broadside.

The juggernaut bucked and shuddered as the tires smoked across the pavement. The whole rig began to topple.

Terminator held on as the side of the cab rolled and became the top. With an unholy scream, like the unoiled hubs of Hell, the whole rig slammed on its side at sixty miles an hour toward the mill. A sheet of sparks forty feet wide trailed behind it on the pavement. A Fourth of July destruction derby. The tickets would have sold well at any price, because this was just the overture. . . .

John saw what was behind him, then snapped around to see the building quickly looming. The huge rolling doors were only partly open.

No choice.

He steered right through them, clipping the sides of the already compressed pickup, right into the mill, as Terminator, with one second to go, leaped from the cab, flying through the open doors as the tanker hit the building with a resounding clang.

Terminator fell with a thud to the floor of the mill's main aisle and rolled as only a few yards behind him the tanker-trailer smashed into a massive concrete support at one side of the doors.

There was a thunderous carnage of twisting metal. The tanker split wide open, spewing a river of liquid nitrogen, pouring out at minus two hundred and thirty degrees.

John hit the brakes on the old pickup, sliding out of control on a patch of slick water. He managed to slow almost to a stop before plowing into a steel support column head-on. He and Sarah were thrown forward, hard.

Terminator, still clutching the M-79 blooper, slid across the floor and smashed through a railing and bounced up against the base of a massive machine.

The semi's cab swung around the trailer wreckage, into the building, and shuddered to a stop. Liquid nitrogen sprayed over the cab, flooding out around it in a hissing wavefront of ultracold. Freezing vapor swirled everywhere, obscuring the wreck.

Terminator lay still for a moment. He came back on-line after an emergency internal damage check, then rose on one elbow to survey the scene.

In the wrecked pickup, John stirred. He was stunned, blood running from his swelling nose. Dazed, he realized he was in a steel mill. There were sirens, and he could see men running . . . shouting. He turned to see what they were running from. . . .

The wall of nitrogen vapor spread from the demolished tanker, providing a strange vista of fire and ice. The huge smelters poured out orange light and fire from the sides of the huge gallery, while the freezing vapor rolled down the center in a white liquid frost.

Deep inside a billowing gray cloud, John could barely make out the shape of the tanker's ruined cab. A figure emerged, pulling itself out. The T-1000 staggered a few steps away from the wreck as the hissing, boiling river of liquid nitrogen flowed around its feet. The T-1000 staggered, moving slowly, as if stuck in thick molasses. It had finally been affected by something. Its feet were freezing to the ground as it strained to continue toward John.

The boy watched in awe as—*CLINK!*—one of its feet broke off at an ankle crystalized by the intense cold into glassiness. It stumbled forward, and its other foot snapped off. As it caught its balance on the stump of its other ankle, the whole lower leg shattered with the impact. It toppled to its knees, catching itself on one hand. Liquid nitrogen flowed around the hand. The hand became stuck to the pavement. The T-1000 pulled and—*CLINK!* —the hand snapped off at the wrist. It looked stupidly at the glassy stump of a wrist. For the first time there was an expression on its face John knew to be a true one . . . pain. But not human, or even cyborg pain. This was liquid-metal agony. The molecular structure of the T-1000 began to go rigid, and the energy-flows firing through them thickened and slowed to a stop. Its mouth opened in a soundless scream as the hoarfrost raced up its legs and across its body.

And then it stopped moving altogether.

Frozen in place.

A mask of furious outrage locked forever on the rigid face.

The lethal killing device had become an icy statue, kneeling in the frozen vapor.

The liquid nitrogen drained out of the tanker and began to rapidly evaporate. Terminator, just beyond the boundary of the cold, could see the T-1000 clearly. He drew out his .45 and aimed. "Hasta la vista, baby."

K-POW! The single shot impacted on the crystallized metal man, releasing the tremendous molecular tension within and blasted the T-1000 into a million diamondlike chunks spraying up into the air. They shimmered across the ground for twenty feet in all directions.

Terminator lowered the gun and tried a crooked smile. It might have worked better if more of his face had been operational.

He looked like he needed a long vacation.

In the pickup, Sarah was in bad shape. Conscious, but very weak. John tried the door. It was jammed. He kicked it open. "Okay, Mom, we gotta get out now, come on. That's it."

He helped her slide down from the seat of the battered cab. Her knees gave way. John tried to take a lot of her weight while reaching in the pickup and grabbing the riot gun off the seat. They turned and hobbled toward the Terminator. John yelled, "Is it dead?"

On his knees, Terminator looked into the dissipating cloud of vapor surrounding the T-1000. The heat of the furnaces had by now evaporated most of the liquid nitrogen.

The T-1000's shards were melting, liquefying into hundreds of drops of mercury, spattered across the floor. The orange glow of the enormous blast-furnaces danced on the liquid metal.

Terminator struggled to rise. One arm was shattered, the hand smashed and nearly useless. A couple of leg-servos were damaged, but repairable. For now, however, he could barely stand. As John and Sarah reached him, he said, "We don't have much time."

"What? Why?"

Terminator pointed. John and Sarah watched as several of the closest T-1000 droplets began to creep toward one another. A moment later, they were fusing into larger blobs. These pools shivered and ran together into larger ones, quickly forming a central mass.

Sarah could see all this through a haze of semi-consciousness. For the moment, she was operating on half-strength, but she knew the horrible implications of what was happening, and she whispered it into John's ear with utter despair. "It's not over."

John believed her. "Come on! Let's go!"

Terminator put one of Sarah's arms over his shoulder and they stumbled away, deeper into the mill.

Behind them, something was moving. A silver head was forming up out of a pool of mercury. It rose higher as shoulders formed, hunching up from the liquid mass. It turned to look straight at its prey.

John looked back in new terror as—

The T-1000 rose to man-height. It was still the mercury form, but its features were forming rapidly. It took its first step after them.

Sarah stumbled. They hastily pulled her up and kept going. Terminator had a pronounced limp, dragging one leg with a shattered ankle joint. John was the one pulling, straining, driving them onward. They rounded a corner into an aisle between towering, glowing furnaces. It was a maze of monstrous machinery. The heat was tremendous and the air shivered with a pounding roar. Sarah cried out in pain and stumbled again.

"Come on, Mom," John urged. "You can do it! Come on!

They dragged her up and staggered on. Her leg was bathed in blood and she was deathly pale. John glanced over his shoulder.

In the main gallery, the T-1000 took a step, now fully formed into Officer Austin. The hell-fire light glinted on its impassive cop-face. It walked forward, seemingly unaffected by its crystallization, but as its hand touched a railing covered with O.S.H.A. yellow-and-black safety tape, it began to turn yellow and black, the color fading to normal at the elbow. It ripped the hand from the railing with difficulty, with a sound like adhesive tape ripping off a surface.

The T-1000 looked at its yellow-and-black striped hand, willing it back to normal. Ripples of "static" or system noise moved subtly over the surface of its body. It was experiencing imperfection. The T-1000 was "glitching." But not just the hand . . .

With each step, the pattern of the tile floor "invaded" its lower legs, Fading as the foot was lifted. Returning as it was set down. The foot was trying to meld with the floor. The chameleonic function had been disrupted and was now out of control.

The T-1000 moved forward, scanning ahead. Glitch or not, it was on a mission, and it could still kill. It turned the corner, entering the aisle between the furnaces.

Terminator saw the silhouette of Officer Austin closing on them through the smoky gloom, breaking into a loping run when it spotted them.

Terminator handed Sarah over to John. "Keep going."

John shook his head no.

The T-1000 was running full-out, his footsteps clumping on the concrete.

Terminator shoved Sarah and John farther ahead. "RUN!"

John obeyed, dragging, half carrying Sarah as best he could. She was straining to remain conscious, half running, delirious. Her foot slid across a cable and she dropped to her knees. John pulled, but she couldn't summon the strength to rise.

John was crying, pleading, "Come on, you gotta try . . . please, Mom. GET UP!"

Behind them, Terminator was trying to load the M-79 with his shattered hand. He could barely maneuver his last grenade into the breech. The T-1000 lunged the last few steps and smacked the weapon out of his hands. It clattered to the floor. The grenade spun across the floor, rolling under a furnace.

Terminator flung the T-1000 against a wall with all his weight. The battle was joined.

John and Sarah reached the end of the aisle.

A cul-de-sac.

Blocked by the base of an immense smelter crucible. They turned to watch the titans battle, backlit by the molten sparks falling from the furnaces above. The battle that would decide the fate of tens of millions.

Terminator grabbed the T-1000 and hurled it with awesome force against the opposite wall of the narrow alley. In less time than it would take to turn, the T-1000 morphed back through itself, from front to back . . . face emerging from the back of its head, coming off the wall straight at Terminator. To ward it off, Terminator smashed his good fist into it. The pile-driver blow

buried the cyborg's fist almost to the elbow in the mercurylike face.

But the T-1000's head morphed in a split-second into
a hand that gripped Terminator's wrist, and the head
"emerged" somewhere else, the geometry shifting faster than Terminator could follow. The T-1000 slammed
Terminator into a large conveyor motor, jamming his
arm into the moving works. A massive sliding bar scis-
sored his arm, smashing it into junk at the elbow.

Terminator strained against the machine pinning
him. His servos whined with overload. The T-1000
turned and loped off toward its target.

Sarah saw the thing coming at them full bore and
screamed, hurling John into a gap between the
machines. He fell into a maze of pipes and girders.

John turned to see her in the narrow gap. She could
follow after him, but she hesitated. A dark mass moved
toward him. John gasped as a huge steel counter-
weight, driven by a chain several inches thick, slid toward him. He rolled out of its way. When he looked
back, he could no longer see the opening.

"Mom! MOMMM!"

Terminator strained to reach a steel bar lying near
him. Steel workers used them to move the red-hot ingots around. He got hold of the end and wielded it as
a lever. With titanic effort, he spread the massive components that were holding him, and withdrew his arm.
It was severed at the elbow, dangling junk hanging
from the crushed joint.

Sarah lost sight of John.

As much of a good-bye as they would have, she
thought as she turned to face the T-1000, swooping toward her like a scythe.

Half slumped against the sooty machines, looking
barely conscious, Sarah struggled to load a shell into
her empty weapon. At the last instant she whipped up
the riot gun and fired.

The T-1000's face was blown open, but quickly reformed as it reached out for her. She frantically fumbled to get another shell into the magazine but—

THUNK! A steel needle slammed through her shoulder, pinning her. The polymorphic killer cocked back its other hand. The index finger extended as a gleaming needle, toward her eye, angling to slash through her frontal lobe and up through her upper medulla. It said in a smooth, chilling voice, "Call to John. Now."

Sarah had survived one metal motherfucker, only to be skewered by another. She was terrified, but more than that, she was mad. She couldn't stop herself from screaming through her gasps of pain, "Fuck you, asshole!"

Once it successfully concluded its request had been denied, the T-1000 went into termination mode and arched back to deliver the killing blow.

WHAM! Something whistled down on the T-1000 with such force that it cleaved its head and body in two down to the navel. The steel bar was imbedded in its body. Terminator flung the killer off Sarah.

The T-1000 bounced off the wall and pulled the steel shaft out of itself, lunging back at Terminator, attacking him in an unbridled blur of motion. Swinging again and again. Hammering Terminator back. Terminator fell back against the wall, his system overloading, disrupting in bursts of static, from the pummeling.

Behind the T-1000 was an enormous I-beam, hanging from two chains, used to lift ingots into the smelters, running on linear tracks. The polymorph grabbed the I-beam and sent it rolling down the track. Straight at Terminator. The two-ton girder smashed into his chest, crushing it.

The T-1000 pulled the I-beam back and then heaved it forward again. Terminator wrenched himself sideways to take the second blow on the shoulder. Metal crunched and pieces broke loose inside the savaged cyborg. He sagged, turning to grip the wall. . . .

The visual array was collapsing inward and ballooning out rapidly, and the man/machine's sense of balance was gone. It tottered as the third blow bashed into his back, smashing his spine and pelvis. Servos ratcheted, freezing up in buckled mounts, failing with a protest of clattering steel. Terminator dropped to his knees, crucified against a wall of machinery.

The T-1000's fourth blow was centered between the cyborg's shoulder blades. His skull was partially caved in. Terminator slid to the floor.

Prime core disruptions fired through the wafer-circuit brain. Memories spun loose from their electrical moorings. Terminator had no real life to see flash before his eyes, but there was data. And other people's lives. The chaotic pattern of human emotions spun out inside its head like a tangling audiocassette as it saw glimpses of the past few days. Sarah and John, kneeling, holding one another as they wept. John trying to hide his tears. Sarah facing the T-1000 with an inappropriate weapon. The T-1000 itself, emotionlessly reacting to changing operational environments. And for a microsecond, a weird fusing caused a gestalt grasp of its entire existence, the meaning of human interaction, and from this mushrooming explosion of cross-reffing came one single entity that the cyborg had not been programmed to experience.

Feeling.

Terminator fell back on the concrete, energy firing like misdirected rockets through his synthetic mind. As the cyborg convulsed in machine-death, he learned his most profound lesson about organic life.

Too bad he didn't have time to analyze it.

Terminator was a pathetic shape on the floor, a lump of scrap-heap. But the tattered strands of a ripped-apart consciousness sought alternate energy traps inside the fractured CPU. Skynet had designed the terminators to withstand enormous damage and survive with enough consciousness to repair the damage enough to complete the mission. And now, the man/machine's brain found back-up circuits in the onion-peel layers of the wafer-circuit, and despite the total trauma to the outer and inner chassis, it searched for alternate strands of cabling to carry the command to
move
move

MOVE . . .

A spark here. There. And then, a leg joint bent convulsively.

MOVE!

The leg bent.

No mere man could have come back from the brink like this. But no man had such compelling commands programmed into every molecule of its artificial intelligence.

Besides, Terminator had seen the revelation, and now it was going to move. Frozen servos notwithstanding.

The cyborg began to feebly crawl, dragging his malfunctioning legs behind the crushed spine. His arm stump screeched on the tile floor as he inched himself forward. But his exposed machine-eye burned red with determination.

It reached out for the immediate solution to its problem: the M-79, with the breech still open, cradled in the crook of his ruined arm lying nearby. His good hand, the exposed steel one, was reaching for the last grenade, visible under the skirt of the massive smelter base. His metal finger reached out for it.

You see, Terminator had not completed his mission.

But neither had the T 1000. It raised the heavy steel bar over its head and stabbed it down with unbelievable force. It punched into Terminator's back, through a gap in the shattered armor. The T-1000 levered it back and forth, widening the hole. Then it raised the pointed bar again and slammed it down, punching right through, emerging from Terminator's chest.

And into the floor.

The cyborg was pinioned.

All it could think of was a last futile response.

Strategy nine thousand eighty-five.

Terminator desperately held onto the thought as his head sagged face down and he stopped moving. The light in his eye went out.

The T-1000 looked down at the cyborg and concluded it was no longer a tactical concern. It shifted its attention to its primary target and went off to find it and execute its mission.

John scuttled like a rat through the guts of the smelter. Above him, vast machines churned untended. He heard a voice calling out low and urgent. "John? John? Can you hear me? Where are you?"

It was his mother.

He crawled out of the shadows, looking for her, stepping onto a landing next to one of the massive smelter crucibles. Molten steel flared in the furnace. Heat shimmered the air, giving everything a hallucinatory glow.

Then John saw her nearby, limping toward him. She could barely move, her leg bathed in blood. He ran toward her as she moaned, "Help me, honey . . ." She hobbled forward, reaching out, grinning. But John began to slow as a shape rose behind her.

It was his mother, holding a shotgun aimed seemingly right at him.

The boy skidded to a stop, eyes wide with confusion. Which was which? He looked down. The first Sarah's feet were melding with the floor, sucking and fusing with the tiles as she walked. They had the color and pattern of the tiles up to the knee.

John shouted, "SHOOT!" and then dove to the side. The Sarah-form spun around, changing into Officer Austin. Sarah started unloading the shotgun into the T-1000.

BOOM!

It staggered back.

K-CHAK. She chambered another round.

BOOM! It staggered again.

K-CHAK.

BOOM!

And again.

And again.

The T-1000 was blown back a step with each blast, Sarah advancing after it. The erupting craters in the

T-1000's body "healed" more slowly now. Its power was waning. She fired again, her eyes blazing with feral intensity.

She walked it back, right to the edge of a pit of molten steel.

K-CHAK . . .

CLICK.

She was empty!

The T-1000 stood at the edge, wavering from the reverberations from the last hit. In a second it would recover its composure, as its crater hits closed. She had failed again. Now it would kill her and then John and Skynet would have its victory. Sarah screamed the last of her fury, preparing to rush the thing and go with it into the fiery death waiting below.

But as her legs tensed to launch herself at the recovering polymorph, steel fingers slid a grenade into the bore of the M-79.

Lying on the floor among the machines, Terminator raised its head.

Strategy nine thousand eighty-five.

Play dead.

Half human-flesh, half chrome-skull, the red eye gazing like a malevolent beacon, he snapped the breech closed with a flick of its wrist and and he pulled the trigger.

The T-1000 took the round directly in the belly. The grenade exploded inside its body. A huge hole drilled clean through it, and ripped the torso open, peeling back, half inside out.

Its center of gravity radically shifted, the T-1000 toppled off the edge into the molten steel. John ran up to Sarah and they watched in horror as the thing's head and upper body reappeared above the molten steel.

It was screaming. A terrifying, inhuman siren of a scream, as all its molecules were searching for the right channels back into its proper structure, but the intense heat and volubility of the molten metal around it confused them. It was changing, morphing, transforming so rapidly into anything and everything it had ever been, John and Sarah could barely follow. . . .

Janelle **Voight** checkered with linoleum tile colors, Lewis the guard with knives exploding from his face, other faces, switching at a stroboscopic rate, a face every eyeblink until they merged into one face—

The chrome figure howled one last time and slipped beneath the surface of the molten steel. Liquid silver ran in dissipating whorls over the superheated surface . . . until they vanished into the glowing mass.

Into nothing.

It was gone.

The empty shotgun fell from Sarah's fingers, clattering to the floor. Her good arm slipped around John's shoulder and they embraced, their bodies shaking.

The crippled cyborg was trying to rise. Its servos pathetically whined and stuttered as he tried to lift himself to a kneeling position. The cyborg collapsed, then tried again.

John saw and ran over, lifting for all he was worth. Sarah joined them, helping as best she could. The crippled machine barely managed to stand on his feet. With their support, he limped to the edge of the pit.

Terminator looked down and saw for himself that it was over. John unzipped Sarah's backpack and took out the hand of the first terminator. "Will it melt in there?" he asked.

Terminator answered, his voice strange, softer, almost human, probably from the damage. "Yes. Throw it in."

John tossed the relic and it sank in the lava.

Terminator added, "And the CPU."

John took it out of his pocket and tossed it into the smelter.

Sarah watched it almost immediately melt away. She took a painful breath, and said softly, "It's over."

"No. There was another chip."

He touched a metal finger to the side of his head. Terminator looked at Sarah. They both knew what must be done.

John's eyes went wide as he suddenly understood

what he meant. He shook his head as his eyes began to fill with tears. "No!"

Terminator faced John. A hideous visage, with all the punishment it had taken, but somehow noble . . . . . . kind.

The man/machine said, "I have to go away, John. It must end here . . . or I am the future." It turned a little so that the battered human side of his face was in shadow. John saw the chrome skull and the red eye.

Still, John pleaded, "Don't do it. Please . . . it'll be okay. Stay with us—"

Terminator put his hand on John's shoulder. "I must complete my mission." And as he said that, the human side of his face came back into the light. He reached toward John and his metal finger touched the tear trickling down his cheek.

It was the revelation.

"I know now why you cry, although it is something I can never do."

He turned to Sarah and said, "Good-bye."

"Are you afraid?"

There was the briefest instant before he responded. "Yes," he said. Not because he was going to cease functioning as a terminator, but because he had sensed a vision beyond his programming of a cosmic order vast beyond even Skynet's comprehension. And it gave him the sense of his first feeling.

Fear.

Of where he was going next, if anywhere.

Of course, he hadn't been asked for further details on his answer, so he didn't say any of this. He simply turned and stepped off the edge.

As Terminator fell, time stretched, and a flash of light engulfed his mind. He was floating down a tunnel, following the flash of light into something like oblivion.

Or salvation.

The artificial brain was seared when the chassis hit the molten steel. Almost all electrical activity was stopped.

Almost.

As the chromed skeleton was dissolved into the same primal stew as the T-1000, Sarah and John watched Terminator sink into the lava, the metal hand going last. . . .

At the last second it formed into a fist with the thumb extended . . . a final thumbs-up.

Then it was really gone.

Mother and son watched the molten metal for a while. Then John remembered Terminator's other arm back down the row of smelters, and ran to get it. It was a pile of useless, twisted metal, but the metal was from the future and this time they weren't leaving anything to chance.

When John tossed the pieces in, one by one, he and Sarah felt a shudder deep within the bowels of the earth. As if a massive pivot were turning.

Of course, later, John would think back and assume it was merely the huge machines pounding away in the mill.

He would be wrong.

History had been reborn.

JUDGMENT DAY

The sun glowed pure in a bright blue sky. Stretched out below it was a lush park. People were casually dressed, having summer fun. Cycling, reading . . . children were playing in a playground, swinging on swings, sliding down slides. The jungle gym was neither melted nor burned, but full of kids swinging and yelling raucously. A bright-eyed little boy pumped the pedals of a tricycle.

Timeless things that decades of technical advancement would not change.

Beyond the line of trees, the alabaster skyline of Washington, D.C. rose up, punctuated by the famous dome of the Capitol and the white spire of the Washington Monument.

But there were other buildings that had not existed before—tall skyscrapers that channeled the winds of change. People of modest income lived in them, thanks to several new government bills recently passed by a brash young senator. The apartments were not handouts. The occupants had to work for them. But the price was adjusted according to the abilities and capacities of each tenant.

And it was fair.

237

August 29, 1997 had come and gone. And nothing much had happened. Michael Jackson turned forty. People went to work as they always do, laughed, complained, watched TV, made love.

There was no Judgment Day.

Sarah Connor had held her breath the entire twenty-four hours of that day. And when the sun had risen and she was sure, she wanted to run down the street yelling . . . to grab people and say "Everyday from this day on is a gift. Use it well!" But they would have thought she was crazy, and she'd had enough of that, thank you.

So she got drunk instead.

She had many male friends, of course, and some of them quite handsome, but she had never married.

And she wasn't sad about it, or bitter. Because Kyle was not dead. And his mission had not been a failure.

If time had twisted into a loop, it was he more than anyone who had, by his sacrifice, caused it to untangle. He was the center of the circle. For he'd come out of the ruins carrying the genetics that helped him survive and seed the forces that would alter history. But . . .

Where did he come from? Who was his mother? Where was his family now?

She even hired someone to look for him, the alternate him, anyway, the one who, like the rest of the world, would be born and survive and never know that there had been, on one time line, a nuclear war and a desperate battle for survival.

Kyle was not dead, but living somewhere in her world, probably married to a nice woman, maybe with a few kids, doing something ordinary.

Of course, he would not know her.

Or love her.

Or understand why she would look at him with eyes filled with tears of love and gratitude.

Because he was not that Kyle Reese, the one she had loved, and who had gone back in time to die before he was born.

For her.

For humanity.

And for John Connor.

So she called the investigator off the case and let it go.

So she couldn't marry anyone.

Or love another man as she did Kyle.

That was thirty years ago. But the dark future that never came still existed for her, and always would, like the traces of a dream lingering in the morning light. And the war against the machines still went on. Or, to be more precise, the war against those who built the wrong machines, for the wrong reasons. For Skynet had just been the natural extension of humanity's own self-loathing and fear. It found a solution that was behind all the oppression the world has ever known. Annihilation.

Some men still wanted to build their Skynets. Other men fought them. And so far, those other men had won. And although there was still occasional war, famine, government corruption, people had taken a step forward on the evolutionary scale, a step they never realized had been taken, except by a handful of them who had defied Fate, or, as Sarah now thought of it, steered it a little toward a more healing path.

And so, through the years, Sarah had become a graceful beauty with strange scars, and a bittersweet gleam in her eyes.

And men loved her in vain.

There was one man she adored, of course. She was sitting in the shade of a tree, watching him now, a man in his early forties playing with two small children nearby.

John Connor had the same stern features as he had in Uptime, but there was no eye patch, no scarring. He was far from the haggard man of grim destiny he was in the world that might have been. But there was still penetrating intelligence in his eyes. For his character had been forged in the fires of love and beaten into wisdom on the anvil of will.

Sarah smiled at him, with a mother's pride, of course, and spoke into a small digital recorder. "John fights the war differently than it was foretold. Here, on the battlefield of the Senate, the weapons are common sense . . . and hope."

She lowered the recorder, remembering the first tapes she had recorded for her son before he was even born, so long ago on that windswept Mexican road. And of the Book she had recorded through his years of growing up. She still had them, of course, and was even now adding to them.

An oral history that would stay in her family, and be passed down through the ages, probably until it became bemusing myth.

Or relevant fact . . .

. . . when humanity finally found out how to time travel.

A pretty four-year-old girl ran to her and pointed at her shoe. "Tie me, Grandma."

Grandma Sarah smiled warmly and bent over as the little girl put her foot up on the bench. When all finished, the girl gave Sarah a peck and ran off to play with her father.

There was no need to weep for Sarah. For she had love. And now she had time to reflect and put it all into perspective, while her son carried on the fight for her and Kyle.

She picked up the recorder again and continued speaking into it, while her eyes went skyward, to the deep blue richness of an atmosphere healing from pollution. "The luxury of hope was given to me by the Terminator. Because if a machine can learn the value of human life . . . maybe we can, too."

She clicked off the recorder and settled back to feel the gentle winds caress her face.

ABOUT THE AUTHOR

Randall Frakes worked as editor of the Army's 16th Signal Battalion newspaper while stationed in Europe, during which time he won the *Stars and Stripes* journalism award for an investigative report on conditions at Mannheim stockade.

After returning to civilian life, Frakes studied film writing and production at Columbia College in Los Angeles and supported himself by writing fiction for *Analog, Fantasy and Science Fiction*, and *Fantastic* magazines.

After college, he worked as a cameraman for Roger Corman in Venice, California, creating photographic effects for *Escape from New York, Battle Beyond the Start*, and *Galaxy of Terror*.

He eventually went back to writing, collaborating with his writing partner, William Wisher, on the screenplay *Last Thirty Days of Liberty*, and the novelization for James Cameron's *The Terminator*.

Frakes also co-produced and wrote a futuristic comedy adventure, *Hell Comes to Frogtown*, and the script for Marvel Comics' dark superhero "Deathlok."

He recently completed the screenplay for Fries Entertainment's *Diplomatic Immunity*, and is developing a novel and several screenplays. He lives in Sylmar, California.

It is five years after the destruction of the Death Star,
and the triumph over the Empire.
But new challenges to galactic peace have arisen,
and Luke Skywalker hears a voice from his past...

Beware the Dark Side....

STAR WARS™
HEIR TO THE EMPIRE
Volume 1 of a Three-Book Cycle
by Timothy Zahn

Here is the science fiction publishing event of the year, the exciting,
authorized continuation of the legendary **Star Wars** saga. Picking up
where the movie trilogy left off, Heir to the Empire revels the tumultuous
events that take place after the most popular series in motion-picture
history.

Heir to the Empire begins five years after the end of **Return of the Jedi**.
The Rebel Alliance has driven the remnants of the old Imperial Starfleet
back into barely a quarter of the territory that they once controlled. Leia
and Han are married and have shouldered heavy burdens in the
government of the New Republic. And Luke Skywalker is the first in a
hoped-for new line of Jedi Knights.

But thousands of light years away, the last of the Emperor's warlords
has taken command of the remains of the Imperial fleet, and he has
made two vital discoveries that could destroy the fragile new
Republic....

A towering epic of action, invention, mystery
and spectacle on a galactic scale,
HEIR TO THE EMPIRE
is a story worthy of the name **Star Wars**.

Available now in hardcover
wherever Bantam Spectra Books are sold.
Also available as a Book-on-Tape from
Bantam Audio Publishing.

AN245 – 6/91